Murder in the Family

Murder in the Family

An Eve Appel Mystery

—

LESLEY A. DIEHL

CAMEL
PRESS
Kenmore, WA

PRESS

A Camel Press book published by Epicenter Press

Epicenter Press
6524 NE 181st St.
Suite 2
Kenmore, WA 98028

For more information go to:
www.Camelpress.com
www.Coffeetownpress.com
www.Epicenterpress.com
www.lesleyadiehl.com

This is a work of fiction. Names, characters, places, brands, media, and incidents are either the product of the author's imagination or are used fictitiously.

Cover design by Scott Book

Murder in the Family
Copyright © 2021 by Lesley A. Diehl

ISBN: 978-1-60381-763-9 (Trade Paper)
ISBN: 978-1-60381-764-6 (eBook)

Printed in the United States of America

To my family who had the good sense to raise me on a farm. I still love the smell of fresh cut hay and the sounds of a rooster crowing in the morning, but I especially appreciate the love of nature life on the farm taught me.

ACKNOWLEDGMENTS

THE FIRST EVE APPLE MYSTERY WAS published in 2013, but the character of Eve and her best friend Madeleine first appeared several years before in the form of a short story entitled "Gator Aid." The story placed first in the Mystery Writers of America Florida Chapter short story competition and gave me the confidence I needed to go ahead and create a series with Eve as the protagonist. I've gotten to know Eve throughout these eight books and three short stories. She is always entertaining and keeps me on my toes since I can't always predict what she will do next. She's a good friend to have, loyal, funny, sassy and the perfect blend of a fashionista turned country gal.

Also by the author from Camel Press:

A Secondhand Murder

Dead in the Water

A Sporting Murder

Mud Bog Murder

Old Bones Never Die

Killer Tied

Nearly Departed

Short Stories in the Series

"The Little Redheaded Girl is my Friend"

"Thieves and Gators Run at the Mention of her Name"

"Gator Aid"

PROLOGUE

THE HEAVY GOLD CUFFLINKS GREW WARM in his palm as he rolled them around listening to the click of the metal as they touched. He held them up to examine them, the deep yellow hue glowing in the sunlight which streamed through the window and bounced off the water surrounding the mangroves outside. He couldn't toss them into the garbage bag where he had thrown his expensive silk pants and shirt. His grandfather has given them to him, and they were all he had left of the man he loved and admired and who served as his role model. Now his grandfather was dead. He had been told the man died of old age, but he knew this was not true. Someone had intervened and killed him in his own home. Worse yet, there was nothing he could do to avenge the death. His hands had been tied.

He clenched his fists in rage, but then dropped them to his sides in a feeling of impotence, turning his attention to the Rolex watch on his wrist. He'd had the timepiece designed for himself and, although it cost more than most people made in a year, it had no sentimental value for him. He threw it in with the other items, all of them the paraphernalia of a life he no longer lived. He put the cuff links in his tee-shirt pocket and patted it to make certain they were safe. Now there was nothing in the houseboat to connect its owner to the man who had wielded power for so many years, commanding the respect of those who worked for him, creating fear in those who worked against him.

Hefting the garbage bag onto his shoulders, he locked the door to the moored boat and headed toward the rusted pickup truck which sat on a patch of gravel next to the road.

His neighbor, a scrawny man who occupied the old, battered craft with peeling paint docked next to him sat in a twisted metal chair by the canal, rod in the water.

"Catching?" he called to the angler as he got into the cab of his truck.

"Nah. You going to the dump?" The neighbor nodded at the bag.

"No. Taking some items to Goodwill."

He didn't know the man's name and didn't want to. This was a community of boats that almost never left their dockage. Many of them sat askew in the water and were no longer seaworthy. The people who lived on them left one another alone. He suspected that like him, the boats' inhabitants found anonymity to their liking and preferred to keep to themselves. On week nights they might walk down the road to the bar and grill for a beer or two, but none of them chanced spending weekends there. Those days were left to the tourists or visitors who rolled in from Miami on their expensive Harleys and cars. It didn't pay to hang out at the bar then. Someone might recognize you, and the point of this place was to avoid contact with people who might get too curious about what you were doing living here, a backwater place on Card Sound Road, north of Key Largo.

He rolled down the truck window—no AC in this old bucket—and pulled onto the road. He waited at the toll gate to pay his fee and then proceeded up over the bridge. The top of the span afforded a view of Key Largo to his south, but he had no time to slow down and take in the azure water and the mangroves stretching to the horizon. While there were only two cars behind him, he knew the traffic from south Florida on a Friday afternoon would increase and be bumper-to-bumper coming off the twenty-five mile stretch that connected the Keys to Homestead, Florida City and the rest of mainland Florida. He intended his journey to be a quick trip to drop off his items, and then he'd head to the shopping plaza for his weekly supplies.

Joining the traffic on US 1, he drove for less than a mile south. Just beyond the second light, he turned into a graveled parking lot and pulled up to the large dumpster at the side of the donation center where he tossed the garbage bag into the donation bin. Traffic whizzed by on the highway. Adjusting his rearview mirror to reduce glare, he checked for an opening in the line of cars and caught sight of another car pulling into the charity center. The car stopped, and a figure jumped out and raised the lid of the bin. Although the shadow from the dumpster hid the individual from view, the mirror provided him a momentary glimpse of someone digging around in the bin. A dumpster diver, he thought. Poor guy, then he remembered that he was, too.

CHAPTER 1

—

"HAVE YOU SEEN NAPPI LATELY?" I asked my father-in-law. "Not since the funeral for his grandfather," Lionel replied. "Nappi seemed preoccupied at the service, didn't you think?"

Lionel shook his head and gave me a look of frustration. "His grandfather is dead, the man who raised him, almost the only family he has left. How did you expect him to be?"

"Filled with grief, but it felt to me as if his thoughts were elsewhere, not on honoring his grandfather's life." I didn't mean it as a criticism. I noticed how distracted he was at the funeral, but I'd shoved the concern to the back of my thoughts until now.

Lionel and I were chopping vegetables in the kitchen of the house my husband Sammy had completed for our family this past summer. The window overlooked the back yard which was bordered by the canal. I waved as my three boys beached their canoe and helped my daughter Netty out of the back of the craft. I marveled at how fast she had grown. She was no longer a toddler, but a little girl of almost five, who loved to spend her time with her three older brothers. In the fall she would attend kindergarten. Her brothers all had horses, and Netty had nagged her father and me for one of her own. She was too small for a horse, but we had talked about getting her a pony. We wanted to wait for her birthday, but knew we'd have to give in to her demands sooner than that. Young as she was, she had a way of bothering people when she wanted something. She could be persistent in her requests and "later" was a word she didn't understand. She reminded me of someone—maybe me. A pony, if we could find one with a gentle nature, would fit her for several years. I'd called a nearby horse rescue facility, filled out permit papers, and we had been cleared for an adoption. They promised to call me when a pony arrived.

The children rushed into the house, hungry after their paddle on the canal. Sammy and I had adopted the boys when Sammy's half-brother had been killed and the boys were left orphaned. Jason, the oldest, was a senior in high school. The middle boy, Jerome, had just celebrated his twelfth birthday. Jeremy, our youngest, was 10. They were full-blooded Miccosukee like their biological parents and would grow up to be as handsome as Sammy, with black hair and the brown skin of their native ancestors. Netty was Sammy and my child. She was already tall for her age like both of us and had Sammy's dark hair and my blue yes. Unfortunately, she also had many of my personality traits including my impatient and somewhat bold nature. I'm Eve Appel Egret, and I've inherited all the bold, brassy, snoopy traits that gallop among the women in the Appel family. Pity the man who would wed Netty when she grew up. There wasn't another man on the face of the earth who could handle an Appel woman like Sammy could.

Netty opened the fridge door and pulled out a container of milk while my youngest, Jeremy, searched in the back of the cupboard and grabbed the package of cookies I thought I had hidden away from hungry kids. I've got a bit of a sweet tooth, and it's almost impossible to keep anything sugary in the house with growing kids and me competing for snacks. Lionel handed glasses to them, and they settled at the kitchen table for their snack.

"You might close that cupboard door," I called to Jeremy, who popped up from the table and slammed it shut.

"It's time for a break," said Lionel and took a seat at the table with them. I continued to work at the counter.

"I meant for you to take a break also, Eve," Lionel said, getting up and pulling out a chair for me.

Lionel Egret, a full-blooded Miccosukee and my husband Sammy's father, spent much of his adult life living in the swamps, hiding himself from his family because he felt responsible for the death of his best friend.

He wasn't. The friend's death was the unfortunate result of the two young men's silly bet over who could find his way home if lost in the swamps. The friend had miscalculated the severity of an approaching storm and died. Lionel felt guilty for letting him take the chance. Lionel emerged from his self-imposed exile several years ago and began to make my life miserable with his stern disapproving judgment of me. He wasn't keen on white folks and, with my six-foot-tall frame, spikey blond hair and penchant for fashion, I'm about as white as you can get. But Lionel and I had come to tolerate and even respect each another, bonding over the love we shared for Sammy and the children. Somehow the fact that my mob boss friend Nappi liked Lionel also swayed my acceptance of the man. I trusted Nappi's judgment of people. He'd seen a lot of bad ones in his years as a "Family" man.

But this solicitous behavior on Lionel's part? That was new. I was suspicious.

I sat and tried to catch Lionel's eye, but he wouldn't look at me, directing his attention to the boys as they told of seeing a big gator north of here on the rim canal, the large canal that surrounded the Big Lake. Netty sighed in that four-year-old going on fifty way of hers.

"Gators are boring," she pronounced.

Lionel's gaze traveled from the boys to Netty, then landed on me, and dropped to my stomach. He knew. How he knew, I had no idea. No one else in the family, not even my grandmother or Sammy knew I was pregnant.

The pregnancy was no real surprise to me because Sammy and I had applied ourselves to making it happen by spending long evenings in our little love shack in the swamps. The cooler early fall weather made for an enjoyable paddle in the canoe out to the shack where the nights filled the swamp with the noises of alligators, frogs and small animals such as raccoons foraging for food and otters slipping into the water to frolic with one another.

My thoughts drifted to my detective work at Crusty McNabb's agency. Business was slow following our last case helping identify a sexual predator for a business owner and discovering the person responsible for the attempts made on the life of the uncle of my best friend Madeleine. Madeleine was also my partner in our consignment shop. Sammy's mother Renata, separated from Lionel for years, had flown out from Las

Vegas for a long vacation and helped at the shop, freeing Madeleine and me to spend more time with our families. Since Madeleine's twins, little Eve and David Jr. had begun kindergarten in the fall, she was thankful for the hours she spent with them before the school day took them away from home.

I knew the letup in my detective work, Renata's help and Madeleine's presence at the store created a hiatus that couldn't continue. We needed another shop clerk on a permanent basis. Our seamstress and part owner Shelley had her hands full with tailoring, and my grandmother Grandy, who spent a few hours each week working in the shop, and her husband Max were enjoying more weekends in the Keys with their friends.

Lionel gave me a piercing look. "You're right to be worried with the extra responsibility. Family time and your work will conflict. You know that."

I threw up my hands in frustration. Lionel, like many of my Miccosukee family, my grandmother Grandy and close friends, read my thoughts with ease. Was I that transparent, or simple?

"An ad in the paper might work," he said, rising from the table. "Who wants to come with me to fish? Catfish for dinner?"

The three boys jumped up from the table and followed Lionel to the canal's edge where they threw their lines into water and settled down to chat. That left me with the vegetables to finish cleaning and chopping. I didn't mind. My thoughts would be my own. At least for a while.

After I finished prepping the veggies, Netty rushed into the house carrying something in her hand.

"Look, Meemie. I caught a fish. Fry it for my dinner." She held up a catfish about three inches long.

I hated to tell her the fish was much too small to be eaten and should be tossed back into the canal.

Lionel followed her in the door. I gave him a questioning look.

"A Netty sized fish," he said.

She was so excited about her catch that she jumped up and down and dropped the wriggling fish on the floor. I picked it up and handed it back to her.

"Since it's your first catch, we'll cook it, but you know what the rules are. You catch it, you clean it."

Netty looked at her grandfather.

"I'm not cleaning it, my girl, but I will teach you how to do it." He led her out the door, her tiny trophy wriggling in her hands.

Through the open kitchen window, I saw Grandfather Egret, Lionel's father and the patriarch of the Egret clan, walk across the yard from his house to the canal where the kids continued to fish. A small stringer of fish lay on the canal bank.

"Better pick those up. There are enough for dinner tonight. We don't want to be greedy and take more than we can use," Grandfather said. "And fish lying there are a temptation for a gator. Gators aren't welcome this close to the house."

A medley of baked, mixed root vegetables and fried catfish fresh from the canal were on the menu tonight. Netty ran from the fish cleaning station next to the air boat dock holding her dinner entrée in her hand. It looked to be about an inch and a half long. Hardly a mouthful.

"She's learning." Lionel and Netty delivered the small specimen to me. I could see the pride on his face as he laid his hand on Netty's shoulder.

I took the morsel from her and set it in the fridge. The other fish would soon join hers. What a difference this dinner was from those I ate years ago when I lived on the Sound in Connecticut. In those days I didn't cook. Instead I dined in fancy, pricey restaurants. My days there were a lifetime different from my existence here in rural Florida.

"You're different, too," said Grandfather, coming into the house to stand beside me. "Do you miss your old life?"

I thought about the question. Did I? Did I miss shopping in stores featuring designer fashions? I still wore my signature stiletto heels. Three-inch heels of every style and color lined my closet floor, and high-end shirts, jeans and dresses hung on the racks. The difference now was that my clothes were from second hand stores like the one Madeleine and I owned here in town. No matter how proud I was of the business she and I had created, I was even prouder of the life Sammy and I shared with our children. This ranching community on the shores of the Big Lake in rural Florida had become more than a place where Madeleine and I started our business, where I had come to get away from my first husband Jerry to think over my life. I'd become a part of this community. For some folks here I remained that crazy Yankee woman with the odd hairdo, but most accepted me. Of course, I'd never change what was uniquely me, my need to tell the truth regardless of the consequences, but I had mellowed a bit and now did my truth telling in smaller bits, allowing people to adjust to me over time. This was home, where I wanted to continue my work and where I wanted to raise my family. Friends, family and a sense of belonging, something I hadn't found in all my years up North. My hand went to my abdomen, and I caressed the bump growing there.

"You know I wouldn't trade this life for anything. What's to miss? Traffic, high prices, concrete, air pollution? Here I have all of you and my friends. There's nothing to miss."

"I thought so." Grandfather patted my arm. "Do you want me to fry the fish?"

"You're a lot better at it than I am," I conceded.

"There is something missing, you know," said Grandfather as Lionel brought the cleaned fish in.

"Nappi," I said.

Lionel's eyes darkened with concern. "Eve and I were talking about him. He's not come around lately. Usually he stops by here to talk and have coffee."

"Or he calls, and we meet at the Burnt Biscuit for ribs." My mouth watered at the thought of a rack of meaty, juicy meat and a side of fries and cole slaw. Much as I love catfish, nothing could compare with ribs and sides. "I'll give him a call. We've got plenty for dinner, and there's leftover peach cobbler for dessert."

Lionel's eyes twinkled with pleasure. "Maybe he'll bring some of those expensive cigars of his, and we can sit out back and have a smoke after dinner. I'll go set up the wood for the fire pit."

My call went to voice mail. "That's been happening every time I try to get in touch with him. I wonder if Jerry knows where he is." I hit the contact for my ex-husband Jerry who worked for Nappi. What kind of work wasn't clear. Kind of a gofer, I guess.

"Evie," he answered. Did he forget I hated to be called that or did he call me that to aggravate me? I guessed it was the latter.

I let a few moments roll by without saying anything.

"You there? I'm sorry. Eve."

"Have you seen or heard from Nappi in the last week or two?"

"No. I've been in Connecticut for the last several weeks. My brother was arrested for stealing a car from an impound lot, so I've been supporting him, bailing him out of jail and finding him a good lawyer."

"Why would he steal a car from an impound lot, of all places?"

"He was doing a friend a favor. The car belonged to a friend of his, but the cops impounded it for evidence in a drug bust. The friend needed it back, so my brother wanted to help him out."

"Jerry, you know there are ways of getting it back without stealing it. What was your brother thinking?" I don't know why I asked that question because I knew Jerry's brother, and thinking was not his best quality. In fact, he seemed not to do much of it.

"It's complicated," Jerry said.

"I'll bet. I don't want to know the details. About Nappi . . ."

"I called him several times, and it went to voice mail. I think he's taking a break from everything and grieving for his grandfather. The guy raised Nappi, you know. Now Nappi has little family left. Just his daughter, and she's traveling somewhere in Europe."

"I'm going to make a trip to West Palm tomorrow to get clothes for the shop. I'll call him and stop by his condo then. Meantime, I'd recommend disentangling yourself from your brother's current mess."

I hung up before I could hear what Jerry's reply was to my suggestion he butt out of the brother's problems.

THE NEXT MORNING, I accomplished my usual chores—threw up twice, and then dropped by the shop to check inventory and see what we needed from our consignors. I called our usual clients as I sped down the Beeline to West Palm. Picking up items from our best customers on the coast was one of the perks our shop offered. It saved them a trip and assured these wealthy matrons that no one would see them use a consignment shop to make a few dollars off their designer fashions. They liked the extra cash, but never wanted to appear desperate for it, or, gasp! be observed by the country club set entering a secondhand shop in the wilds of Florida. Many of the women in wealthy coastal communities consigned with us but pretended to one another that they didn't. That's why we never used a van with our store's name on the side to pick up items. The neighbors would talk. We kept it our little secret, never discussed it with our consignors and acted surprised when one of them came into the shop, as if she wandered off the coast, got lost and decided to purchase some little thing that caught her eye, perhaps a dress for a formal occasion. If we knew the item was consigned by one of her friends, we steered her to another. Everyone stayed happy, and everyone made money, including our shop.

I secured a great haul of merchandise including shoes, clothes and some household items like flat wear and sets of casual dinner dishes. I decided to head for Nappi's condo and call him on the way there. Grieving or not, Nappi needed people he loved and who loved him around him. I felt a bit guilty I hadn't decided to stop by his place sooner.

This time the phone message was different: "The number you have reached is no longer in service." Puzzled, I clicked off as I pulled up to his condo. There was a sign on the front lawn: "Sold."

CHAPTER 2

I WONDERED IF NAPPI HAD DECIDED to leave Florida and return to Connecticut to be nearer friends in the North, but I was hurt he hadn't gotten in touch with any of us here. And why end the cell phone service? I was about to try his landline in Hartford when my phone chirped at me. It was Crusty McNabb, the owner of the detective agency where I was apprenticing as a PI.

"Where are you, Eve? I need you here in the office. We've got a case."

My heart beat faster. Good. At last. Maybe it was more than insurance fraud, the cases I hated because Crusty made me sit surveillance to get evidence on the bad guys. In my condition, I'd never make it through half a morning without the need for a bathroom.

As if reading my mind, Crusty broke in before I could speak. "And, no. It's not an insurance case. It's a case for someone you know well. Your ranching friend, Jay Cassidy."

"He's not hurt, is he?"

"No, but one of his hands is, and a horse is missing."

"I'm in West Palm. I'll be there in less than an hour."

I maneuvered my way out of the condo complex and onto the highway heading north. At this time of the day I wouldn't encounter much traffic unless I counted the pair of sandhill cranes at the side of the road. I slowed to make certain I passed by without frightening them onto the roadway. They were such regal birds who cared for their young with overwhelming devotion and chose their mates for life. Kind of like Sammy and me, I smiled to myself.

When I pulled into the strip mall that contained our consignment shop as well as Crusty's agency, I parked in an open slot next to the black pickup with Jay Cassidy's ranch logo on its side. I hadn't seen him for several months but would have preferred we get together under other circumstances. Hiring a detective meant he had a problem he couldn't solve on his own.

I dashed into the agency and through the door leading to Crusty's office. He and Jay were sitting on either side of the desk, their feet propped on the top. They had cigars in their mouths.

"Crusty McNabb, you know there's no smoking in this office!" I reached around Jay to grab the cigar out of his mouth, then seized the offending tobacco tube out of Crusty's.

"We ain't smoking them. We're holding them," said Crusty. "Give those back."

I looked at the nasty smokes and noted they were not lit. Even so, the smell of them in my hand made me ill.

"Sorry." I tossed them onto the desk and ran into the bathroom.

"Sensitive nose on that woman," I heard Jay say as I bent over the toilet bowl.

I flushed the toilet several times to cover the sounds I was making and emerged from the room feeling better, but shaky.

"You look kind of green," said Crusty. He tilted his head to one side and raised an eyebrow in suspicion. "I hope you don't have the flu."

"No, I'm fine."

"I meant I hope you aren't contagious," Crusty replied.

"I don't think this is catching." I grabbed a folding chair from against the wall, opened it and sat. "What's going on? Someone got hurt? And there's a horse involved?"

"Yesterday I sent one of my hands with a trailer and horse to take a run to Chokoloskee to a ranch near there."

I interrupted him. "Sorry, but I'm unfamiliar with that area. Where is it?"

"It's south and west of the Tamiami Trail."

I shook my head. What I knew about Florida was limited to the two coasts, the area around here and the Keys. I was as naive as the tourists who vacationed in Florida.

"The northern edge of the Everglades." Crusty said. "It's quite a drive."

Jay nodded. "It is. The ranch's owner is a friend of mine who stopped by several weeks ago and saw some of my polo ponies. He was interested in one of my gals, so I told him I'd let him borrow her for a few months to see how he felt about buying her. She's one of the ponies owned by the Argentinian jerk who tried to transport drugs into this country by stuffing them into the vaginas of the polo ponies he brought here. You remember that one, don't you, Eve?"

I did. Eduardo, the Argentinian he'd mentioned, was the husband of the woman whose mother was killed and left on the dressing room floor on the day of the grand opening for our consignment shop. That nasty, reptile-like man fled back to Argentina with a woman whose name I never knew, but who was his female clone—dark hair and eyes and an ice-cold personality. They were uninterested in the welfare of his horses or of the humans around them. I shivered. I didn't know what became of him back in Argentina, but I was certain I never wanted to cross paths with him again. Or with the ice maiden.

Jay continued his story. "Neither the horse nor the driver arrived at their destination. Instead, when we went looking for them, we found the truck and an empty trailer at the side of the road about 30 miles west of here. My driver was spotted wandering down the road a mile from the truck and trailer. He had been beaten and couldn't remember much except he pulled over to help a motorist stranded on the side of the road. Someone hit him from behind and worked him over good. He's lucky to be alive."

"The horse is gone?" I said.

"Yup. That pony was a handful. She wasn't easy, didn't trust anyone much. My rancher friend knew he was taking on a horse with issues, but he's a good trainer. I thought he might be able to gentle her some and get her back on the field as a polo pony."

"If she's the horse I think you mean, I do remember her. She had attitude."

"You would too if you'd had drugs stuffed up your, you-know-what, and then had some vet with rough hands extract them from you. I don't think she ever forgot that."

"Wasn't she the horse that saved my life?" I asked.

Jay nodded. "A tough bird. She could have given anyone who tried to get her out of the trailer a rough time. Maybe they wanted to steal her, but she got loose. No telling where she is now. Maybe off in the swamps somewhere. I hated losing her, but I'd like to treat the person who beat up my man some of the same in return." Jay's eyes turned dark with anger. He wasn't a man to cross.

"You reported this to the police?" I said.

"No, I did not. My reputation is on the line here. I don't want anyone thinking I can't take care of my own horses and the men who work for me. I want this to be investigated, and I want it to be quiet and done well. Top priority. The cops won't see it as that important."

Jay was one of the wealthiest and most influential ranchers in this area. What he wanted, he got. He wanted Crusty and me to track this down. Now.

"Is this agency up to it?" asked Jay.

I nodded. Crusty gave me a look of concern. "Your flu won't stand in the way, will it?" he asked.

"Nope, no, absolutely not."

"Good." Jay got up from the chair and clapped his Stetson against his leg. "I expect to hear from you soon."

Crusty and I sat in silence for several minutes after Jay left.

"You thinking what I'm thinking?" asked Crusty.

"We need information about Jay's friend, the guy who was to receive this horse. And we need to interview the driver to find out what he knows about the motorist he stopped to help."

"I can't believe the driver would be in on this, not if he took as severe a beating as Jay said, but we start there. You talk to the driver who is in the hospital, and I'll pay a visit to the friend." Crusty removed the two cigars from the top of the desk and grabbed his hat off the wall hook. "I'll see you back here tonight." He stuffed the cigars into his shirt pocket. "No sense letting these go to waste. I don't smoke anymore, but I could give them to one of my pals."

That was a lie. Crusty didn't smoke in the office anymore, but he hadn't given up the stinky habit when he was out on the lake fishing.

"Sure, "I said.

On the drive to the hospital, I tried Nappi's Connecticut number.

"That number is no longer in service," repeated the recording. It was as if the man had left this planet.

AT THE HOSPITAL, JAY'S DRIVER WAS making a slow recovery from his beating. He was covered in bandages and his right arm was in a cast. He could add nothing to what Jay had already told us. Because the blow came from behind, he never saw his attacker. As for the horse, he confirmed that she was willful and would have given any stranger who tried to get her out of the trailer a difficult time.

"When she got to know you, she was more trusting. I hope Mr. Jay finds her." The driver sighed and laid back on his hospital bed. A nurse came in and signaled me he needed rest.

I patted his hand and left the room. To continue to beat him after he lost consciousness seemed senseless especially since he wouldn't have been able to identify his attacker or attackers. How could someone have been that angry at the driver, or did the attacker have some issue with Jay and took it out on the driver? Why? The attack seemed cruel, almost sadistic.

Back in the car, I decided I should drop by the consignment shop. Madeleine was working until three when she needed to pick up her twins from kindergarten. Shelley was supposed to take over the shop then, but, since I was free for the afternoon, I decided I'd give Shelley a break.

My cell rang. The caller ID said it was Madeleine.

"Hi, Eve. I'm wondering if you can come by here a little early. We need to talk."

"I'm coming to the shop now. What's this about? It sounds serious."

"We'll talk in person." She ended the call.

Oh, oh. It was serious.

The expressions on Shelley and Madeleine's faces told me I wouldn't like what they had to say.

Madeleine stepped forward, but Shelley put her hands on Madeleine's shoulders and moved her to one side. "I think I should tell Eve."

"Tell me what?" You aren't ill, are you?"

"No, no. I'm fine. This is hard to say, but I've decided I must leave here and do what I said I was going to do several years ago. I'm going to New York City. You know I always thought my career in design should be there, not here. I've been using the internet to look for a position, and I found one in a small design house. I applied and was accepted. I'll be an apprentice. The money is lousy, but I've saved up, and I'll be sharing an apartment with two other young women."

This was much worse than I expected. I was taking on a new case with Crusty, and I was expecting another baby. I had counted on Shelley's help in the shop.

"I thought you were happy working here and being a part owner?" I'm certain the shock and disappointment showed on my face. I mentally kicked myself. I was being selfish. This young woman needed to follow her star, not spend the rest of her life wondering if she had missed a chance in the design field. "Sorry. How silly of me to assume this place could provide you all you dreamed of." I reached out and hugged her to me. "We will miss you, you know. Do you want to sell back your share of the shop? It will give you a nest egg for the city."

"Would you buy it back?" Shelley looked at Madeleine for her support.

Madeleine nodded. "Of course. And if you find the city is not right for you, you can always come back here."

"When will you leave?" I asked, my mind already racing with the issues this would create. How could we find another seamstress? Hiring help in the store was something I thought could be put off for the immediate future, but now it seemed crucial to hire someone right away. Madeleine and I exchanged worried glances.

"I wouldn't leave you with all this up in the air. I have several friends whom I met at the design school in West Palm. I'll give you their names. I know they'd be interested in a part-time position as a tailor. As for shop help, I'm not certain they'll be interested in clerking also, but you can ask them. I know this puts you in a bit of a jam, but . . ."

"But, this is your chance. Do it. We'll work this out. Don't worry. Huh, Madeleine?" I turned to my partner who was walking back to the office. "Madeleine?"

"She's angry because I'm leaving."

"She's surprised because this is all so sudden. Don't worry, Shelley."

After Shelley left and as Madeleine was walking out the door to get her kids, I stopped her. "You're upset."

"Of course, I'm upset, Eve."

"But this is Shelley's future."

"I'm not mad at her. I'm mad at you. As usual, the burden of this shop will fall on my shoulders while you spend your time chasing down crooks."

I reached out to touch her, but she wrenched her arm away from me.

"I'm late." She slammed through the door, making the bell on it jangle loudly.

"Okay then. We'll talk later," I said to her retreating back. I was too shocked by her outburst to say more, even if I had been given the chance.

What a pickle I was in. Madeleine was right about my love of taking down the bad guys. I always thought she understood, but I had been distracted these last years by detective work. I guess I had ignored how much my distraction with being a PI had left her the bulk of the burden with running the business. And now what she didn't know was this pregnancy meant family would have to come first. I wasn't going to tell her until I had worked out how to deal with the shop.

I grabbed my cell phone to see if I could connect with Grandy. She always came through for me. I stopped before I hit the call button. That was the problem, wasn't it? I always counted on someone else to come through to make it easier for me to juggle the demands of my life. Grandy had always advised me to reach out to others rather than go off like the Lone Ranger, my preferred way of operating. I'd thought I'd gotten better at that, but all I had accomplished was to shift the responsibility of the shop to someone else. This was one of those situations where I would have loved to talk everything over with Nappi. Maybe it was better he wasn't available to me. I'd gotten it wrong. Shifting my load to someone else was not the same as collaborating with others. I'd do better, but first I would let Madeleine have her space and talk with her about the shop later.

WHEN I GOT HOME, SAMMY WAS sitting outside and called to me to join him. I grabbed an iced tea from the fridge and dropped down on the outside chair beside him, tucking a cushion behind my back. He pulled me closer, and I buried my nose in his shiny, black hair inhaling the clean smell of my man.

"How was your day or should I ask?" he said.

I gave him a weak smile. He could always tell when something was bothering me even if I tried to hide it. The people close to me were too darn good at reading me. I told him about Shelley leaving and what Madeleine had said to me.

"Don't tell me she was right. I already figured that out. I told her I would be responsible for hiring someone to work the shop, but I've dragged my feet on that. Having your mother for a few weeks in the store was temporary. She lives in Las Vegas and has no interest in moving back here."

Sammy nodded. The man was an angel. He was letting me work through this issue.

"Okay," I sighed and took a sip of my tea. "Here's the news. I'm pregnant."

"I know."

"You do? How?"

He smiled at me and reached out for my hand. "Do you think I'm that dense?"

"And?"

"It's what we both want, Eve. I couldn't be happier."

"Me, too."

"But?"

"This time I need to find a more permanent solution to the consignment shop. Madeleine wouldn't want to take on the full burden of it. We're partners, but I'm the partner who has been absent. I know I can't be a wife, mother, detective and run the shop. Something has to go."

He gave me a wry look.

I punched him in the arm. "Don't be silly. I'm not about to give up you and the children."

"If you're thinking of letting go of the detective work, I know, and you know you can't do that. It's part of your nature to snoop."

"I need someone to step into my shoes in the shop. Grandy has a right to her retirement with Max. And I don't want to hire a young woman to work as a clerk. I want someone Madeleine will see as responsible and committed to the work. I cannot think of who that is now."

"It will come to you," said Sammy.

"No recommendations?"

"Nope. You'll work it out."

We held hands until the glow from the sun dipped low into the canal waters.

"Grandfather is cooking tonight. Let's go eat," Sammy said.

"It's so pleasant out here maybe we should eat outside tonight," I said.

"I'll lay a fire for later. We can do s'mores with the kids."

My mouth watered at the thought of chocolate.

The shadows on the water almost hid the canoe nearing the shore.

"Your father," I said. "I assume he's joining us for dinner."

Lionel pulled the canoe onto the bank and strolled over to us.

"Did you tell him yet?" Lionel asked.

"Well, if I hadn't, that comment would pique his curiosity, but yes, he knows."

Lionel threw his arm around Sammy's shoulders. "How do you feel about being a father again?"

"I'm getting used to it," Sammy replied with a smile. "Is being a grandfather again good for you as well?"

"I like it. I'd like ten more grandkids."

I groaned. "I'm not a brood mare, you know."

"I know," Lionel said. "You're doing fine."

Lionel almost never paid me a compliment. This wasn't much of one, but it was something from him.

"Thanks, Dad," I said, then reached up and gave him a peck on the cheek.

He cleared his throat as if embarrassed at the affection.

"By the way, don't you think it's time you did something to find your friend Nappi?" he asked.

That was the Lionel I knew, A compliment followed by some kind of jab.

I tossed it back at him. "I thought I'd let you take on that one."

Before he could answer I rushed ahead to catch up with Sammy on his way to the wood pile.

"Out of curiosity," I asked, "who all knows about the baby?"

His dark eyes twinkled. "Oh, almost everyone."

CHAPTER 3

—

E VERYONE? EVERYONE KNEW I WAS PREGNANT? Did I have no secrets? Sammy hugged me as we walked up the steps to the house. "Nappi might not know."

"That's only because no one knows where he is."

"I'll find him," said Lionel, coming up behind us.

"And you'll let me know when you do?"

"Sure."

That didn't sound like a convincing "sure," but it was the best I would get for now.

"Meemie," said Netty, reaching up to be lifted into my arms, "when can we get my pony?'

"As soon as the rescue group calls to let us know they've found the right one for you, we'll go visit them." Maybe I shouldn't have been so certain about finding a pony. Netty took statements like that as solemn and unbreakable promises.

"I want a black one with white spots, and a girl." She grabbed a handful of my hair and tugged. "'kay?"

"It's fine with me, but we'll have to wait to see what pony they find."

"People are so slow." She wriggled out of my arms and ran into the house to join her brothers.

My cell chirped. I read the caller ID before answering.

"Crusty. How did it go with Jay's friend?"

"I don't think he's involved in the assault and the theft. You talked with the driver?"

"I'm certain he's in the clear. Now where do we go?"

"Jay called me on my way back to the office. He's a mighty impatient man, and he's worried someone is targeting him."

I was puzzled. "He didn't tell us that. Why does he think someone might be after him?"

"He thinks the other farms involved in breeding and raising polo ponies might be interested in wiping out the competition especially if it comes from some, as he calls it, 'redneck farmer from the swamps.' Sounds kind of paranoid to me, but it could be the only lead we have. What do you think?"

"Possible, I suppose." It did sound a bit over the top, but when Jay wanted action, he wanted it right now. "Okay. It might be time for a little undercover work. I'll dig out some ladylike attire and tomorrow morning pay a visit to several of the farms. I can pose as a wealthy woman wanting to invest money in a string of polo ponies for my polo playing lover, name and team unnamed. At this point. I'll toss Jay's name around to see what they say about his ponies."

"I bet they have nothing good to say about him. Those farms are pretty toney. They would have no respect for a rancher from this area, no matter how great a breeder he was."

"Oh, I know they'll put him down, but maybe how they denigrate him is more important than that they do. I'll wander around the barns and see if the stable attendants are willing to gossip any. They might be the best source of information." I had done some undercover work at fancy polo farms before. It had almost gotten me killed, but the operative word here was "almost." I was smarter now, and I wasn't dealing with an international drug smuggler this time, was I?

"Are you up to this with your flu and all?"

"I don't have the flu!" I yelled into the phone.

"Geez. Don't get so mad. I'm worried about you, that's all."

"What have you heard?" I asked, trying to keep the suspicion out of my voice. I hoped news about my pregnancy hadn't reached him yet or he might be less willing to let me take on major responsibility in this case.

Lionel had heard my end of the conversation and knew it was Crusty. He leaned toward me and said into the phone. "She's not sick. She's hatching another baby. She'll be fine."

I groaned.

"Is that so?" asked Crusty.

"It could be, but it's not the flu. I'll get back to you as soon as I find out anything."

"Maybe you should take my gun with you," offered Crusty.

"No. Not gonna happen."

"Okay. I've got another idea."

"What?" I asked, but he'd ended the call.

THE NEXT MORNING, I WAS UP EARLY to talk with the managers, owners and stable hands at the polo farms. I had selected an appropriate wardrobe for my visit to the area south and east on the lake and was about to hop into my convertible when I realized my car might not be the best choice for this trip. It was too sporty and not sophisticated enough. How I wished Nappi was available. He would loan me something more appropriate. My choices other than my convertible were Sammy's beat up truck or the van. Neither of them said "bored rich gal." Oh, well. I looked at myself in the bedroom mirror. At least my attire said money. I had on a pair of designer jeans, a silk blouse and my usual footwear—black leather boots with four-inch high heels. I'd donned a long brown wig and tied it back with a coral and teal Hermes scarf. Casual elegance. It would have to do.

As I walked out onto the porch, a black SUV with tinted windows pulled up.

"Nappi!" I cried.

The driver side door opened and a man in a taupe linen shirt and brown pants got out, but it wasn't Nappi.

"What are you doing here?" I put as much scorn in my voice as I could muster on no coffee. It was Jerry, my ex-husband, the bane of my existence. You'd think once a woman divorced a guy, he would butt out of her life, but I think I saw more of Jerry since we severed our legal tie than I had when we were husband and wife. Our too frequent contact was not my doing.

"Crusty called and asked for my help. He told me you needed someone to, uh, babysit, I mean, pose as your driver. He said you were doing some snooping at a few pony farms. I have the car for it." Jerry gestured at the expensive SUV.

"Where did you get that?" I asked. "Is it one of Nappi's? Do you know where he is?"

"He gave it to me."

"Why would he do that?"

"Because he likes me. People do like me, you know."

"Well, there's no accounting for taste," I said, then realized I was insulting Nappi, one of my closest friends. "He may have a soft spot for you. Have you seen him recently? You must have if he turned over the car to you."

"Nope. He left the keys in my mailbox and parked the car in front of my apartment one night."

"Aren't you worried about him?"

"Nappi?" Jerry laughed. "He can take care of himself. Why would I worry about him?"

"Someone should. Nobody has heard from him in days."

Jerry opened the rear door of the SUV for me and gestured me into the back seat. "Did you ever think maybe he doesn't want to be heard from?"

Did Jerry know something no one else did? I slid into the seat and thought about what he had said. He had a point. Nappi had always taken care of himself, and many times he had taken care of me, my friends and my family.

Jerry got into the driver's seat and put the car in gear. "Now where would milady like to go?"

"Let's go bother some wealthy horse breeders with silly questions from a lady with too much money and too much time on her hands."

He trounced on the accelerator, and the car surged ahead spinning gravel and dirt. I looked in Jerry's rearview mirror and saw Lionel shaking his head as if he was watching a bunch of hooligans on their way to a drag race.

"A bit more dignity in your driving, Jerry, please." I reached into my leather shoulder bag, extracted a chocolate bar and held it up so Jerry could see it. "Want one? I've got several."

He shook his head. Good. I didn't have to share. I could eat all five of them. Or maybe that was overkill, even for a pregnant woman.

When we arrived at the first farm, the sense of déjà vu overcame me as we pulled into the long driveway leading to the barns. I had visited a horse facility like this years ago. I was in disguise then also, playing the wife of Jay Cassidy, who was posing as a man interested in buying a string of polo ponies to start his own team. Later, Jay did start his own team, but our initial visit to a polo ranch resulted in tangling with Eduardo, the slick, slimy Argentinian crook. Every time I thought about that man a chill ran up my spine. I shook off the feeling of disgust and fear. Today's visit wouldn't be half so dangerous.

Horses grazed in green fields on either side of the road. It was pastoral, not frightening. Jerry pulled up to the nearest barn, opened my door, and I stepped out holding an empty champagne glass. I handed it to him.

"Geez, Eve," he whispered. "Speaking of dignity. It's only nine thirty in the morning."

"The rich have their own rules," I replied in a haughty voice, then in a whisper added, "It's for show, Jerry. There was nothing in the glass."

"Right, but you have chocolate on your mouth." With a flourish, he pulled a clean linen handkerchief from his pocket and handed it to me. "Ma'am," he said.

A young man dressed in tight fitting jeans and a tee-shirt that hugged his chest muscles emerged from the nearest stable and greeted me with a smile.

I held out my hand to him as if I expected him to kiss it. To my surprise, he did. Classy, I thought, and couldn't help the tingle that ran up my hand and arm.

"I may be of help?" His smile broadened.

"Yes. I'm looking for some polo ponies to buy."

He gave a small chuckle. "The lady is interested in playing?"

I returned the chuckle with a soupcon of dismissiveness in it. "Oh, no. I'm buying them for a friend."

"Ah, yes. I assume you want to keep the friend's name confidential?"

I could hear the quotation marks around the term "friend." This fellow was smooth. And sexy. I mentally kicked myself. My hormones must have been in confused disarray. I had my own sexy guy at home.

"Come this way." He gestured me into the barn ahead of him. Jerry followed us. "My name is Homer Smith. I breed polo ponies for some of the best. You know horses?" he asked.

Smith? I raised one eyebrow in disbelief. He ignored the look. I did not give him my name, and he didn't ask. He was familiar with wealthy women who liked to spend their husband's money and wanted to keep a low profile.

Jerry bumped into Smith, causing his smile to slide into a frown.

"Perhaps your driver would be more comfortable waiting by the car," he suggested.

"He's not my driver. He drives me, but he's my financial advisor. My money guy." I winked at Smith. "And he knows something about horses, don't you, Milton?"

Jerry turned to look behind him for the Milton fellow, then realized I was speaking about him.

"Oh, sure. I love horses."

"Loving them and being a judge of horseflesh are two separate things." Smith gave him a severe look.

I turned to Smith and tapped him on the shoulder. "Now that's what Mr. Cassidy told us earlier today when we visited his ranch. There's one fellow who knows horses, huh, Milton?"

Jerry bobbed his head up and down. The smile that Smith had once more managed when learning Milton was the one with the checkbook slid again into a frown, this one accompanied by a shake of his head.

"I know he bought some horses from that Argentinian fellow when he left the country, and I hear they are fine ponies, but I know nothing more about him. He's not part of our, uh, set. I think you would be better off buying from an established farm."

"Like this one?" I asked.

"You can judge for yourself." He flashed his perfect white teeth. "Let me show you and your, uh, Milton." This time he made eye contact with Jerry and put his arm around Jerry's shoulders as if they were old buddies. Money spoke volumes to Smith.

"I'll wander around while the two of you talk hooves or whatever," I said.

Smith, now intent upon convincing Jerry of the superiority of his ponies, gave me a dismissive wave, friendly, but dismissive. Follow the checkbook, huh, Smith, I thought.

I walked out of the barn and into another stable behind it. I wish Grandy had been available to accompany me this morning. Grandy knew horses. She had ridden when younger, but it was something I never became interested in while growing up. I did love the smell of the horses, however. It was warm, earthy, comforting somehow. And I owed my life to the intervention of the horse that Jay lost in the trailer incident, the one he'd bought off Eduardo. I wondered where she got to. Jay was certain no one could have managed to move her into another trailer. Did she run off? Was there a prize polo pony wandering around in the swamps? I had a soft spot for the gal. I hoped someone would find her and return her to Jay.

"Senora Cassidy?" said a soft voice from a feed and bedding storage area.

I turned to see a short, brown-skinned man holding a bale of straw.

Oh, my gosh. Talk about the past haunting me. It was the man who had worked in Eduardo's stables.

"Oh, it's Carlos, isn't it?"

"Yes."

"How did you recognize me?" I asked. It had been years. I'd worn a disguise that day also, but it was different from the one I had donned today.

"I would always recognize you by your shoes and your height. You are so tall, senora."

He was an observant man. And a kind one. He had tried to help the horses that Eduardo's manager and an uncaring veterinarian were abusing.

"You are still working with horses. You told me you loved them. I hope this place treats them better than Eduardo's did."

"Si. Senor Smith is good to the horses . . ." He stopped speaking as if he intended to add something more.

I nodded. "I'm glad to hear that, and I know you must feel better working for someone who cares about the animals as much as you do."

"He's a little, how do you say, full of himself, but he breeds horses full of spirit, and he does it with care."

"That's good to know."

"You are here with Mr. Jay?"

"Uh, no, but I am working undercover for a detective agency." I told him what happened to Jay's horse and driver.

"You think Senor Smith had something to do with that?"

"I have no reason to think so."

Carlos looked puzzled, so I explained my relationship with Jay was not one of wife and husband and gave him a brief run down on my life since I had last seen him.

"I'm sure you won't tell anyone what I'm up to. I want to visit a few more farms around here today with the same story."

"You know you can trust me." Carlos gave me a broad smile, one I found more sincere than Smith's.

I nodded and patted his hand. "It was good to see you and to know you are happy here. I think I'd better see what Smith and my friend are doing." It had occurred to me that Jerry was enough of an idiot to arrange to buy a few ponies. I needed to stop him before that happened.

As I started to leave the barn, Carlos stopped me.

"I don't know if this is important, but another woman came here a month or so ago asking questions about polo ponies. She mentioned Mr. Jay's name and asked if he was still in the business of raising them."

"A woman? Did she talk to Smith? Do you have a name?"

"No name. Senor Smith was not around. She talked to one of the other grooms."

"What did she look like?"

"I don't know. I only heard her voice because I was tending to a horse in a stall and she was outside the barn. I did not like the sound of her voice. It was cold."

"Can you tell me the name of the other groom?"

"He left here a few days later. I think he moved to another farm. I don't know which one. It might be hard to find him. Workers move around a lot." Carlos toed the straw at his feet and looked up at me with fear on his face.

I knew what that look meant. Some of these men were here without papers, illegals.

"I'll keep everything quiet, but I'd like to find him if I could."

"Juan Mateo. That's the name we knew him by."

I knew it might not be the name he would continue to use when he went to a new position. I was curious about that woman. It sounded as if she knew something about Jay and wanted to know more. I had to find a way to ask Smith about the man without arousing his suspicions.

Smith and Jerry walked into the barn. Carlos turned away and carried the bale of straw into a stall at the far end of the barn.

"You and Carlos talking?" asked Smith.

"Yes. He seems so fond of the horses and his work. He's the kind of man my, uh, the man for whom I'm inquiring about horses might want in his employ, but your man, Carlos, is it? says he is happy here. He did mention another stable hand who left here a few days ago and might be looking for work."

"Who?" Smith asked.

"Juan Mateo."

Smith's face darkened. "Carlos is right. He's no longer here. He left without giving me any notice, so if you find him you might think twice about hiring him."

"Did you find anything, Melvin?" I asked.

"I thought your name was Milton," said Smith.

"Melvin, Milton, whatever," I said with haughty snootiness as if the names of underlings didn't count.

"Yes. Several ponies." Smith replied. "You have my card. I'll hear from you in a few days then?"

WE TRIED SEVERAL OTHER PONY FARMS but learned nothing of interest. Everyone knew Jay's name, everyone respected him, and all the breeders told me how superior their horses were to ones raised on a ranch in the rural community of Sabal Bay. No one seemed to dislike Jay enough to steal one of his horses or harm his driver. It was a wasted morning, unless I could talk to that stable hand from Smith's place and ask about the nosy woman inquiring about Jay's horses. That was probably a dead end also. I slumped down in the back seat as Jerry drove me back to Sabal Bay. I was tired, hungry and disappointed. I rummaged around in my bag and took out another chocolate bar. Grandy would kill me if she knew I was eating all this sugar, but she was in Key Largo and would never know. I took out another bar, but decided I needed real food. I'd wait until we got back home.

My cell rang. It was Jay.

"My driver is out of the hospital, and he's remembering something. The car broken down on the road, the one he stopped to help? A woman was driving it."

"Did he describe her?"

"He didn't get a good look at her before someone hit him. The doctor said his memory for the incident has been affected, but he said he thought she had an accent."

"That's vague. What kind of accent?"

"He's not certain, but maybe he thought it was like those he hears from the workers around here from Guatemala. Central or South American, I'd guess."

Maybe it was the same woman inquiring about Jay at Smith's farm. Many people living around here were Mexican or from countries where their first language was Spanish. I knew Jay was trying to be helpful, but the information wouldn't get us far in the case.

When Jerry dropped me off at my house, my friend, Detective Frida Martinez was sitting on Grandfather's porch with him.

"It's been a long time since we've seen you." I pulled my wig off and dropped into the rocking chair next to her. "Anything new?"

"You go first, Eve. What's with the wig and the chauffer?"

"It's Jerry."

"Since when do you let Jerry drive you around? And where did he get that car?"

"It's for a case Crusty and I are working on. That's all I can say."

"I'm working on something interesting, too."

I waited.

"That's all I can say."

"You're being mean because I won't tell you about my case."

She gave me a wink. "We found a dead body in one of the small canals out in the Deer Path area."

"Anyone we know?" I asked.

"He had a receipt for a money order he sent to Mexico. It was difficult to read because it had been in his pocket and in the water for a while, but the name was Juan Mateo."

CHAPTER 4

———

JUAN MATEO. A NAME I'D HEARD THIS MORNING.

"Interesting," I said to Frida. "What's the story on this guy?"

"I don't know. We checked with the dairy farms and ranches around here. No one recognizes the name. I'll get some of the herd managers and ranch owners to look at the body. I have no other information on him."

I scrutinized her face. Was she telling me this because she was curious about how I might react?

"You think I know something about the guy?"

"You're always poking around. I thought you might have heard something I could use."

I turned over in my mind whether I should tell her what I knew about Mateo. I would tell her, you bet I would, but not right now. How could I explain the circumstances under which I heard the name without revealing why I was nosing around a polo farm? It was too complicated to tell the whole story. I had to keep Jay's name out of this. Could I do that? I decided to talk with Jay before I said anything to Frida. The murder of a man who talked to a woman who had asked about Jay Cassidy as well as the assault of Jay's driver and disappearance of the horse a few weeks later had to be more than coincidental.

"Let me think on this and get back to you," I said.

Frida got out of the chair with reluctance and a disappointed look on her face. She knew I was holding something back but decided to let me reveal what it was in my own time. "I've got to run, but I'll look forward to hearing from you, Eve."

"Sure. Nice to see you."

"Yep." She got into her car and waved goodbye to Grandfather and me.

"What are you keeping from the detective?" asked Grandfather.

"How do you know I'm keeping anything from her?" Well, that was a dumb question. Grandfather could tell what I had on my mind sometimes before even I could.

He smiled and tapped his pipe against the floor of the porch. "Netty and the boys took out the canoe. We might have a mess of fish for dinner tonight."

I rolled around the thought of fried catfish or bass and came up with a big yuk. There was too much fish on the menu of late. I knew it was good for us, but not again. Tonight felt more like a macaroni and cheese night—familiar comfort food to settle my stomach.

"If they catch fish, I'll let you cook them. I'll make something to go with them."

"I'll bet you miss having Nappi stop by here and ask you to join him for ribs and slaw, don't you? Grandfather asked.

I did miss that, but I vowed to eat in a healthier manner with this baby. I'd begin tomorrow.

"I think we all miss Nappi," I said.

Grandfather nodded. "He's a good man. I'll check out the greens in the garden to see if we have some for dinner."

Collard greens were never one of my favorites. Another food good for the diet, but . . . but . . .

"You can have a salad," said Grandfather, again reading my distaste for greens tonight. "Along with your macaroni and cheese."

"I give up," I said. "I have no idea how you do that."

"Do what?" he asked, a twinkle in his eye.

"Know what I'm thinking. That's what."

"You're so easy, Eve. You're almost transparent."

"Okay. What do I want for dessert? Tell me that?"

"Chocolate ice cream, as usual."

As usual, he was right.

SAMMY SOMETIMES BROUGHT HOME BIRDS from his part-time position working at David and Madeleine's game ranch. Today he had procured two quail, so we added roasted bird to our dinner along with the fish and macaroni and cheese.

As we sat down to eat, I noticed Lionel was absent. Had he not gotten wind of the chocolate ice cream, his favorite?

"Where's Lionel?" I asked.

"He told me he had an errand to run and wouldn't be back for a few days," said Grandfather.

"Did you ask him what it was?" asked Sammy.

"He made it clear he didn't want to talk about it," Grandfather said.

"Into the swamp?" I said. He hadn't gone off on one of his journeys to be alone for several months. Maybe he figured it was time again.

Grandfather shook his head. "No. I don't think so. I watched him walk toward the road. A few minutes later, a car stopped and when I looked to see who it was, Lionel was gone. I think he caught a ride. No telling where he went."

"Maybe somebody kidnapped him." I was joking, but inside I had the unsettled feeling Lionel might have followed up on my comment that I'd leave it up to him to find Nappi.

I shoved that thought to the back of my mind, helped clear the table after dinner and loaded the dishwasher.

"Do you want me to build a fire out back?" Sammy asked. "We can have our coffee there tonight."

"Sure. I'll join you in a minute. I've got to check in with Crusty." I took my cellphone to the front porch while Sammy and the rest of the family headed out back.

When I connected with Crusty, I told him what had transpired this morning at Homer Smith's polo farm as well as Frida's mention of the murder of someone called Juan Mateo.

"Coincidental that name coming up at the farm and on the dead man? You don't believe in coincidences any more than I do. I think it's time we have another talk with Jay, don't you? Frida should know about Juan Mateo, and I can't tell her without revealing the circumstances surrounding my hearing the name. We don't want to be impeding a murder investigation, do we?'"

Crusty made unintelligible noises at the other end of the connection.

"Are you chewing on a cigar?" I asked, suspicion clear in my voice.

"I'm chewing on it. Not smoking it," he shot back.

"Oh, good. That way you won't get lung cancer. Just mouth cancer."

He ignored my snide remark. "I'll call Jay tonight and see if he can meet with us tomorrow morning. Are you free?"

"I'll be there in the morning." I would, after I threw up a couple of times, now my morning routine.

AS IT TURNED OUT, MY STOMACH FELT FINE the next morning. I avoided caffeine and drank a glass of orange juice with my scrambled eggs and toast. Crusty had called earlier to say Jay would be in the office at nine. Since we opened the consignment shop at ten, I had time to talk with Jay and be in the shop. I hadn't heard from Madeleine since she had stormed out angry at me, accusing me of saddling her with the burden of the shop because of my pregnancy. I hadn't called her because I felt she had unfairly judged my commitment to our business. I was committed to the shop, although I hadn't given any thought in recent weeks to hiring someone to work the shop, had I? No. I had not. She was right. I assumed the issue would go away or that she would find the solution. Or, as she had said, that she would increase her hours as I incubated the baby and then did newborn duty. I was a bad friend and a worse business partner. I wasn't looking forward to seeing her this morning, but there was nothing I could do about the issue now. I had to focus on Jay's problem. And then there was the nagging worry in the back of my mind about what had happened to Nappi. Where was that man? I was once more in Eve overload. Okay, Eve, I chided myself, get a grip. You can't always count on others to solve your problems. You can work this out. One issue at a time.

Crusty gave me one of his worried looks when I entered the office.

"Wipe that look off your face. I'm not going to throw up all over your boots or your desk or Jay. I'm fine." Maybe this pregnancy would be easier than the last one.

It was a stretch, but Crusty and I were in accord about there being a connection between what I learned at Smith's ranch yesterday and Frida finding the body in the canal. It was time for Jay to talk to the authorities about the hijacking. I suspected Jay's driver had made up a story about how he received his injuries, but, because they were suspicious, I knew the hospital would report them to the police. Frida must have interviewed him and would follow up with Jay. We needed to convince

Jay that he couldn't keep the event under wraps. He had to understand we were giving him our best detective advice.

When Jay appeared in the office, and Crusty and I tried to be persuasive about the importance of him telling Frida about the hijacking, he wasn't convinced. Until I told him what he already knew.

"Your reputation as a rancher, breeder and trainer of polo ponies is golden. No one would suspect you of anything underhanded. Even the hoity toity rich boys on the polo farms I visited yesterday said your stock was great. They may have told me you were a country boy, but they didn't denigrate your expertise. If there's any negative feeling toward you, it's jealousy at how well you're doing in only a few years in the business. This could be part of something bigger." I'd keep the matter to myself for now.

Jay shifted in his chair and looked down at his boots as if he *was* a humble country boy. His pose didn't fool me. He knew he was good.

"So how about it?" said Crusty. "Can we bring Detective Martinez in on this now?"

Jay nodded. "Give her a call. I'll talk to her about my driver and the missing horse. I guess there's no sense in paying for your expertise if I won't follow your advice. Seems a stretch to me, but you're the detectives."

"I'll leave you to it. I've got to mend a few fences," I said.

"Why does that not shock me?" said Jay.

I gave him a look of surprise. We had once disagreed about land use here, but I thought we had made up. Was I wrong?

"Kidding, Eve," he said, giving my arm a friendly pat as I arose to leave.

"He means it's your aggravating manner. We've all been there with you," said Crusty.

I was not aggravating. I was decisive. Opinionated.

WHEN I LEFT CRUSTY'S, I mentally prepared myself to talk with Madeleine, to tell her she was right about how I took her for granted and to promise her I would do better. I expected to find her alone, setting up the cash register for the day's business, but there was another woman with her. Her back was to me, and she was hanging newly consigned dresses on a rack. Had Madeleine hired someone without consulting me? When the woman turned around, I couldn't believe my eyes.

"Renata! What are you doing here?" I rushed over and threw my arms around her. Sammy's mother had left here not long ago after paying us a visit. At that time, she had helped us in the store and had proven herself to have a good eye for the kind of merchandise that would sell here. She was so good, in fact, that I let her visit our clients in West Palms to pick up what they had to offer. She managed to talk many of them out of items they might not have let go of, and she encouraged them to convince their friends to consign with us.

"I got back to Las Vegas and settled in to my position as a dealer again, but then decided I'd had enough of the gambling life." Her tone of voice said it was more than the need to move on from a casino position.

"What's up?" I asked her.

Renata was about to reply when the bell on the front door tinkled and a customer walked into the shop.

"I'll take care of this," Madeleine said, touching my arm as she passed. "You two need to talk."

I led Renata to our back room and closed the door.

"I quit my job at the casino." She threw herself into a chair.

"Okay." I didn't want to say anything to interrupt her story. I gave her a tiny smile of encouragement.

"I'm too old to be fending off the advances of customers, to be dressing in low cut blouses and to be making nice with drunks. I'm tired. I need a better life. Would you consider hiring me here? I understand you need help."

Oh boy. Did I.

"And," she continued, "the casino changed hands. The new boss is a creep who can't keep his hands off any of the female employees. All the gals need the work, so they don't want to make waves. I'm willing to take my case to a lawyer, but meantime, I don't need to deal with the boss man one moment longer. I'm out of there. I'll go back if the case goes to trial and I need to testify, but for now, I want to be here with my family. I miss all of you."

"Even Lionel?" I said, chiding her.

I thought for a moment she wasn't going to answer me. She dropped her gaze and shifted around in the chair as if the seat had become uncomfortable, then she met my gaze. "Well, no, but when I arrived here yesterday, I got in touch with him and told him I was here, perhaps on a permanent basis. He didn't like it, but he has no say over my decisions. How are you and he getting along?"

"We've reached an armistice."

"Good."

"Uhm, I'll have to run this by Madeleine. We need someone here, that's not an issue, but I can't make that decision without conferring with her."

The door opened and Madeleine stepped in "No sale. She was browsing. Did you offer her the position, Eve, or do I have to do everything?" She said it with a straight face as if she remained angry at me, but the corners of her mouth twitched, and she broke into a grin.

"You're hired," Madeleine and I said in unison, and we grabbed one another for a group hug and did a little threesome jig across the room.

I felt as if the three of us were meant to be coworkers.

"I'm curious, Renata. How did you get in touch with Lionel? He doesn't have a cell." I also wondered why she had talked with him but hadn't gotten in touch with Sammy and me.

"That's kind of funny. I rented a car at the airport and was on my way to the house, about to turn into the drive when I saw Lionel at the side of the road, so I stopped. He said he needed a ride to the bus station, so I offered to drive him back into town to catch the next bus."

"A bus? To where?"

"You know how he is. He doesn't like to reveal much and particularly to me."

Renata and Lionel had once been married—I didn't know if they had divorced--but Lionel fled to the swamps after their son Sammy was born. Renata tried to live here and to teach Sammy tribal ways. She was lonely and felt she couldn't raise her son as she should, so with Grandfather's blessing, she left Sammy with him. Lionel may have married a white woman, but he had little use for white folks in general. I think the only white person here he liked was Nappi.

"You don't know where he was going?" I asked.

"Well, don't be silly. I know. You're not the only gal who likes to snoop. I waited until he got his ticket, then pretended to leave, but I hid out behind the station and watched him get on a bus headed for Miami."

"I wonder why he was interested in going to Miami," I said.

Renata shrugged. "After all these years, I've stopped wondering why Lionel does anything."

I wondered if his abrupt departure had anything to do with Nappi. Was he trying to find him?

The doorbell jingled, and Jay stepped into the store. The storm clouds in his expression told me he wasn't here to shop, but I ignored the warning of a bad mood.

"Looking for a dress or something more intimate like a nightie?" I asked.

"Don't play with me, Eve. This is all your fault."

"What's up?" I asked.

"Frida came into Crusty's right after you left. I took a call while she was there. It was from my friend in Chokoloskee. I told him I could send another polo pony his way, and he wondered when I might do that. Frida overheard the call and said I should hold off until she investigated the hijacking in greater detail. She also thinks there might be some relationship between a body she found and the hijacking. You and Crusty didn't tell me about that. Did you put that idea in her head?"

I tried to give Jay my best innocent look, but I knew it wasn't working, so I decided I had to deny involvement in anything Frida said. "Frida's got a murder on her hands as well as the hijacking. Two crimes in this area? Unusual, wouldn't you think?"

Jay would not be placated. "I assume your wild imagination put this together, and you roped Frida into thinking in a similar vein. The point is I can't delay getting another horse to him. Who knows how long her investigation will last? I'm in the business of selling horses, not twiddling my thumbs while the police follow some silly lead, a lead you gave them." Jay was so spitting mad that his face reddened, and he swung his arms around like a crazy man. He accidentally hit one of the dress rounds, knocking the hats which sat on top of it off onto the floor. It teetered on one of its legs, then righted itself with a shudder.

Jay gave the scene a glance, shook his head in disgust and banged through the door. We watched him jump into his truck and lay rubber out of the parking lot.

"Got yourself in the middle of some murder case?" asked Renata.

"Of course," said Madeleine.

The two of them returned to organizing the shop.

"I'll take care of the mess," I said.

"No, I will," said Madeleine, taking out her cell and punching in a number.

I couldn't hear what she said, but when she was finished she disconnected. "Jay will be back here in a minute to straighten up the mess he made."

Jay's truck pulled up outside, and he once more entered the store. This time, his eyes were downcast with a look of utter shame on his face.

"Sorry, ladies. My temper got away from me, as Mizz Madeleine pointed out to me." He began picking up hats and making certain the dress round was back in the correct position and that it was stable.

Once finished, he tipped his hat to us and walked toward the store exit. On his way past me, he whispered, "It was all your fault, you know."

"Oh, sure. Thanks for your patronage and come again." I turned my back to him to hide my smile.

CHAPTER 5

—

"**W**HAT DID HE SAY TO YOU ON THE WAY OUT?" asked Madeleine. I tossed a pair of panties onto the shelf. "He says it's my fault." "You think the apology wasn't real."

"No, it was. He was embarrassed at how he behaved toward you two, but he's angry at me. He'll get over his mad. He always does." I leaned back against the counter and smiled at Renata. "I have an idea. How would you like to accompany me to the coast to pick up some merchandise this afternoon? I'll have to make a stop at the horse rescue facility before we do that. They called this morning to say they might have a pony for Netty."

"Good idea," said Madeleine.

"Great," said Renata.

ON THE WAY OUT OF TOWN, I kept looking at Renata. She seemed distracted as if she wanted to say something to me but wasn't sure she should. Maybe she hadn't heard I was pregnant. It seemed as if everyone already knew, but she had arrived last night.

"Something on your mind?" I asked.

She shook her head.

"I guess I should tell you . . ."

"Oh, I know you're pregnant again, Eve. That's so great. You look healthier this time." She leaned over and kissed my cheek.

"I guess everyone knows, and I didn't tell anyone. Odd, isn't it?"

"It's this family. The Egrets have a way of seeing into your . . ."

"Soul?" I asked.

"Yes."

We drove in silence until we hit the Canopy Road to the coast.

"I'm so happy about the pregnancy," she said.

"You already told me that. What's up?"

"You must be wondering why I didn't stop by the house after I dropped Lionel at the bus station."

"I guess I assumed you wanted to surprise me at the shop."

"That's not it."

"Oh. Then what?"

"Lionel and I didn't go right to the bus station. We stopped off for something to eat and we got talking and . . ."

Why couldn't she come right out with it? "What?" I yelled at her.

"We kind of renewed our acquaintance."

Huh? I had no idea what she meant. They had no "acquaintance." They parted ways when Sammy was small. They lived in separate states. The only time they were acquainted was in the first years of the marriage when they had Sammy. Could it be . . . "Oh. No. You didn't."

"Lionel and I spent the night together."

I slammed on the brakes and pulled off onto the narrow shoulder.

"It doesn't mean anything. Honest."

"How could it not? You hate each other for decades and then you jump into bed with him. Your ex-husband?"

"We never got divorced."

Right. Why would you divorce a man who barely talked to you, wandered off into the swamps for twenty-five years, and left you with a son to raise? That's what I would do.

"You're angry," she said.

"No, no. I'm shocked." And maybe a little disappointed in her judgment.

Someone blew their horn from behind and then swerved around us, giving me a rude hand gesture on the way past.

I pulled back onto the pavement and continued down the road in silence.

"Eve, say something."

"I don't understand."

"Either do I," Renata confessed.

We looked at each other and then burst into laughter.

"Oh, those Egret men," I said.

"I'll work it out," Renata said, but her tone was less than convincing.

At the rescue facility, the manager showed me a little, brown pony with a blonde tail and mane.

"She wanted a black and white one," I said.

The manager sighed and gave me look that said she had better things to do other than deal with me. "We're a rescue facility, not a department store for selling horses."

"I know, and I'm sorry, but she was very specific," I said. "I may be into saving a pony, but she's . . ."

"She's kind of spoiled, and her older brothers got the horses they wanted," said Renata. "Sorry, Eve, but you know it's true."

I sighed and nodded.

"I get it, but if you turn down this one, I don't know when we'll get another pony. I do have another family who wants a pony, but you're first on the list. What do you say?"

I could tell the manager was getting to the end of her patience.

"I'll give you a few minutes to talk about it. I've got a horse coming in soon, and I need to get a stall ready for her." She walked away, muttering to herself and shaking her head.

"Netty will be so disappointed, if she doesn't get a pony soon." I didn't add that everyone would be disappointed if they had to listen to her whining for much longer.

"I know my granddaughter. She won't be happy with a brown pony. And I'm pretty sure this is a boy not a girl," said Renata.

I hesitated several more moments then decided the pony deserved someone who wanted him, not another pony. I caught up to the manager and told her what I thought.

"That's smart of you. All rescues deserve the best families, ones who feel as if the horse was meant for them. I'll be in touch." She turned to watch a horse trailer pull into the drive." I think that's the horse I told you about." She hurried away, signaling the driver to follow her toward one of the barns.

"I'm glad I didn't tell Netty I was stopping by here today to check out the pony."

"Something will come up. If not a rescue, we can go to a livestock auction. They must have one around here close," said Renata. "I could ask . . ." She stopped midsentence.

"I'll ask Sammy," I said, knowing she was about to indicate she'd talk with Lionel about an auction. I figured there were more important things they should talk about.

"Look," she said, noting the concerned look on my face, "I don't understand what happened with us either, but I need time to think about it, so don't tell anyone, especially not Sammy."

I wouldn't say a word, but given the Egret family's ability to read minds or something like it, I couldn't promise that Sammy or his grandfather didn't already know.

WE PICKED UP A FEW ITEMS from some of our usual consignors. I introduced Renata to the ones she hadn't already met on her earlier visit and informed them she would be working with us and stopping by for merchandise. They gave her the once over as wealthy matrons often did, but she won their confidence when she began talking about designer clothing and high-end furnishings.

On the way home, I thought what a find for the shop Renata was. We didn't get a pony for Netty, but I counted the trip a success, and smiled to myself. Maybe Renata getting involved with Lionel wasn't so bad. It could mean she would like to relocate back here for good. I mentally slapped myself. I was being selfish.

I made my turn onto the Beeline from the turnpike, and we headed north. I was exhausted, but it was emotional fatigue. I'd be happy to get back to the shop and drop off the merchandise. My cell chirped. I looked at the caller ID. It was Jay.

"You calling to say you're still mad or did you come to your senses and forgive me?" Did I sound too smug?

"Let's not talk about that now. As I said, I need to send another horse to my friend, and I'm thinking I need a tough guy to do the driving. And I thought to myself, who survived in the swamps alone for decades and took a bullet rescuing his family and survived?"

"Lionel? You want Lionel to drive for you?"

"What do you think?"

"I think it's a horrible idea. I think you should let this whole thing go until the police have found who beat up your driver and took your horse."

The line sent dead for a moment.

"Are you there, Jay?

"I talked to Crusty about this. He liked the idea."

"No, he didn't. He told you to tell Frida what you were planning, but you're not going to, are you? You don't think she can do her job, do you? Is it because she's a woman?"

"Now, don't go getting Yankee uppity on me, Eve. I want to know how to get in touch with Lionel. I called Grandfather, but he says he hasn't seen him today, that he left yesterday and hasn't been back to the house since then. For some reason, he thought Renata might know where he is."

"You told Grandfather Renata was here?"

"No. He already knew."

I glanced over at Renata. "Your story is already in the wind."

"Can I talk to her?" asked Jay.

I rolled my eyes and turned the phone over to Renata. She listened for a minute, then said, "I'll tell him you want to talk with him. He can take it from there."

She handed the phone back to me, but Jay had disconnected.

"Let's drop the merchandise at the store and then you can come with me to the house. It's obvious everyone already knows you're here."

She nodded. "Do you think Lionel is as tough as Jay believes?"

Without hesitation, I said, "Yes, I do. Don't you?"

"That's always been his problem. Sadness, anger and mistrust hidden behind a skin of steel." She turned her face to look out the passenger's side window.

I wanted to tell her I believed there was more behind the steel, that Lionel was also a man of compassion and love for his family. Oh, not that those were dominant attributes, but they were emerging. Otherwise why had he left the swamps? He came back for Sammy and now he had his grandchildren. I screwed my face up in a grimace. I found the man so, so annoying.

SLEEP ELUDED ME THAT NIGHT. Perhaps it was because of the excitement of having Renata here and Sammy's and the children's happiness at seeing her and knowing she would stay, if not forever, then for the foreseeable future. I sat on a log at the water's edge and watched the moon rise over the canal. Someone touched my shoulder and I jumped, almost falling off my seat.

"Lionel. What are you doing here?"

"I live here, you know. I'd think you'd be smart enough to stay away from the canal at this time of night. This is when the gators like to hunt. You'd be a stringy piece of meat for them, but they might be desperate."

I couldn't make out the features of his face in the shadows, but I thought I heard him suppress a chuckle.

"Renata was here tonight, but I'll bet you already know that and have been hiding out all evening instead of coming in and joining us."

"I already saw her."

"So I heard." I patted the log next to me. "Sit down. You can protect me if a gator comes along looking for a snack."

He sat and stretched out his legs in front of him, arms crossed over his chest.

"You want to see Nappi?" he asked.

AT BREAKFAST I TOLD THE FAMILY that I had gotten a call from Grandy who wanted me to come to Key Largo this afternoon to pick up some items for the consignment shop.

At the shop I told Madeleine I would work this morning and leave for Key Largo around noon.

"Will that work?" I wanted to make certain Madeleine didn't view my trip as ducking my responsibility at the shop.

"I don't recall Grandy being into designer wear other than what she buys from us," said Madeleine.

I gave a nervous laugh, "She was given some clothes from a friend, Tommy Bahama stuff."

"Who will be the consignor? Grandy or the friend? I think you should meet the friend in person, don't you, kind of get a take on who she is?"

Oh, oh. She was suspicious about my trip and was trying to find out more about it.

"Are we running a background check on our consignors now?" I knew that would put her off the scent.

"I guess your hormones are running the show this morning. You're in a twitchy, bitchy mood," said Madeleine.

It wasn't my hormones that were dictating my behavior. I had lied to the family and to Madeleine. Grandy hadn't called me. I had called her to arrange for a boat Max could captain. Lionel said he would meet me at the marina in Key Largo. No one was to know what we had planned. Not even Nappi. Especially not Nappi, who both of us knew would find himself another place to hide if he thought we were coming.

"Sorry," I said to Madeleine.

"Don't worry about it. I know what you're going through. Tell Grandy we miss her." Madeleine gave me a big smile. Was that a smile of encouragement and understanding or a suspicious smile? My guilty conscience was getting to me.

I TOLD LIONEL LAST NIGHT I'd drive him to Key Largo, but he insisted he didn't need the ride.

"I have a few more arrangements to make down there," he said.

I thought about what I was getting into. Lionel had been short on details and long on insistence that this was the one chance we'd have of finding Nappi. I wanted to believe him.

"If he's smart, he'll move in a few days," he said.

"Why would he do that?" I asked.

"Because he'll be giving this a lot of thought and will arrive at the conclusion that I'll find him. Or that someone will," Lionel replied.

"Who?" I had asked last night, but there was no response. Lionel had left me alone by the canal.

Now I had a million questions and no answers. How could Lionel find Nappi if no one else knew where he was? I dismissed my doubts. If Lionel could find his way around the swamps of Florida, he could find his way to our old friend.

I parked my convertible in the lot next to the marina in Key Largo where Max and Grandy said they'd meet me. I locked the car, got out and smelled the fresh sea air, then strolled down the line of boats docked there.

"Hey, Eve," yelled Grandy, waving to me from several boats down.

We hugged each other and stepped aboard the boat, an older Chris Craft inboard cabin cruiser.

"Whose boat?" I asked her.

"A friend's," she replied.

Max came out of the cabin, and I gave him a kiss on the cheek.

"Thanks for this," he said. "I don't know what you have in mind, but this gives me a chance to captain this old tub. I've always admired it and told my friend I'd take care of her while he spent some time visiting his daughter up north. I might want to buy the old gal. She's a beaute, isn't she?"

I'm not much one for boats, but she was lovely with her teak wood trim, a cabin that slept four and a small galley.

"Is Lionel here yet?" I asked as I settled onto one of the deck chairs.

"Lionel?" Grandy said. "What would he be doing down here?"

The boat dipped as someone stepped on board.

"Permission to come aboard, captain," said a man dressed in a colorful tropical shirt, white slacks and deck shoes. His hair was tied back in a low pony tail.

I couldn't believe my eyes. It was Lionel all duded up in yachting garb. If not for his height, he could be taken for a rich Cuban from Miami.

He shook hands with Max and gave Grandy a warm embrace. I received a mischievous grin.

"Do you like my disguise?" he asked.

I nodded in mute astonishment.

"Where are we going?" Max asked.

Lionel pulled one of the charts from the storage pocket by the helm. "Here," he said pointing to a point north of the Keyes. Lionel looked around the small boat. "I hope you have a small rubber raft stowed here somewhere. We're going to need it to get ashore."

"We could dock here." Max pointed to a spot on the chart.

"I know, but I don't want anyone there to know we're around."

"There's no raft aboard, but I'll run down to the Randalls's and borrow theirs. Back in a jiff." Max jumped off the boat.

"You told me I couldn't ask any questions, but . . ." I began.

"Maybe she's not allowed to ask anything, but I will." Grandy stepped forward and confronted Lionel. It was an incongruous sight: my short, chubby Grandy toe-toe with someone aa foot taller than her. "What's going on?"

"We're on a treasure hunt for a man who doesn't want to be found because he thinks he's protecting everyone," Lionel said.

CHAPTER 6

—

"THAT SOUNDS LIKE SOMETHING YOU DID, Lionel," I said. Lionel knew what I meant. He hadn't wanted to be found when he left for the swamps.

"I was as wrong to abandon my friends and family as is he," said Lionel.

"That almost sounds like an apology for what you put Sammy through all those years."

Lionel turned on me, and I thought for a moment the anger I saw on his face might erupt into something physical, but instead he dropped his gaze and spoke in a low voice. "That's between me and Sammy."

"No, it's not, Lionel. What you did affected the whole family, and it left such an impression on Sammy that it haunts him to this day. And you know that."

"And now it also haunts you because you love Sammy," Lionel said.

I nodded.

"I cannot undue those years, but I can do better now. Finding my friend and yours is part of how I can make it up to you."

Any anger I might have been harboring for Lionel was swept away by the sincerity I saw on his face and heard in his words. "I appreciate it, Lionel. More than I can say."

Our gazes locked for a moment. "I hope Nappi appreciates my efforts," Lionel said.

"How can he not? You and he shared a hospital room together. You're buds. But I'm curious, how do you know this is where he's hiding?"

"Because he brought me to this place once. I promised I'd never tell anyone. He expects me to keep that promise, but I'm willing to betray him because I think he needs us."

MAX RETURNED, HAULING A SMALL RUBBER DINGY which he pitched onto the boat deck. "Tie that down, and we'll get under way."

It was a beautiful day to be on the water. The sky was a brilliant blue, the water calm as we made our way north from Key Largo. Had we not been on a rescue mission, I would have enjoyed the ride. As it was, I didn't understand what was going on with Nappi and why he had abandoned all his past to hide here. I think Lionel understood his impulse to hide and reckoned it had to do with protecting others, but he didn't understand what Nappi was hiding from.

I watched as the bridge which crossed from the Keys onto Card Sound Road appeared ahead of us. It arose out of the mangroves on either side. At its northern end, I spotted boats docked at the bar there, and I could hear music coming across the water. We were too far out to see if the place was busy today, but, since it was a weekday, I suspected it would be quiet. The establishment got most of its trade on weekends. The locals who lived aboard some of the beaten-up houseboats docked on the nearby mangrove canal and a few fishermen stopping by for a beer on their way back from a morning on the water hung out at the bar and restaurant during the week.

Lionel directed Max to maneuver the boat behind one of the mangrove islands. No one from land could see us anchored here.

"Let's go, Eve." Lionel threw the dingy into the water and steadied the craft while I stepped off the dive platform on the boat and into the smaller craft. He handed me a paddle and joined me in the dingy.

"You know how to paddle?" he asked me.

Well, no, but I'd never admit that to him.

"Oh sure." I dipped the paddle in the water.

"You might want to use the other end of the paddle. It works better."

I shot him an embarrassed look and tried the broader end. He was right. It worked like a charm.

"We'll beach the dingy on the other side of the bar between it and the first house boat."

"You mean the boat that's half underwater?"

"Yep. We won't be seen by anyone at the bar because we're hidden by the garbage dumpster. There's no one living on the half-sunken house boat."

We tied the raft to the rickety dock by the houseboat and stepped ashore.

"Oh, gator guts," I said.

Lionel looked as I held up my foot.

"Something bite you?' he asked.

"No, I stepped in the mud. My shoe got sucked in, and I lost it. Do you have any idea what that shoe cost me?"

Lionel shook his head. "No, and I don't care."

"Well, not that much. I bought them at a yard sale." I shrugged, pulled off the other and tossed it into the backpack I wore. "I'm not digging through all that muck to find it." One shoe lost in the mud was understandable, but if I'd tossed the other in after it, it would be littering.

I stepped carefully through the weeds at the water's edge, up the bank and onto the sand. We kept to the cover of the spindly cabbage palms and Norwegian pines that edged the road and walked without a sound past several houseboats that also looked abandoned until we came to one where dingy laundry hung off the back. We crept by, tiptoed onto the boat next to it, and tapped at its door.

"This is where he is?" I asked in a whisper. "I can't believe that." My dapper, well-dressed friend in this dump? No way.

The door opened a crack. A steel gray pistol materialized through the opening. It was ugly and deadly, not at all what I was expecting.

"Go away," said a voice coming from the full-bearded man behind the gun.

"Is that you, Nappi? It's me. Eve. Lionel is with me."

The door swung open and a hand pulled me into the boat. Lionel shouldered his way in behind me.

The man under all that facial hair had Nappi's brown eyes, but that was where the similarity ended. He was dressed in cut-off jeans, a yellowed shirt that I guess had once been white and was bare foot.

"Put down the gun," said Lionel. "We're here to help you."

"You can help me by getting out of here. Did anyone see you?" Nappi pushed a thin curtain back from the window to scan the boat next door.

"I don't understand, Nappi. All the ways I used to contact you are dead ends. What is going on?" I asked.

Nappi placed the gun on the table and sank onto a chair.

"This is it. This is all that's left of me. I own nothing else, and if you check, you won't find my name on this boat either. Nappi Napolitani doesn't exist any longer."

The man in front of me wasn't the man I knew. This man appeared to be utterly defeated, alone, sad and cut off from the world.

I reached out to encircle him with a comforting embrace to bring back my old friend.

"Tell us what's going on," I said.

Lionel snorted. He was having none of it. "I don't want to hear a story filled with self-pity. I didn't come here to spend my time holding your hand. I came to help get you out of this mess. I've been where you are. I know you think you're doing the right thing, but I know you're not. What's up? And can you get Eve here a glass of water? She's worried and exhausted."

"And pregnant," I added.

Nappi jumped out of his chair and rushed to the sink where he ran water into a glass and handed it to me.

"You okay?" His brown eyes filled with concern.

"I think I'm getting the hang of this pregnancy thing. I'm not so sick this time."

Before he and I could say more about my condition, Lionel broke in. "What do you mean you don't own anything? You're one of the wealthiest men I know."

"Not any more. All my accounts have been closed, my properties in foreclosure, some sold already. Even my off-shore accounts are no longer mine. I have no idea how this happened."

"Get off your duff and take action. Your friends will help you and so will the men who worked for you," Lionel said.

"I can't. I've been warned off. Whoever is doing this got to my grandfather. Someone made his death look natural, but it wasn't. I got a letter from him before he died. He told me he was being watched. I think that someone wanted me to know his death was murder. It was a warning that they could get to me also. Then I received a note saying I should not interfere in your lives or those of my family and business associates.

'Interfere'? That's an implied threat." He barked a derisive laugh. "How could I? I've got nothing I can use to be of help to anyone."

"You're going to sit back and not find out who killed your grandfather or who was responsible for removing your identity and everything associated with it?" asked Lionel.

"I think the responsible party believes I'm out of the picture. If I stay that way, I don't think they'll do anything to you or anyone I know."

If Nappi thought his inaction was fending off whoever was behind this, I didn't. There was something nasty and evil about all of this. "You can't think doing what they want will mean everyone is safe. I don't think they want just your money. They're after something else. Whoever did this to you isn't finished. This is the beginning. Staying here and hiding out isn't going to save anyone."

"You're so certain, Eve." said Nappi. "Has something happened?'

"Not that we know about, but don't you feel as if something is coming? Because you've so effectively disappeared, whoever is behind this must be frantic to locate you. They'll want to make certain your hands are tied. They'll find you. We did," said Lionel.

"I've been careful. Only you know about this place," Nappi said, but his voice didn't sound as certain as I would have expected.

"The person responsible for doing this to you has an agenda we can't see yet. I'll bet they are looking for you right now. They'll want to see you suffer, and they know removing your money and influence is not enough. What's most important to you is what's important to all of us. Family and friendship. Loyalty."

Nappi said nothing for several minutes. He walked to the window over the galley and looked out over the water.

"I think you're right, Eve. It feels to me as if there's more involved here than making Nappi a poor man." Lionel put his hand on Nappi's shoulder. "We've got to do something."

I agreed. But what?

I joined Nappi at the window and scrutinized the mangroves. Had the people involved found him already? Had we led them to him without meaning to? Perhaps we were already in the middle of this macabre dance.

"This is all conjecture, Eve." Nappi put his arm around my shoulders.

"Call it what you like, conjecture, a hunch or whatever. I think she's right," said Lionel. "She's a durn snoopy woman who's often right."

Nappi looked into my face. "You know there are plenty of reasons why people would want to target me."

I pulled away from him. How could I make him understand? I knew there was more than Nappi involved here. "I thought you were proud of my work as a PI," I said.

His forehead wrinkled in an expression of puzzlement. "I am."

"Then why did you insult me by not coming to me to help you find out who is doing this to you, to all of us?"

Lionel nodded. "She's right. You show little faith in her snooping skills."

Nappi swept a hand across his brow. "What can I do?"

"Nothing. Stay hidden. Keep them off guard. They'll continue to look for you. Meantime we'll keep vigilant and make certain everyone is safe," Lionel said.

"Didn't you say you have contacts at the FBI?" I asked.

"Yes, but I'm not certain how reliable they are."

"As in, they might be involved?"

Nappi thought for a moment. "I don't know."

"Well, I need a snoop with credentials. Let me think about this." What I didn't want to share with Nappi is that I might have to reveal Nappi's plight to Frida and hope she would use some of her contacts to dig up information on who might want to harm Nappi. Before I took that step, there was another person I might contact. It was a long shot, because this guy might not be the right position to get information, and he also wasn't a fan of mine. We'd met once. He and his partner rescued me when I had been dumped on a dirt road alongside a canal known to be the favorite habitat of large alligators. My presence ruined a drug bust the two of them had been working. Would he remember me? If he did, was that to my advantage or disadvantage?

"Do you have something up your sleeve, Eve?" asked Nappi.

"Maybe."

"Do you want to share?"

I shook my head. "Not now. It may come to nothing. I might have to use your contacts in the FBI."

Nappi dropped his arm from my shoulder. "I hope not, and I also hope you aren't thinking of contacting Frida about this. You know she thinks I'm a fancy dressed thug."

"She does not," I said, my voice firm. "She thinks you're, uhm, connected."

"Tell her not anymore." Nappi gave me weak smile.

There was a knock on the door.

"Hey, neighbor. I've got some fresh snapper I caught for you."

Lionel and I exchanged worried looks.

"Leave them outside," Nappi called through the door.

"Not a good idea. The sea gulls might swoop down and get 'em."

"I'm busy with something right now. I'll open the door a bit and you can hand them through. Thanks for thinking of me."

"I got somethin' else, A bottle of corn liquor. Bet you never had any, have ya?"

"Guy's insistent, isn't he?" I whispered to Nappi.

"I'll even share with your friends."

"He knows someone is here with you," said Lionel. "We'd better let him in and see why he's snooping around."

Lionel jerked the door open and the guy who appeared to have had his ear up against the wood to listen, jumped back.

"You're a big one, ain't ya?" he said to Lionel.

"Who are you?" Lionel's face bore a grim and unwelcoming expression.

"Name's Darby Dunlop." The man, a scrawny fellow, dirty, and with a week's worth of beard, baggy cut-offs and a loose, long-sleeved, faded and torn shirt, stepped inside and plopped a stringer of fish onto the table. He stuck out his hand.

Lionel ignored it. The man managed to sidle past him and approach me. He smelled of fish and sweat.

"Hey there, pretty lady. You this guy's girlfriend?" Darby raised his eyebrows and waggled them at me. "Hmmm?"

"I'm . . ." I started to say, but Nappi intervened.

"As you can see, Darby, I have company, or I'd ask you to stay."

"Naw, don't worry. I want to get your take on this liquor here." He shoved a mason jar containing a clear liquid at Nappi. "Take a swing."

Nappi gave a small sigh and seemed to decide the only way to get the man out of here was to comply with his request.

Nappi unscrewed the top and lifted the jar to his lips.

"No!" I jumped in front of him and grabbed the jar. "Don't be rude. Ladies first."

"Now I know you're eager to taste some, but you're AA, my love. Let me." Lionel removed the jar from my hands. "Let's sit down, and I'll find a couple of glasses. It' not right to drink fine booze standing up."

What was Lionel up to?

Darby smiled an uncertain smile, surprised at Lionel's friendly about-face.

"You folks from around here?" asked Darby, smacking his lips at the taste of the brew.

"No, they aren't. Nice of you to bring by the booze, Darby, but we were on our way out to dinner." Nappi rolled the glass around in his fingers, put it to his lips, but I could see he didn't drink any.

"Going down the road then for some conch fritters? They're the specialty of the house." Darby said this as if he were talking about a fine dining establishment, not a backwater bar and grill.

"I thought I'd take everyone to a place in Key Largo," said Nappi. "We won't want to miss the early bird specials, so we should get going."

"Have one for the road," said Darby, tipping another splash of the booze into his glass and the remainder of the jar's contents into Nappi and Lionel's. He gave me a rueful look. "Too bad you don't get to join us."

"I think that's enough." Lionel's earlier stern manner was back. He grabbed the jar, the stringer of fish and the collar of Darby's shirt and walked him to the door. Lionel reached over and opened the door, then put the fish and jar into Darby's hands, shoved him through the door and slammed it behind him.

Through the window I watched Darby steady himself on the houseboat's deck. He looked back at the closed door and raised his arm to give us a wave of goodbye. The sun through the mangroves glinted off the watch he wore and created bright circles of light which reflected off the water. The watch was large, gold and familiar.

I grabbed Nappi's arm.

"Where's your watch, your Rolex?" I asked, wondering how Darby managed to lift it off his arm without anyone realizing it.

"I tossed it. It wasn't the kind of thing a poor, down-and-out guy living on this dump of a boat would wear."

"I think it's now in the possession of your neighbor. I wonder how he got it?" I said. "It's so showy people would notice it, like whoever is behind all this misfortune."

"No one knows I'm here, so why would the responsible party be nosing around this place?" Nappi asked. "You're being paranoid."

"No. I'm being cautious."

CHAPTER 7

—

My cell rang as Lionel and I were saying good-bye. It was Grandy. "A marine patrol boat has come by here twice. I think they wonder what we're up to. The next time they're going to stop and ask," said Grandy.

"That will draw attention," I said. "We'll be there in five minutes."

I hugged Nappi and told him we would be in touch. He'd ditched his cell phone so communication wouldn't be easy, but we promised we'd make contact somehow.

"I don't think we should chance coming here again," said Lionel. "and I recommend you keep an eye on your neighbor. Darby is too nosy. He might go down to the bar and blab."

Nappi smiled and nodded. "I can take care of myself, even without money and contacts."

As we paddled out to the boat, I said to Lionel, "Are you worried also? Did we make a mistake coming here?"

"Whoever is after Nappi or us has far reaching influence. It couldn't have been easy doing what they did to Nappi. Eventually, they'll find him."

"We need to find out what's going on and who is behind this." I dipped my paddle in the water and stroked with all my strength.

"You're getting good at this," Lionel said. "For such a skinny gal you've got arm strength."

Nice compliment, but I knew I'd feel it in my shoulders tomorrow.

"We're glad you're back." Max helped haul the raft on board. "There's the marine patrol boat returning for another look."

"Anyone else?" I rolled my shoulders to relieve the ache building there.

"A few other boats came by, but then headed south or circled around the island as if they were heading toward the bar. Other than the marine patrol no one has given us much attention," Grandy said. "Oh, wait. There's the Boston whaler that came by earlier."

The boat flew by us on plane giving us a wide berth. The fellow piloting it waved, then the boat sped on by heading for Key Largo. I noted the name on the boat, *Eddie's Plaything*.

Max had Lionel pull anchor, and we also headed for Key Largo.

We tied up at the marina, and Max returned the raft.

"Something to eat before you head back?" Grandy knew me. I was always willing to eat.

"Lionel?" I asked.

He grunted, which I took for a yes.

"There's a place right here on the canal that has good food," said Grandy.

"Do they have barbecue, fries and slaw?" I asked, swallowing the saliva filling my mouth at the thought of food.

"No, but they have red snapper, mahi and shrimp." Grandy must have seen the disappointment in my face because she added, "And great burgers."

I ordered the biggest burger on the menu and gobbled it down before the others finished. I followed up with chocolate ice cream. All the food groups satisfied—fat, protein, carbs and chocolate. I felt almost satisfied although I missed being able to have my favorite—Scotch.

Grandy gave me a disapproving look as I wiped my mouth.

"What? I'm eating healthy. Didn't I forgo the fries and order my burger with double tomato and lettuce? That's a lot of veggies."

She rolled her eyes. We finished our meal, paid the bill and walked out of the restaurant. "That's not what I meant, and you know it. You're eating for two now. You need to think of what impact your diet has on your growing baby. I'm sure your doctor told you that."

"Don't you have something to say about how I eat, Lionel? Tell her how Grandfather cooks for the family?"

He said nothing.

"Well?" I spun on my heel to see whether he heard me, but he wasn't there.

"Where did he go?" asked Grandy.

I suspected I knew, but thought I'd keep it to myself. The fewer people who knew what Lionel was up to the better. I assumed Lionel planned to make his way back to the houseboat and hide there, keeping an eye on Nappi.

Lionel and I had told Max and Grandy we needed the boat to contact Nappi but left out his specific location and what the three of us talked about. I knew they wouldn't volunteer the information to anyone, but if they didn't know anything, no one could get it out of them. I shivered to think about the possibility. Nappi hadn't wanted to believe there was more to his situation than removing his money and influence, but, when we left him, the worry lines on his face had deepened. I knew he was half convinced I was right about his situation being the beginning of more to come.

"Lionel is the most aggravating man, going off without a word. You'd think he'd ditch the disappearing act now he has his family around him and Renata is back." Grandy shook her head and hugged me goodbye. "I don't know what's going on, but I hope Nappi will be okay. Him I like."

As I drove north off the Keys, I called Sammy at the exit off the turnpike onto the Beeline Highway.

"Grandfather said there was a possibility you were up to more than visiting Grandy. He thought there was something else going on, and it involved my father. And maybe Nappi." Sammy did not sound pleased.

"I should have known I couldn't fly below Grandfather's radar. I'll tell you what I can when I get home."

"Is Dad with you?"

"No, Lionel had work to do. He'll be back as soon as he can."

Oops, I thought to myself after I ended the call. I had told Madeleine I was going to Key Largo because Grandy had some items for our consignment shop. How was I going to cover my lie with no clothes in my trunk? I'd find some story to tell her when I got to the shop tomorrow.

I became aware of how stiff and sore my shoulders were as I drove home, moving them around to ease the tightness setting in from rowing the raft. Maybe I could call a friend of mine who lived in a condominium park with a pool and a hot tub. Submerging myself in bubbling hot water sounded heavenly. I glanced at my watch. Too late for that. I wanted to get home to my family. One day without them, and I missed them. How must Nappi feel isolated from everyone he cared about, not knowing when or if he would see them again? I hoped I never knew what that felt like. I was determined to make certain I could help end his ordeal without jeopardizing him or those he loved—me, my family and my friends and his.

I reconsidered my earlier thoughts about contacting Frida to get her help and cancelled the idea for the time being. Tomorrow I'd call the drug agent whose case I'd messed up and see what he could offer, other than a hang up once he knew it was me.

AFTER HUGGING THE KIDS, I drank a cup of chamomile tea and filled Grandfather and Sammy in on the day's events. I might have preferred to keep them in the dark to protect them, but Grandfather was so good at reading my thoughts I knew it was not possible to shut him out of my head.

I propped my elbow on the table and leaned my chin on my hand. I was so tired . . .

"Eve. Eve." Sammy shook me awake. "We need to get you in bed. We can continue this tomorrow."

Grandfather patted my shoulder and left for his cabin next door. Sammy half carried me into our bedroom.

"I missed you," I said as he removed my clothes, "but not right now, my love."

I heard him chuckle. "That's not what I had in mind. Go to sleep."

"Umm," I turned on my side. The next thing I knew I smelled bacon frying.

"Oh, yum." I popped out of bed and into the shower where Sammy joined me and, because we were both wide awake, we took up where we left off last night. I don't know which I noticed first, the smell of burning bacon or the shower turning cold, but breakfast was not what I had anticipated.

"I sent the kids next door to Grandfather's. I assume they're having a better breakfast than this." Sammy grimaced as he shoveled cold cereal into his mouth.

The house land line jingled as I was about to leave for the shop.

"Where's Lionel, and why aren't you answering your cell?" It was Jay.

"So nice to talk with you too," I said.

"I need to get my horse on the road, so what did you do with Lionel?"

"What you need to do is change your tone of voice with me." I wasn't about to put up with Jay's authoritarian side at any time of the day but particularly not at this hour in the morning.

"I've got a business to run." His tone remained cold and demanding.

"First off, I'm not kidding about your manner. And no one 'does anything' with Lionel. You know what he's like."

"Okay. Okay. I'm out of line, but things are falling apart here. I've got a driver who can't work because of his injuries, and one of my stable hands quit yesterday. I'm down to Antoine and one other hand who's a newbie. If I can't find Lionel, I'll have to drive the horse myself. Help me out here, Eve. Please?"

"Better, but I'm not certain I can do anything for you. Have you told Frida what you intend to do?"

"No."

"Or Crusty? Our agency requires a little cooperation from our clients."

"No."

"Call them, then get back to me."

"But . . ."

I disconnected.

"Where is my cell" I asked.

Sammy pointed out the window. "Try the seat of your car. I think you left it there when you came in last night."

"Thanks." I planted a light kiss on his lips, but the kiss soon turned into more of a body hug. I knew what both of us were thinking. Without breaking kiss contact, we headed back into our bedroom. The kitchen door banged open, and three boys plus Netty barged through. So much for an encore this morning. I sat down in the family room with them, and we caught up on yesterday's events.

"I got to ride one of the horses," said Netty, her voice filled with excitement. "I want my own horse."

"Pony," I reminded her.

She shoved out her lower lip in a pout. "Horse."

"Ask your father." I grabbed Sammy's arm and shoved him front and center to explain to Netty about the pony versus horse situation.

I blew everyone kisses as I walked out the door and got into my car. There it was. My phone, on the passenger's seat.

I scrolled the list of unanswered calls. Two were from numbers I didn't recognize. Both left messages.

The first call was brief, a few seconds. I heard Lionel's voice.

"Call me at this number."

I returned his call. He answered after one ring.

"You don't have a cell phone. Whose phone is this?" I asked.

"It's a burner," he replied.

"A burner? What do you know about burners?"

"Because I spent decades in the swamps doesn't mean I'm stupid. I know all about burners."

"Learned by hanging around Nappi, no doubt."

I heard him snicker. "No, from hanging around with you and hearing about all the bad guys you've encountered. It rubbed off. A useful learning experience, but it's one of the many reasons I don't much care for people today. They're too detached from what's important."

"Okay. I know what you think of most folks. You've made it clear over the years."

"I'm getting to like you better, Eve."

"Don't try your sweet tea southern charm on me. What do you want?"

"Two things. First, to let you know I'm keeping an eye on Nappi and I'll keep you updated."

"You know he wouldn't like it if he knew you were snooping around, babysitting him."

He ignored my comment and pushed ahead. "I also want you to talk to Renata for me."

"Call her yourself. From what I hear, the two of you are in contact now, close contact."

"She doesn't have a cell phone. She doesn't like them either."

"Call her at the store during the day, but don't make it a habit." I was half serious, half joking.

"I don't want to talk to her. I want you to talk to her for me. Tell her the other night wasn't what she thought it was."

I could tell Lionel was embarrassed by spending the night in bed with his almost ex-wife. I was enjoying his discomfort. I'd never heard Lionel so ill at ease before.

"Let me see if I get this. You and Renata had sex, but you want me to tell her it wasn't what she thought it was. What was it then, Lionel, if it wasn't sex? Bingo?"

"You're not going to help me out, are you?" Now he sounded as if he was angry, but I was not getting involved in this.

"No, I am not. Whatever you call it, you need to deal with it between the two of you and not through a third party." Time to change the subject. "Now, how's Nappi? Anyone around?"

"No one here except for the nosey neighbor, that Darby character. I don't like him. He's too interested in Nappi. He may have brought in a stringer of fish yesterday, but I don't see him as much of a fisherman."

"I agree. And the watch I saw on his arm? I'm sure it was Nappi's custom-made Rolex. I wonder how he got it. Nappi said he put his into a bag he gave to the thrift shop. I guess Darby could have bought it there."

"The thrift shop would have sent it on for pawn. No one coming into a thrift shop could afford to pay what it was worth. Nappi should have tossed it into the water if he wanted it to disappear."

I hoped Nappi's watch wouldn't come back to haunt him, or worse, somehow become the link leading to his location.

"Keep me posted. And maybe you should toss this burner and get another one every few days—to be cautious."

"Good idea," said Lionel. Nice. I was sharing paranoia with the man who was its major stockholder.

"Are you doing okay? Enough food, someplace to stay?"

He laughed and disconnected.

It was a dumb question to ask a man who had survived for almost three decades in the swamps.

Before I could pull out of the drive onto the road, my cell twittered again.

"It's Melissa Andrew, the manager at the horse rescue facility. This is sheer luck, but we have a black and white pony, a female. She came in today. Someone mistreated her, and she's skinny with a dirty and matted coat, but I think we can get her in good shape in a week or so. Do you want to come look at her today? Maybe this afternoon?"

Did I? Yes, I did. How fortunate for Netty. I didn't want her to get her hopes up, and Ms. Andrew was cautious also, not wanting my daughter to see the pony in bad shape, but I would look at her today.

I hit the accelerator and sped toward the shop. On the way, I thought over the events of yesterday and again remembered I had no items to show for my supposed trip to pick up used merchandise from Grandy. I needed a good reason why I came back empty handed.

"Where are the clothes you were supposed to get from Grandy?" asked Madeleine when I walked into the shop.

"Oh, shucks. Grandy and I forgot because we were having such fun." Simple, but elegant and not completely untrue.

Renata was in the back inventorying new arrivals. She signaled me to come join her.

The bell on the door jangled, signaling a customer.

"I'll handle this," Madeleine said.

"Can I have a word with you alone, while Madeleine is busy?" asked Renata.

"Sure," I said. "Do you mind if I sit? I'm tired from yesterday."

"You're okay?"

"Yeah. I think I'm getting good at this pregnancy thing. With my first, I was sick all the time. With this one, I'm exhausted. I think I'll stop with two. The third one might be sick and exhausted." I slid into a chair and remembered there was another message for me on my cell.

"Let me clear this off my phone first." Since I didn't recognize this number, I thought I'd delete it, but I was curious. If I had deleted the other one, I'd have missed Lionel's contact.

I hit messages and listened. The message was short and ominous.

"He can disappear, but you can't. There's more to follow. Expect it."

CHAPTER 8

—

"Eve? Are you alright? You're so pale." Renata bent over me and peered into my face.

"What? Oh, it's nothing. I'm fine. A message I need to take care of, but not right now." But soon, very soon. I was right. The message confirmed it. This was about more than Nappi. I glanced toward the window afraid I might spot someone in the alley outside. I shook myself free of the feeling and directed my attention to Renata. "There's something you wanted to tell me?"

"If you want to go home and lie down, it can wait. You don't look good."

"No. No." I reached out and pulled Renata into a chair next to me. "Tell me."

"It's about Lionel. And me. The other night."

Oh, no. I wanted to stay out of this. First Lionel and now Renata wanted to drag me into it.

"I've been thinking about it and, well, you know how sensitive he is . . ."

Sensitive? Thin-skinned maybe but Lionel was not what I'd call a 'sensitive' man.

"I think we made a huge mistake doing what we did the other night. Can you talk to him and tell him I've had second thoughts? I don't want to hurt his feelings, but I think it's better we be friends and nothing else."

Friends? Now that would be new. I never thought of her and Lionel as friends.

"I think you should talk to him yourself. It's not my place to get into the middle of this thing, whatever it is, between you and Lionel. If the two of you don't talk, you'll never be able to resolve this. No one else can do that for you."

Renata hung her head. "I know you're right. I'm such a coward. I don't want to face him and maybe break his heart. It took a lot for him to reach out to me."

"Tell him."

She nodded. "Okay, but where is he?"

Advice I could give her, but I wasn't willing to divulge Lionel's whereabouts nor what he was doing, so I kept it simple. "I can't say."

She interpreted it the way I was hoping she would.

"Will you let me know if you find out?"

"Sure." But I wouldn't.

"Is this private?" Madeleine stuck her head around the door to tell me one of the young women Shelley had recommended for the position of seamstress for the shop had come in for her interview.

"Right." For a moment I had forgotten we'd hired Renata on a temporary basis making it clear we would go ahead with the interviews of the women Shelley had recommended who, like her, had design experience. "Renata can take over out front, and the two of us can talk with her back here. What's her name?"

"Mona Street. Here's her resume." Madeleine handed me a sheet of paper with Mona's credentials and experience on it. We both looked it over, and then Madeleine asked her to come back. I introduced myself, and the three of us talked for a while.

After she left, we both agreed she was competent, but worried she didn't have Shelley's design vision.

"We'll never find anyone who's as good as Shelley. I think we're setting the bar too high by believing we'll find someone who can redesign dresses like Shelley did. Let's go for someone who can do the basics," I said.

Madeleine agreed. We decided we'd interview the other candidates recommended by Shelley and decide by next week.

"I overheard your discussion," said Renata. "Maybe I could help. I'm self-trained, but I think I have an eye for design."

From what I had seen in her work with our patrons, I believed her.

Her recommendations were always tasteful and her own clothes, while not designer brands, fit well and were tasteful and chique.

"I thought you dealt Black Jack," said Madeleine, who then looked embarrassed. "I mean, I didn't think you were into clothing." Her face continued to redden. "Oh, boy. I'm getting this all wrong."

Renata reached out and patted her hand. "Don't be upset. I'm not offended. It's a secret I've kept for years. I make my own clothes. I learned to sew from my mother years ago. It's the one thing she taught me. I can't cook worth a darn and neither could she. Sewing came in handy altering the outfits I wore in the casino. I did adjustments for the other employees too."

Madeleine and I exchanged looks. Did we luck out or what?

To be fair to the other women recommended by Shelley and who were interested enough to apply for the position, we had Renata fill out an application, and we asked her to do an interview. Her work experience was odd for a permanent position in a consignment shop, but we couldn't fault her background in dealing with the public. While Madeleine and I talked, Renata went back out front.

"If we hire her, we need to tell Shelley, and I'm worried what she'll think. She owns a share in this business. She knows the other candidates, but we should bring her in here when we interview Renata."

"I'll talk with her," said Madeleine. "I'll do a better job of it than I did talking to Renata."

"If you don't mind I'd like to pop next door and talk to Crusty. I won't be but a minute," I said.

I entered Crusty's waiting room and found the door to his office closed, meaning he was doing something he shouldn't be, like smoking.

I tapped but didn't wait for an answer before I opened the door.

"It's you. Hi. I was about to come over to see you." He shoved something in his top desk drawer.

"About to light a cigar?"

"Well, like I said, I was leaving the office to step next door."

"And you thought you'd light up on the way. What you don't realize is the smoke stays in your clothes and you carry it wherever you go. It's a smelly habit, and it's unhealthy."

"Don't nag. I get enough badgering from Margie."

"Who's Margie?" I asked.

"A woman I met the other week at the Rusty Nail. We went to dinner last night. And don't give me that look. We're friends. Friends." He cleared his throat and reached into the desk drawer. "Gum?"

I shook my head.

Crusty took a stick out of the packet and began to unwrap it, but then tossed it back into the drawer. "What I wanted to talk to you about was Jay. He called me about the wisdom of transporting another horse. He thought Lionel was the man for it, but it seems he can't be located. Is he off on another trek in the swamps?"

"I'm not his keeper, but until Frida finds out what happened to Jay's driver and the horse, I don't think transporting another horse is a smart move."

"Yeah, Frida said the same, but Jay is convinced it was a onetime thing."

"I'm not. I received a phone call I think was a warning to me and my family and friends. I'll play the call for you."

Crusty listened, pulling at his beard and mustache, a habit he had when he focused on something.

"It's about Nappi's disappearance and . . ."

". . . and a warning no one around me is safe and the caller is about to begin making moves against us. I can't see how the incident with Jay's driver and horse is related, but I'll bet it is."

"I agree. This is something I think our detective friend Frida should hear."

I shifted around in my chair. "There's more, but . . ."

Crusty narrowed his eyes with a suspicious look. "I'll bet it involves Nappi and Lionel somehow. Have you seen Nappi?"

I used my favorite line when I avoided giving a direct answer. "I can't say."

"Okay. We'll keep Frida out of it for now, but if more happens, we might have to bring her in."

Crusty said he would talk with Jay, but he was certain Jay was determined to find someone to drive the horse south.

Madeleine was ending a call when I walked back into the shop. "That was Shelley."

I raised one eyebrow. Madeleine signaled me to follow her into the back room, out of ear shot of Renata.

"Shelley recommended young women who could do tailoring, but she wasn't certain any of them wanted to work on the floor of the shop selling. If we hire one of them, we'd also must find someone to work as a clerk. Shelley is cool with what we do. She said she'd leave it up to us who we hired. 'I'm the one who's leaving the position open,' she said. 'I don't think it's up to me to decide who you hire even if I do own a part in the place. I trust yours and Eve's judgment.'"

"Does she want to be in on the interviewing at all?"

"Nope. Our call." Madeleine smiled and shrugged. "We've lost a real gem in Shelley, haven't we?"

"Yep."

"I'll take charge with inventorying back here if you want to talk with Renata. I do think to make the process fair, we should ask her for a resume like we did the other applicants."

"I agree. I'll let her know."

"Oh, I almost forgot. Sammy called. He wants you to call him. It's something about the two of you going to lunch." Madeleine gave me a quizzical look. "Sammy doesn't do lunch. It must be important."

I stepped out into the alleyway and called the game ranch, hoping I'd catch Sammy in David's office and not out with a group of hunting clients.

David answered. "Sammy's right here. I'll put him on."

"Lunch? Something's up."

"You are so suspicious, Eve," Sammy said. "Can't I ask my woman out to lunch?"

"Yes, but you never ask me out to lunch. What is going on?"

"Suspicious and impatient, my favorite characteristics in a woman."

I could tell he wasn't willing to tell me what he had in mind over the phone. "Can we meet at the Palms Café?" he asked.

"Kind of a girlie-like place for you, isn't it?" I chuckled.

"Maybe, but it's quiet. See you there in half an hour?" He disconnected before I could ask him again about this get-together.

SAMMY, LOOKING UNCOMFORTABLE and out of place among all the lunching ladies and businessmen, sat at one of the café's tables, a wrought iron ice cream parlor kind of thing. His long legs didn't fit under it, so he had stretched them into the space between tables and was trying to keep them out of the way of the wait staff who moved in and out of the small area taking and delivering orders.

"Sorry ma'am." He grabbed his hat off the table top as a waitress swept by and almost toppled it with her elbow onto the floor.

"My fault." She gave him a smile. Women always smiled at Sammy. The man was so handsome.

"What's going on?" I pulled out the chair across from him.

"Nice to see you, too, Eve. I ordered herbal tea for us." He arose from his seat to help me into mine and almost knocked over his chair in the process of getting up. He grabbed for it before it toppled, and at the same time he tried to reach out and pull the other chair out for me. We bumped heads.

"You're having herbal tea?" I said. "When have you ever drunk herbal tea?"

"I'm flexible," he replied.

"Well, I'm not." I waved at the waitress and mouthed, "we're leaving."

I grabbed Sammy's hand and pulled him up and out the door.

"I don't know what's happening but making yourself so uncomfortable is silly. We'll sit on one of the benches in the park." I suspected he was going out of his way for me because he wanted something, something he knew I didn't want.

We crossed the street and entered the grassy area between the two major streets in the downtown. Trees shaded the benches there, and we selected one nearest the less busy thoroughfare. "Okay. Tell me. I know it's something I'm not going to like."

"Jay was in touch with me this morning."

"Looking for Lionel, right?"

"Kind of." Sammy spoke so softly I almost couldn't hear him.

Oh, oh.

"But not really?" I waited for him to explain. He wouldn't meet my gaze, and he shifted around on the bench as if he was as uncomfortable here as he had been in the restaurant.

He shook his head. "He asked me if I would drive one of his horses to Chokoloskee."

"No. You won't."

"I already told him yes. He offered a lot of money. We could use the extra cash to build a barn and a bigger corral for our horses. The one we have is too small, and we're going to need more space for the pony."

"No."

"Eve. Listen to me. I can take care of myself. I'll carry my pistol and take the shotgun."

"No." I got up and walked back across the street, then got into my car and drove off. When I checked my rearview mirror, Sammy sat on the bench his head in his hands.

I drove to the sub shop and bought lunch for everyone. I dropped one off to Crusty and took the others to Madeleine and Renata.

"Lunch," I said. "I got mixed subs for everyone. I hope you're all okay with my choice." I placed two of the sandwiches from the bag on the counter, then went to the back room and sat down. Madeleine followed me and wrinkled up her forehead in a look of concern. When she opened her mouth to say something, I held up my hand. "Don't ask."

"I wasn't. I wondered if there's extra mustard." She pointed to the bag which I cradled in my arms as if it contained precious cargo and not a deli treat.

I looked up at her and began to cry. Soon I was blubbering, snot running from my nose and down into my mouth.

"You and Sammy had a fight." She dropped into the chair beside me and put her arms around me and hugged.

"You're smushing my lunch," I said.

"Always the food first, huh, Eve?"

We both began laughing, although my laughter was mixed with sobs. Renata must have heard the ruckus because she peeked into the room and then closed the door. Madeleine shoved a tissue box at me and, after using most of it, I finally could talk enough to tell her about Jay's offer to Sammy and Sammy's acceptance.

Madeleine continued to hold me and make those maternal comforting sounds.

The words she used were, "You should eat something." I took her wise advice. I ate my sub, of course, I did. Crises never put me off my feed.

Later, after I couldn't shed anymore tears, I said, "I've got to see a person about a pony. Thanks for not telling me I behaved like a crazy woman."

"Do you think you should go the horse rescue place today? How about putting it off until you feel more up to it." Madeleine said.

"You think I should find Sammy and we should talk, don't you?"

"Eventually."

"I will . . . eventually, but right now there's a pony I need to consider for my daughter. She can't wait. Sammy can." I grabbed my purse and was off.

I crossed my fingers this pony was the one for Netty. I knew she had her heart set on a pony and getting her one would please her as well as make the family happy.

MANAGER ANDREW GREETED ME as I got out of my car. "I think this little gal is what your daughter wants. As I said she's a little skinny, but her temperament is wonderful. She likes people and she's not a biter, a characteristic many ponies have. I put a saddle on her this morning and she appeared eager to go. If you don't take her, well, I have others who will. Let's go look."

She led me to the stable and down to the last stall on the right. She was right. The little black and white pony's ribs were showing, but she seemed to be intent upon remedying her bony condition by eating happily at the hay placed in her stall. She raised her head when I stuck out my hand and clucked at her but lowered it back to her lunch and once more took up munching.

"Hungry, isn't she?"

"It seems eating is all she's been doing since we got her. She'll soon be plump and her coat shiny. What do you think?"

"I think she's perfect."

"Great. We'll work with her for another few days and see how it goes. You said your daughter is eager for this pony, right?"

"You have no idea. We're all eager for her to have one."

"She should be ready to travel soon. Can you arrange to have someone transport her?"

"My oldest son can take our horse trailer. He's good at handling the animals."

"I've got some papers for you to fill out."

The two of us began to walk back through the barn, but one of the volunteers stopped us and wanted to talk to Ms. Andrew. The two of them walked off a short distance while I leaned up against one of the stalls. I felt a soft nibble on my shoulder. I turned in surprise and gazed into the soulful eyes of a horse who had put her head over the top of the stall.

"Well, well," I said.

The rescue facility manager ran over to me. "You've got to be careful with her. She's a handful. She's been suspicious of everyone, has bitten several of the volunteers and lunges at anyone entering the stall. It's going to take a lot of work to get her calmed down."

The horse continued to gaze at me.

"I think I know this horse."

"Yes?" said the manager. "How?"

"She saved my life."

Chapter 9

—

"There has to be a story there." Andrew's face was alight with interest. "You tell me how she saved your life, and I'll tell you how this facility got her. This horse has to be special."

The animal nuzzled my neck in a friendly manner, and I reached up to pat her nose.

"You have a way with horses," said the manager.

I shook my head. "Not at all. I've never been much for horses, although my grandmother rode a lot, and now my sons have horses. I've never ridden, never been interested. To be honest, I'm kind of scared of them. They're so big. Sometimes I get the feeling they're smarter than me and know I'm frightened." I gave a nervous laugh as the horse gave my ear a light nibble.

"Maybe it's time you learned to ride. Tell me your history with this animal."

"She's a polo pony from Argentina brought here to play but abused by a nasty owner and his veterinarian. When the veterinarian and the owner tried to harm me, this gal gave the vet a lesson in hoof play by almost crushing his skull. If she hadn't backed him off, I wouldn't be here to tell the story."

"I wondered if she might have been trained as a polo pony, but with her temperament I assumed the owner wanted to get rid of her so he dumped her hoping the swamps would take care of the problem." Her eyes darkened with anger, and she shook her head. "I hate the way some people treat animals. Anyway, a guy was driving along a gravel road southwest of here and saw her standing by the road. He alerted us and we sent a trailer for her. It sure wasn't easy getting her in the trailer."

"If you knew how she'd been treated by her previous owner and the abusive vet, you'd understand why she has trust issues. For the past few years she's been at a friend of mine's ranch near the lake. He's been working with her. He was sending her to another rancher south of the lake when his driver was hijacked and the horse disappeared from the trailer. I guess she sensed something wasn't right when the robbers tried to kidnap her. She got away. My friend thought she had been stolen and he'd never find her. I know he'd like her back."

The manager frowned. "I'm not sending this horse anywhere until I know who's going to be taking her. Tell him to call me."

I gave her Jay's name and assured her he was a reputable rancher and a well-respected horse breeder and trainer.

"We'll see," she said. "I assume he has papers to show he owns her."

I was certain Jay did have papers on this gal and told the manager he would be calling her today to talk with her about the horse.

With a final pat of my old life-saving equine friend, I got in my car and connected with Jay on my cell.

"I'll be right there," said Jay. "Stay put. Your presence could be helpful if she's in doubt about me."

"Before you rush over here, I've got something to say to you."

"Sammy talked to you." There was a note of hesitance in Jay's voice.

"Oh, yes. And now I want to talk to you."

"Listen. We can talk later. Right now, I need to get over there and claim my horse." He disconnected, the coward.

Jay arrived less than a half hour later and jumped out of his truck when he saw me. "Where is she?" His face looked like a bank of thunderclouds—threatening.

I stopped him from heading into the barn. "I suggest you adjust your attitude some. These people had nothing to do with taking her. In fact, she's alive because someone found her wandering near the road and brought her here. These are true animal lovers who want the best for the horses they rescue. Take it down a notch and be cooperative. I'll introduce you to the manager." I took Jay's arm and walked him into the barn.

The manager approached us. "Is this the man who says he owns the horse?"

Jay's face got red. "I do own her."

I kicked Jay's ankle, and he backed down.

"This is Melissa Andrew. She's the manager here. My friend, Jay Cassidy."

She gave him a glance from head to toe, then reached out her hand and shook his. "Melissa."

"Jay. Sorry I got so huffy," he said, "but this horse means a lot to me. I've worked with her for years and realized a friend of mine south of here might be able to do more for her than I could, so I was sending her to him when my driver and the horse trailer were hijacked. The driver was beaten unconscious, and I feared the horse was gone forever. She's a great horse and has potential as a polo pony, but I'm not putting her in play unless she's ready."

Melissa listened in silence, scrutinizing the expression on Jay's face.

When he finished explaining the horse's background, Melissa seemed to have come to some decision. She nodded and said, "Come see your horse," and led him into the barn.

By the time I followed them in, She and Jay were talking, their expressions relaxed and smiling. The horse was nuzzling Jay's hand as he patted her nose.

"She knows you and likes you," said Melissa. "I'll trust you to transport her back to your ranch as soon as you like. There will be some papers to process first, and I'll need to see some proof you own her . . ." At this comment, Jay's face flushed with anger, "A formality. We're licensed by the state. and they require us to be certain everything is in order."

Jay relaxed and smiled. "I understand." He put out his hand, and they shook again.

"See," he said as we walked back to our vehicles, "I can be nice."

"Yeah, well, nice isn't going to get you out of the jam you're in with me. Sammy is not going to drive a horse trailer down south for you."

"It seems to me Sammy makes up his own mind about what he does. He already said he would drive for me, and I promised my friend I'd send him a horse."

I turned my back on him and got into my car. I rolled down the window. "Not with Sammy driving, and that's final." I started the engine and was about to stomp on the accelerator when I thought better of spinning gravel in the horse rescue drive. Melissa and I were in a good place with the pony now. I didn't want to jeopardize anything for Netty. I gave Jay an icy smile and eased my foot down on the accelerator. I could be nice, too.

WHEN I GOT BACK TO THE SHOP, Madeleine and I set up a time to interview the remainder of the applicants for the tailoring job. I left Madeleine and Renata to work the shop while I continued to inventory new items having arrived at the shop in the last week. Madeleine stuck her head back around the door. "Call Sammy. The inventory can wait."

"I'll see him tonight at home."

"Now, Eve. Talk to him now." Tiny though she was, Madeleine could be as authoritarian as a general when it came to giving orders.

"Yes, ma'am." I gave her a mock salute.

I tried the office at the hunting ranch thinking I might catch Sammy there again, but David answered and told me Sammy was in the field leading a group of hunters for a quail hunt.

"What did you do to him?" he asked. "He came back her like a man who had been lassoed, roped and tied."

"He deserved it."

"Look, Eve, I know you don't want Sammy to take unnecessary risks, but Jay is paying him well. I wish I could pay him as much, but I can't, and he says you need the money to build a barn for your horses. And I understand you're trying to find a pony for Netty. You'll need a place to keep the three horses and Netty's pony, too."

"I don't think the hijacking was an isolated incident. They might try again," I said.

"What do you mean?"

"I can't say more, but please talk to Sammy and tell him not to do it. We'll find another way to get the money."

"I'll tell him you called, but I'm not going to intervene for you. You need to talk with Sammy. I think Sammy can take care of himself. I wish you had the same conviction." David ended the call.

Why was no one on my side? Why couldn't they see how dangerous it was for Jay to send another horse south not knowing what was happening? Jay was angry at me and so was Sammy, but I had hope this could be remedied.

I called Jay, and when I connected, I didn't let him say a word before I started talking.

"You found your horse, and she'll soon be back with you, but she needs some time to mend. She's the one you want to send down to your friend, right?"

"What is this all about, Eve?"

"Here's the deal. You get her back to your ranch and you let her settle in a bit, then you can send her south as planned, but wait a while."

"That was what I planned."

"Yes, but I'm asking you to wait longer, at least until we find out more about the hijacking."

There was silence on the other end.

"My friend wants another horse from me, and he wants it soon."

"You told Melissa a story about your horse. You didn't want your friend to work with her. You wanted to sell her to him. It's all about money, isn't it?"

"No. I did want him to work with her, and I did think he might want to buy her, but he's eager for another pony soon. I'll send her down there when she's in better shape and has recovered. I'm telling you the truth. He could buy both horses."

"Why do you need the money now?" I asked. Jay was wealthy. Why the rush? He could get his friend to hold off.

There was silence on his end. I heard him sigh. "Okay. How long do you want?"

"Maybe a month."

"I'll give you a week, and you explain to Sammy why he's not getting his money sooner." He disconnected.

His decision was not what I wanted to hear, but it gave me a week to work out what was happening with Jay's horse and how it was connected to Nappi's plight. Or was it?

I decided I had to kick this investigation into high gear.

I left the back room and tapped Madeleine on the shoulder as I went by her. "I'm going out for a few hours if it's okay with you."

She gave me her Cheshire cat grin, looking as if she knew what my absence was all about. I was tempted to confess it wasn't about meeting Sammy and making things right between us, but I thought I should leave her believing good things about me. I slammed out the door and dashed into Crusty's. His private office door was closed, so I put my ear to it to listen for voices. I heard laughing. Odd. PIs never left their clients laughing. They left them with a report on the investigation and a bill.

To be polite, I knocked, then turned the knob to open the door and stepped in. Good. Crusty was not holding a cigar. He was holding a woman on his lap. Both of their faces were wreathed in smiles.

"You must be Margie, Crusty's new friend." I held out my hand as I approached the desk. Thank goodness the two of them were fully clothed. I didn't think I could tolerate the sight of Crusty without his bolo tie.

The woman got out of his lap and patted her blond hair in place. She was almost as tall as me but bustier.

"Howdy." She grabbed my hand and shook it so hard I thought my teeth would rattle loose. "Oh, gosh, I'm sorry. I shouldn't shake so hard. Crusty told me you're pregnant. Or is the pregnancy a secret?" she asked.

"Nothing is secret around here when it comes to my life, it seems. It's as if I took out an ad in the local newspaper announcing it."

"Aw, Eve. I didn't think you'd mind my telling Margie," said Crusty.

"It's fine, and it's nice to meet you, Margie. I hope you know what you're doing hooking up with this guy."

"I think I can handle him," she said.

The determined look in her eyes left me no doubt about her ability to manage him. "Sorry to interrupt, but I need to talk with Crusty. Business."

"No problem. I've got to leave. Meet you later at the Rusty Nail." Margie planted a loud kiss on Crusty's forehead and waved goodbye as she left.

"Nice gal. I hope you treat her right," I said to Crusty, dropping into a chair.

"Long day?" he asked.

"Not so long as it was complicated. Is there something about me men find offensive?" I asked.

"Not just men," he said. I knew he was joking, but I shot him a warning look.

I'd never admit it out loud, but I was sometimes, often, almost always, to be honest, aggravating.

"Let me ask you a question. Do you know any Drug Enforcement Agents in West Palm?"

"Why?"

"Answer the question."

"No," he said, pulling his mustache and beard.

"I know you're lying."

"Let's say I do, so what do you want me to do?"

"Well, a number of years ago I met two of them by accident. I was tied up and ditched at the side of a dirt road, left as dinner for swamp denizens. These DEA guys rescued me. Now I'd like to talk with them."

"Talk with them."

"I don't think I left a very good impression on them."

He waited for me to explain.

"They claimed I messed up a drug bust."

Crusty groaned. "Sure you did."

"It wasn't my fault. I didn't ask to be dumped in the middle of nowhere, at a meet-up for drug sellers."

"You want me to talk with them because . . ."

"They would hang up on me if I called."

"I need more information." He propped his boots up on his desk and leaned back in the chair.

"It's connected to Jay's missing horse, which I found today."

He looked interested.

"I'm certain this is related to Nappi's disappearance and the warning message I received on my phone. Somebody has it in for me and everyone surrounding me."

"I don't see how a DEA agent can help."

"I want someone with federal connections, someone who might be able to get information through the FBI without alerting anyone there. Nappi had friends in the FBI and I would go straight to them, but Nappi told me he's not certain if they can be trusted, so I thought I another agency might be able to extract info. What do you think?"

"It's a stretch."

"My other alternative is to try to use Frida to see if she can find out anything with her law enforcement connections."

"Involving Frida would be my last choice. She's is a friend, and we work closely with the cops around here. I don't want to burn bridges on a hunch." He tipped his chair forward. "Here's another thing. It sounds like you've been in touch with Nappi. I thought he'd disappeared."

Oops. I'd said too much. I ignored his implied question. "As you said, a hunch." Someone rattled the doorknob to the back door.

"Are you expecting someone?" I asked.

"No." Crusty waved me to one side of the door, opened his desk drawer and pulled out the pistol he kept there.

I leaned against the wall to the left of the door, reached out, and in one motion flung it open.

The afternoon sun didn't penetrate the alleyway, and I couldn't make out who stood outside the door, but I could see it was a man, a tall man, broad-shouldered and big.

"Stop right there or I'll shoot," warned Crusty. I grabbed the broom standing by the door and slammed it down on the man's head as he stepped into the room. He went down like a rock.

"Did I kill him? I swatted him with the broom. "The guy must have a soft head."

"I think you broke my arm."

"Lionel? What are you doing here?"

"I know I'm not your favorite person, but what a mean way to greet a member of the family, Eve."

Crusty reached out and helped Lionel off the floor. "She doesn't like you? I never noticed."

Lionel made a sound like a growl and shifted his shoulder around. "Yep. Broken."

"Sit down." Crusty helped him into the desk chair.

"Don't be silly. I hardly touched you. And I repeat, what are you doing sneaking around the alley? I thought you were . . . somewhere else." I stopped myself before I could reveal Lionel's last location was on Card Sound Road.

"Bad news," said Lionel. "Other than my injured shoulder. It's about Nappi."

I gave him a warning look. Only Lionel and I knew where Nappi was. Nappi wanted us to keep his location from everyone else, and I had assured him I wouldn't reveal his hideout.

Lionel shook his head. "Nappi's missing."

Crusty snapped his gum and gave me a PI look signaling I'd been hiding something critical from him.

"He left the houseboat?" I said.

"Maybe. It could be someone found him and took him," Lionel said.

CHAPTER 10

———

"I SAW THE LIGHTS GO OUT in his place around midnight last night, and I continued to keep watch until I was certain he was asleep. This morning I saw no sign of him. Each morning he brings his coffee out onto the back of the houseboat to sit on the deck there and drink it. This morning he didn't. I remained watching for an hour past the time he appeared, and he didn't show. I decided to take a closer look. I didn't spot any movement inside. I took a chance and went in. He wasn't there."

"He gave you the slip while you were snoozing," I said.

Lionel looked embarrassed. "I fell asleep thinking he was asleep too."

"He must have known you were babysitting him. I knew he wouldn't like having someone spying on him, even if you are a close friend," I said.

"I know. I tried to be careful."

Oh, no. This was what we didn't want to happen. I had felt a sense of relief when Lionel found Nappi. I guess I thought knowing where he was hiding was protection for him, but, if he left on his own, he must have thought knowing where he was had put us in danger. "It's beginning as the message said it would. I hope they didn't grab him. He was so certain he was safe staying off the radar. He thought he was protecting his family and us." A tear worked its way down my cheek.

Crusty put his arm around me and led me to a chair. "Sit down, Eve. Here." He extracted a white handkerchief from his pocket and wiped my face as the tears began to flow in abundance freely.

"Hormones," I said. "I'm usually better at taking bad news."

"Well, I'm not," said Lionel. "I was so miserable when I found Nappi was gone I almost punched the wall, but then I realized the place wasn't mine to destroy."

"Tell me the whole story," said Crusty. "Why was Nappi there?"

I filled him in on Nappi's situation. "He thought if he made himself invisible—like he had any choice given the dire straits he was in—whoever was responsible would ignore him and leave everyone he knew alone."

"But you didn't, did you?" Crusty turned to me and gave me a half smile. "I don't know if it's pregnancy hormones or the kind of gal you are, but your hunch was right on. The warning on your phone and Nappi's disappearance confirm it. Now the question is, what can we do?"

"We need help more than ever." I gave a final swipe to my face and blew my nose. Time to shift my brain into high gear. I pulled my cellphone out of my pocket. "I'm calling the DEA contact in West Palm. I hope he's still there. Or at least I think I hope he's still there and doesn't hang up when he hears my name."

"Here, give me your phone." Crusty reached out and took the phone. "It's ringing. Who do I ask for?"

"Ask for Agent Bud."

Crusty explained who he was and said I worked with him, then turned the phone over to me. "He's, as you guessed, not happy to hear from you, but he said he'd listen."

The best way to get Bud's cooperation was to be honest with him, so I laid out the whole story. He listened without interrupting, then said, "I think we should meet. I've got something going in Indiantown this evening. I'll meet you in the parking lot in the town center there, around seven." He didn't wait for me to agree but disconnected.

"Rude man. He didn't say goodbye."

"We are asking him for a favor," said Crusty. "And, from what you told me about pulling you out of the swamps, it sounds like you already own him one."

I did owe the guy. Not only had he rescued me from dying alone in the swamp trussed up like a Thanksgiving turkey, but I'd messed up his drug bust by being present at the scene. I could apologize, but it wasn't my fault someone had tossed me there. Things happen, I thought, often to me. I shrugged and tossed the phone in my purse.

"I've got some other fences to mend right now. I'll check in when I get back from the meeting with Bud tonight."

"I don't think you should go alone, Eve. Take Lionel with you tonight."

"Why don't you come along?" I asked.

"I've got a date with Margie, remember?" said Crusty.

Lionel who had been silent for my crying jag and the recovery from it spoke up. "I've got something also. I'll be in touch." He walked out of the office.

"What does he mean?" asked Crusty.

"I'm not sure." Maybe he had an idea where Nappi went. Or he could be contacting Renata to talk with her about their recent get together. Naw, that would have been too sensible.

He stuck his head back in the door. "Did you have the talk I asked you to have, the one with you-know-who?"

"No. I told you. It's your life and your talk to have."

"Women." He slammed back out the door.

"If I didn't know better, I'd say Lionel sounds like he's having some kind of a lover's spat." Crusty grinned, delighted with the idea Lionel might have troubles in the romance department.

I rolled my eyes. "Lionel? Nope."

Outside Crusty's office, I connected with the office at David and Madeleine's hunting reserve. Once more David answered the phone.

"Is Sammy back yet?"

"Back and gone again. He said he was going to Jay's ranch."

Was he driving the horse today? Maybe I could catch Sammy at the ranch, and we could talk there. I didn't want him to go off on Jay's errand without being able to work things out between us.

I called Jay. "Is Sammy there?"

"Eve? He left a few minutes ago with my truck and trailer."

"No, no, no."

I ended the call, poked my head in the shop and told Renata I had something important to do, then I jumped in my car. Maybe I could catch Sammy before he left town.

I sped down the street and turned south on the highway leading to the west of the lake. The road led out of town like a flat ribbon of concrete, so it should be easy to spot anything ahead, but no other vehicles were in sight. I pushed down on the accelerator and crossed my fingers no cops would spot me with their radar and clock my speed. Before the road curved left, I spotted the trailer ahead. It had to be Jay's. I put on more speed and caught up, honking my horn to get Sammy's attention. An arm reached out the driver's side window and signaled me to pass. I pulled out and was even with the truck when the face of an older white man in a red cap appeared in the window. He yelled something at me and then gave me a digital sign of anger. Not Sammy. I mouthed "I'm sorry" and dropped back into my lane. Could Sammy be this far ahead? The turnoff to our house and the airboat business was ahead on the right. I slammed on my brakes before I raced past. There was a horse trailer in our drive. Sammy!

He was getting out of the cab when I drove up. I jumped out of the car and ran up to him. I almost knocked him down as I threw myself into his arms.

"I am so, so sorry." I hugged him tight to me.

"Eve, Eve." He hugged me back and whispered in my ear. "Everything is fine."

"Yes, it is. Now turn the trailer around and take the horse back to Jay's."

Sammy pulled away from me. "Horse? There's no horse in there, not yet. Since I was willing to drive his horse south and you put up such a fuss about it, he said he told you he was going to wait a week, but in the meantime, he wondered if I'd like to make a little money picking up two horses from Clewiston tomorrow. I took the truck and trailer today so I could get an early start tomorrow."

"I asked him to give me more time to figure out what went on with his driver and the other horse, but I wasn't certain he would. By the way, I located his horse today at the horse rescue facility. Did he tell you?"

He nodded. "You look tired and stressed, Eve. I think you should go into the house and take a lie down."

I grabbed his hand and smiled up into his face. "Good idea, if you join me."

He returned my smile with one of his lop-sided sexy grins. "What do you have in mind, lady?"

I began walking toward the house pulling him with me. "I'm so happy you decided not to drive the horse for Jay. I know this won't be as much money, but we'll get by."

I felt a tug as he stopped following me.

"Tomorrow doesn't change anything, Eve. I'm determined to drive the horse for him next week."

Things are never simple for Sammy and me, are they?

We didn't get around to talking about whether Sammy would drive to Chokoloskee for Jay. Talking didn't seem important, but I managed to find a few minutes to tell him about finding a pony for Netty.

"Now we need a barn big enough for the pony and the other three horses."

I didn't comment. It was an argument we didn't need to resume in our bed.

"I've been thinking. Grandy's birthday is coming up in a few days. She used to love to ride. Wouldn't it be great if we could get her a horse of her own? She sometimes rides one of the boys' horses when she comes, but I think she'd be here more often if she had her own horse."

"Are you trying to wean her off Key Largo?"

"Not completely. I could only accomplish that if I broke up her marriage to Max. As much as he likes fishing the lake, he's as much wedded to blue water as he is Grandy. He needs his ocean fix. Besides, they have long-time friends in Key Largo."

"I think buying her a horse is a wonderful idea, but it means we need even more money and increases the urgency of a barn to stable the horses. If this keeps up, we'll soon be buying a horse for you."

"Not me, not in my condition." I patted my emerging baby bump.

He was right. We would need another horse. When this baby was old enough, he or she would ride Netty's pony, but then Netty would need a horse. Horses, barn, feed. It all cost money. I thought about the job Jay offered to Sammy. I might feel good about it if I found out what was going on with the threat and all it entailed, and I was certain it included Jay and his horses. The ponies were Jay's life. The enemy was someone who understood taking his horses would wound him to his core. I had a week to find out who wanted all of us injured or maybe dead.

I told Sammy I had an appointment in Indiantown after dinner, and I was honest about what it was about.

He repeated what Crusty had said. "I don't want you going alone."

"I'll be fine. It's not as if this DEA guy is a threat"

"I'd better come along."

"You have to get up early tomorrow to pick up Jay's horses, then you've got a full morning schedule for the airboat business, and you told me David booked a large group of hunters in the afternoon."

Sammy was as overcommitted with jobs as I was.

GRANDFATHER AGREED WITH ME. At dinner, he also vetoed Sammy accompanying me tonight. "Sammy needs his rest if he's going to take that horse early tomorrow. Maybe I could go along."

Did no one think I was competent enough to go on my own?

In his usual way, Grandfather read my annoyance. "Like you, we believe the threat you received is real. We want to protect you and the little one on the way."

Sammy slipped his arm around my shoulder. "Grandfather will stay here. I've already thought of someone and called. He should be here in a few minutes. Wait. I think I heard a car pull up."

I peeked out the window and recognized the black SUV.

"Not Jerry." I groaned and shook my head. "Anyone but Jerry."

"I heard what you said, Evie." Jerry stood in the doorway. "You think I can't help you out?"

"I suppose you have a gun with you?" I hoped he would say no. Jerry and guns were a lethal combination. He was a poor shot, worse than me, and he even kept his eyes open when aiming.

"Right here." He pulled a pistol from his pocket.

"Get the gun out of my house. There are children here," I said.

"Sorry." Jerry placed it back in his pocket. "I'll meet you in the car."

"My car. I'm driving." I also found Jerry to be a bad driver. I'd tolerated his chauffeuring me to the polo farms, but that was enough. He was too distracted by anything happening at the side of the road. A sidearm and a steering wheel in the same hands, Jerry's, were a duo I didn't favor being around. I grabbed the car keys to my convertible.

"I'll be in bed when you get back," said Sammy accompanying me to the door.

"Want me to wake you?" I gave him a suggestive smile.

All our boys got the implication of my offer and groaned in chorus.

"Wake *me*, Mommy. Wake *me*," sang Netty. I lifted her in my arms and gave her a hug and another kiss.

JERRY SAT IN THE PASSENGER'S SEAT with his arms crossed and a scowl on his face. "I know you're not happy to have me go with you, but Sammy insisted."

"Right," I said. "My problem will be how to explain your presence when I talk to my contact."

"I could pose as your driver. Pull over up ahead, and I'll take the wheel."

"This wheel stays in my hands. The convertible is my baby."

"I thought that was your baby." He nodded toward my stomach.

"Oh, would you be quiet? I don't want to talk."

"We could have had kids when we were married, you know."

"You? A father? I don't think so."

"You're hurting my feelings."

"Why are you bringing this up now? We went our separate ways long ago."

"I know. I think I made a mistake letting you go."

I gritted my teeth to hold back my exasperation. I wanted to throw him out of the car. I struggled to get my irritation under control. I tried deep breathing for several minutes and was able to hold my irritation in check. The way out of this annoying conversation was on my shoulders, so I decided to be the bigger person. As annoying and clueless as he was and as bad a husband as he had been, he had come through for my family and friends many times. I pulled over at a side road.

"Look, Jerry. There's no point in regretting what might have been. You'll find a nice gal, and the two of you will marry and have kids of your own."

His face lit up at my words. "You think so?"

"Sure. I'm sorry I was so harsh with you. It must be baby hormones." I smiled and tapped him on his hand. "With the right partner, you'll become a good husband and father."

"You're saying our breakup was as much your fault as mine.?"

"Don't push it, Jerry." I pulled back onto the road.

It took enormous control for me to say what I did, and it wasn't a lie, well, not much of a lie. He had some good qualities. I had married him . . . against the advice of everyone I knew. Jerry was quiet the remainder of the drive, an inane smile on his face.

I wasn't certain I'd recognize Bud. It had been years, and extreme emotions like my fear I was about to become a gator's dinner tended to wipe out memory, but he recognized me when I pulled into the town center lot. I rolled down my window, he saw me and walked up to the car, his eyes dark with suspicion.

"Hi, Bud. Thanks for seeing me."

Bud returned my greeting with a question. "Who's he?"

Before I could reply, Jerry leaned forward. "I'm her body guard."

Oh, boy. Who would believe that? And yet, Bud seemed to buy it.

"I guess this must be serious if you think you're in danger. How can I help?"

I wouldn't say his demeanor was friendly, but his voice sounded less hostile than it had on the phone.

"Can we find somewhere comfortable to talk? How about the Italian restaurant? I could go for a slice anyway."

"I thought you had finished dinner right before I picked you up," Jerry said.

"I can always eat." And a restroom would be just the ticket about now.

We all trooped in and found a booth in the back. On a weeknight the place wasn't crowded with a few late diners finishing their meals.

"We're about to close, Bud," said the waitress.

"She knows you?" I asked.

"I drop in here from time to time. The place is aware I conduct some business around here, but they don't know what kind. The staff gives me privacy, so we don't have to worry about being overheard."

He waved away the menus she was about to hand us. "Got some pizza left? A few slices are all we need," said Bud. "And a couple of iced teas."

"Make mine water. And I'll take two slices if you have them."

Bud gave me a stare of disbelief. "You finished dinner little more than half an hour ago, and you're up for two slices? What are you, eating for two?"

"Yes."

He was silent for a moment, then said, "Congratulations," but his tone of voice said he was in some doubt as to whether my pregnancy was a good thing or a bad thing. His facial expression said he was sorry I was about to become the poor baby's mother. I couldn't blame him. It had to be difficult to believe I was the same woman he hauled out of the swamp. My first impressions are not always the best ones.

"I've done this before." I hoped to reassure him I had experience in the mothering department.

He cleared his throat and said, "Great," but his tone was unconvincing.

The pizza arrived in a few minutes, and I wolfed down one slice and then reached for the other one. Bud and Jerry had eaten half of theirs. While they finished, I restrained myself from stuffing the other slice into my mouth and putting it down like a bear out of hibernation.

"Here's my dilemma, Bud. I have a friend who has mob connections, or he did. He also has connections with the FBI. Don't ask. It's a long story. He's fallen on misfortune of late and has no idea why. We think someone is after him, well, I think they're after me and want to get to me through him."

"I see what you're saying," Bud said, wiping his mouth.

"Anyway, I received a warning message on my cell, which said my friend's misfortune is the beginning of a lot of trouble planned for me, my family and friends. I'm not going to sit and wait until something else happens, so I think the place to begin is to find out who severed my friend's ties to his money and property. I talked with him and asked him why he didn't go to his contacts in the Bureau, but he said he wasn't certain he trusted them. I need someone at the federal level who can look into whatever might be happening to my friend."

"I'm your choice?"

"Yes. Please." I picked up my half-eaten slice before it got cold and started to finish it off.

"Your friend wouldn't be Nappi Napolitani, would he?" Bud smiled.

CHAPTER 11

━━━

I DROPPED MY SLICE IN ASTONISHMENT. "Nappi is the first name that came to mind? How do you know him?"

Bud gave me a sly smile. "He's been helpful to the DEA at times."

I hadn't expected Nappi had so many federal level contacts. I almost asked Bud if Nappi knew the president.

"He's an interesting guy, you know," Bud added. "He's rumored to be mob connected, but he has no use for illegal drugs. My kind of fella. There have been some rumors circulating he's dropped out of sight."

"He did because someone removed all his assets. He thought by flying under the radar he could reassure whoever was responsible for his misfortune that he was no threat to them. I knew where he was hiding, but while one of his friends was keeping an eye on him, he disappeared. We think he might have been taken against his will."

"You say you received a threat also. Has anything happened to you?'

"Not yet, but as I said, I know something is in the wind. I want to know what." I couldn't control my anger at Nappi's situation. I slammed my fist down on the table, jarring my water glass. Bud reached across the table and caught it before it slopped into my lap.

"You want me to snoop around to see what I can find out?" Bud took the last sip of his drink.

"Yep."

He sat back in his chair and crossed his arms over his chest.

"Well?"

"Don't rush me. I'm thinking about it."

He leaned forward, and I could tell he wasn't happy about whatever decision he had reached.

"It's against my better judgment, but I'll see what I can do."

"Oh, I could kiss you. Thanks."

He put up his hand as if to stop me from getting up from the table and delivering a kiss. "I'm not doing this for you. I'm doing this for Nappi. There's something about the guy. Mob connected or not, and there's some doubt about the connection, he's a decent human being. If something has happened to him and I can help him out, I will."

I gave Bud my cell number and asked him to call with anything he discovered. After I had asked the waitress to wrap up a calzone for me, all of us got in our cars and left.

"When are you going to eat the calzone?" asked Jerry.

"It's not for me. It's for Sammy." I had gotten it for Sammy, but the smell of sausage and sauce made me reconsider. Jerry wouldn't know if I ate it when I got home.

I pulled out of the lot ahead of Bud.

"Success." I relaxed into my seat.

"Watch your speed here, Eve. The railroad crossing is coming up."

I heard a train whistle blow as we approached the crossing. The signal lights flashed, and the gate dropped. I applied my brakes. They felt sluggish, but the car stopped short of the gate, and we waited for the train to cross.

"I think I need to have my brakes looked at. They're kind of spongy."

"Better do it soon. Bad brakes are nothing to play around with."

I remembered the brake incident with Madeleine's uncle's daughter-in-law a few months ago. Someone had cut the brake lines, and she had run into one of the canals running along the Canopy Road to the coast and almost drowned.

"I'll take it slow. We're too far from Indiantown to turn around. Nothing would be open back there at this time of night anyway."

I slowed more and tapped the brake. "I've got no brakes now. I'd better pull over. Someone will be along soon. Meantime, I'll call Madeleine."

"Why not Sammy?" asked Jerry.

"He needs his sleep. He's got a long drive tomorrow."

I kept my foot off the accelerator and moved the car to the side of the road. A gravel pull-off appeared ahead. We coasted onto it.

"We're in luck." The car came to a complete stop short of the end of the pull-off.

Headlights appeared behind us. Jerry stepped out to the side of the road and signaled the driver. The car began to pull over, but before it did, it sped up and flew by us.

"What the . . .? said Jerry.

"Never mind. There's another car right behind him."

This car drove up behind us and stopped. Bud got out.

"What are you doing here?" I asked.

"When you pulled out of the parking lot back there, I spotted a puddle of something on the ground where you were parked. I thought it was suspicious because I heard another car start its engine and pull out of the far end of the lot. It seemed to be on your tail. I went over to the puddle. It was brake fluid, so I jumped in my car to catch up with you. If you hadn't slowed down after you crossed the tracks, I'd never have overtaken you."

"If I hadn't had to stop for the train, I'd never discovered my brakes were faulty. That's why I pulled over."

"The other guy acted as if he was going to stop, then changed his mind." Jerry looked up the road, but the taillights of the car had disappeared into the night.

"I'm certain that was the car I saw follow you out of the lot and held the person or persons responsible for tampering with your brakes," Bud said.

Although the night was hot and humid, it felt cold to me. My teeth began to chatter. Jerry noticed and walked me to Bud's car where he put his jacket around me and sat me down in the back seat.

"Now will you let me call Sammy?" he asked.

"Not now," I said. "Tomorrow is soon enough."

"Then I'm calling Frida."

He was right. This was a matter for the authorities. "Here's my cell." I held it out to him with an unsteady hand.

"Your fingers are cold as ice," Jerry said.

Bud walked over to the car. "You called the police?" he asked Jerry.

"Yep. We have a friend who's a detective on the force. Eve has her personal cell number. I got in touch, and she'll be right here."

Bud leaned down to give me a close look. "Your color is funny."

"I think I ate too much pizza."

"Well, don't throw up in my car."

"I wouldn't think of it." I leaned out and tossed up pizza.

"Nice going," said Jerry.

"What? It wasn't in his car, was it?"

Bud looked down at his once-shiny black alligator cowboy boots. "I shined these up this morning."

I knew how guys in rural Florida felt about their boots. "I'll get you a new pair."

Sirens wailed in the distance, and lights flashed. I recognized the approaching car as Frida's, but behind her an ambulance pulled up.

"Who called the ambulance? Are you sick, Jerry?" I asked.

"No, you are." Frida walked over to the car and gave me one of her penetrating looks. "I called them as soon as Jerry told me what happened here." She held out her hand. "Now off you go."

I leaned back into the seat and ignored her. "But I'm not sick."

Frida nodded to the EMTs who helped me out of the car and walked me to the ambulance.

"You need to think of the baby. Let them take a quick look at you."

"In we go," said the female EMT. Her partner, a male, began taking my vitals.

"I think it's best we take a ride to the hospital to be certain the baby is not in distress," said the woman.

"You think the baby is in danger?" My heart did a quick jump in my chest.

"It's a precaution," she said, her voice soothing.

I thought back to my pregnancy with Netty where I had so stressed myself out, I also had made an emergency trip to the hospital and was admitted for a few days. I wanted this to be a normal pregnancy, one where I didn't have to be carted off for medical observation to make certain everything was fine. I thought I was handling this one so well and now, here I was about to take another ambulance ride.

"It's only for the night," the male EMT said, as if he had read my fears.

"You're not Miccosukee, are you, and related to the Egrets?" I asked. It seemed all the Egret clan could read my thoughts.

"Huh?" His forehead wrinkled in a puzzled expression. "How did you know?"

"I'll tell you if you go into my car and get me my calzone. If I leave it, it'll go bad and I might want it for breakfast."

"I'm riding along." Jerry tried to step into the ambulance.

"No, you are not." Frida restrained him. "You are staying right here to tell me what happened tonight."

The ambulance pulled onto the road. "Sorry we had to leave your husband. I'm sure he's worried, but I told him everything would be fine." The female EMT gave me an encouraging smile. "And here's your calzone."

I read her name tag. "Thanks, Deirdre." My stomach growled. I grabbed the calzone out of her hand.

"Better not eat it right now."

"I'm starving."

"Pregnant women always are, and you look as if you could use some meat on your bones," she said.

"I'm always like this. This is my fighting weight."

Both EMTs looked puzzled at my statement. I decided not to try to explain, but I wanted to clear up Jerry's relationship with me. "He's not my husband. We were out having a snack and . . ." What I was saying didn't sound quite right. "We were married, but now . . ."

"The other guy was your husband, right?" asked the EMT with the name badge reading "Tommy."

"No, he joined us at the restaurant, but he's not my husband either. My husband is at home, Asleep."

They exchanged puzzled looks.

Deirdre whispered to her colleague. "Baby hormones."

"I heard what you said. It's not baby hormones. I'm always like this. Just not so hungry."

ONCE IN THE EMERGENCY ROOM, I waited for over an hour before a doctor entered my cubicle. He completed his examination and then gave me an encouraging smile. "You're fine Mrs. Egret, and so is the baby."

"I can leave then?"

He nodded. "There are two fellows here, Bud and Jerry. They're anxious to see how you're doing. Do you want me to let them in here after you're dressed?"

I slid off the examining table and was slipping into my clothes. "Great.

They're my ride home." I fumbled around with the clothes on the chair. "Is this everything?"

The nurse who had given me a gown to wear when I came in, looked concerned. "Are you missing something?"

"My calzone."

"I tossed it in the garbage." She pointed toward the waste receptacle in the corner.

My shoulders slumped in defeat. The calzone and I were not meant to be.

Jerry stuck his head around the curtain. "Ready for company and to go home?"

He and Bud stepped into the room.

I shrugged into my jacket and held out my hand to Jerry.

"What?"

"You've got my cell. I gave it to you to call Frida. Where is Frida??"

"Did I hear someone mention my name?" Frida also stepped into the small cubicle. "I've got Sammy with me."

I hadn't wanted to disturb Sammy, but when he came into the room and wrapped his arms around me, I felt better, as if everything would be all right.

He stepped back and gazed at me through eyes clouded dark with hurt. "Why did Frida have to call me. Why didn't you put in the call, Eve?"

Jerry put his hand on Sammy's shoulder. "Eve didn't want to worry you, and things happened so fast . . ."

"But she's my wife, and it's my baby." The hurt look turned to anger.

"Sorry, old man," said Jerry.

"I'm sorry, Sammy, but I'm fine and so is the baby. It wasn't my idea to call an ambulance."

Sammy's expression softened, and he once more pulled me close. "It's okay, my love."

"Is Eve okay? What about the baby?" A pair of twinkling blue eyes appeared in the opened curtain.

"Grandy? What are you doing here? I thought you were in Key Largo." Max peered over her shoulder.

"Did you think I wouldn't hurry here when I heard what happened?"

The nurse pushed her way into the room. "I don't think there's room for everyone in here."

"There's more family in the waiting room. Let's go home. I'm sure you need rest." Grandy reached out and took my arm.

"How about some weak tea and toast?" Her smiling face couldn't cover the concern in her eyes.

"Tea? Toast?" I found the suggestion a poor replacement for my cheesy, fatty calzone. "How about a nice big slice of cheesecake?"

"We don't have any," said Grandy. "And it's not good for the baby."

"It's good for me."

"Eve, don't create trouble."

I gave in. When Grandy took me in hand, I knew there was no fighting her.

"Yes, Ma'am."

In the waiting room I was greeted by the boys and Netty as well as Grandfather. They ran to me and all embraced me. Netty held her arms out to be picked up.

"Meemie all right?" There was fear in her eyes, and her sweet little mouth curved down and quivered.

"Don't cry, baby. I'm fine." I picked her up and cuddled her to me. "Let's go home."

Frida touched my shoulder as we walked out of the hospital. "I need to talk to you, but tomorrow is fine." She smiled and walked to her car, turning when she opened the door to give me a wave of her hand.

"I need a ride," said Jerry.

"I'll drop you," said Bud.

"I owe you more than I can say," I said to Bud.

"Yes, you do." His tone was serious, but I thought I spotted the side of his mouth tip upward a bit in the beginning of a smile. "I'll be in touch."

Sammy helped me into his truck next to Grandfather who slid into the middle of the front seat next to me. Sammy lifted Netty from my arms, and then buckled her into the car seat in Grandy and Max's car. The boys squeezed themselves into the back seat with Netty. It had been a long night for all of us. Grandfather put his arm around me, and we headed home. Could I have been anymore exhausted? I had difficulty keeping my eyes open.

Through a yawn, I said, "I'll tell you everything about tonight as soon as I get some food in me."

"Food can wait," Sammy said.

I wanted to assure him I needed something in my stomach to be able to give him a full account of the night, but the next thing I knew he was tucking me into our bed. I turned on my side and drifted into sleep.

THE NEXT MORNING OVER A CUP OF COCOA and toast with peanut butter, Grandy informed me Sammy had left with the horse trailer to pick up Jay's horses. "He said he'd be back before noon and to keep you in bed for the day."

"In bed? I'm not staying in bed. I've got work to do."

Grandy pulled her chair closer to mine at the table. "I know you're not staying in bed. Sammy is being overprotective, but I did call Madeleine and tell her what was going on. She said she and Renata would take care of the store today."

"I need to talk with Crusty."

"I already made arrangements. He's coming here for lunch."

"And Frida."

"She'll be here soon. Everything is fine. Now you sit back and enjoy your cocoa."

"Hanging around here all day is almost as bad as staying in bed. I'm not an invalid."

"You're beginning to whine, Eve." Grandy gave me a stern look.

I heard a car drive up to the house. Through the front windows, I saw Frida get out. I opened the door to her.

"Is this a good time to talk?" she asked.

"Sure. Maybe you'd like to take me out for coffee."

She gave me a puzzled look. "We can get coffee here, can't we?"

"Shh," I said, "I don't want Grandy to hear. I'll tell her you need to question me down at police headquarters."

"Okay, but why?"

"Otherwise she won't let me out of the house. She thinks I need rest."

"Don't you after last night?"

"No, I need pastry. Let's go."

Frida did a convincing job of telling Grandy she had left her always present notebook at the station, so we had to go back there.

Grandy allowed me to leave because I was with Frida.

"Do you think she believed me?" Frida said when we got into the car.

"No, but she's not going to question an officer of the law."

"There is something I need to tell you, and it's better Grandy doesn't hear it because it's part of an official case."

"Why can I hear it?"

"Because I think it may be related to something you and Crusty are looking into."

"Okay but get me a donut first. I can listen better with sugar coursing through my system."

Donut in hand, I settled into a chair in Frida's office.

"You know the dead body we fished out of the canal near here?"

I nodded.

"We talked with Homer Smith, the owner of the stable where you said the dead guy, Mateo worked. He said whoever told us Mateo worked for him must have been mistaken. A Juan Mateo never worked for him. We asked him to look at the body. He said he'd never seen the man before."

CHAPTER 12

———

"**S**MITH WAS LYING TO YOU, YOU know."

"I know. I didn't reveal my source for Mateo's name to him. My question is, why wouldn't he tell me the truth? He's taking a serious chance hiding something from the authorities in a murder case."

"I assume you've checked into Smith, and he's legitimate?"

"Yeah, I know the name sounds phony, but it appears he's on the up and up." Frida hesitated, and she dropped her gaze as if she was reluctant to continue talking.

"You have something else important, but you're unwilling to talk to me about it?"

"I hate to admit this, but your pal Nappi always had such great sources of information. If anyone could find out all there is to know about Smith, Nappi could. I haven't seen him around here for a while. Do you know where he is?"

"No, I don't." And I wasn't lying.

"Are you certain? You know how you like to keep things from me."

"Not this time."

"Odd. You always know where he is. Or how to get in touch with him." She waited, but I said nothing.

"How about Jerry? Would he know?"

"Jerry never knows anything." I knew I sounded defensive. "I mean, you know Jerry is out of the loop most of the time."

"Okay, then. Let's go over last night. Bud thinks the guy who sped off right before he arrived was responsible for tampering with your brakes. We towed your car, and this morning our lab confirmed someone did tamper with them. Could this be related to Jay's trouble and Mateo's body? Did anything else happen?"

She was so smart. "No." I reached for another donut.

"You would tell me if it did?"

I nodded.

"Nappi not being around much isn't related, you don't think?"

"You know how Nappi is. He has his own life."

"You know Bud is DEA, don't you?"

I nodded, wishing I had room for another donut to cram in my mouth so I couldn't respond to her questions. I'd only back myself into a corner and wouldn't be able to get out.

"What's the connection with you, Jerry and Bud?'

"What did he tell you?"

"He said he bumped into you and Jerry in Indiantown and the three of you had pizza together. Since when do you and Jerry get together for pizza?"

"We were married once."

"Yes, and I know you have little use for the guy."

"Look, Frida, Jerry and I are working a case for Crusty. I can't reveal the details. I must protect our client. Now, if you would, point me toward a restroom. I drank about two gallons of orange juice and a liter of cocoa."

"I'll take you there. I'll be right outside."

Frida walked me down the hall and leaned against the wall waiting for me. I had considered escaping so I wouldn't have to answer any more questions, but the restroom didn't have a window. I looked at the air conditioning duct, but decided I'd have to confront her sometime. She had been nice enough to feed me donuts and cocoa and orange juice. And more donuts. What a friend.

When I finished, I washed my hands and looked at my face in the mirror, I almost regretted leaving the house without making further repairs, but I remedied my appearance by running damp hands through my hair and swishing with cold water to remove any donut crumbs from my teeth. There. It was as good as it was going to get.

I stuck my head out of the doorway.

"I'm here. You didn't expect me to leave, did you?" Frida tipped her head to one side as if questioning whether I was capable of bolting through the exit door.

"Don't be silly," I said. "I'm not going anywhere. I need a ride home. Besides there's a donut left. My favorite, a chocolate-covered one. Let's go."

Back in her office, we settled back into our chairs. To my regret someone had removed the donut box while we were gone.

Frida seemed to understand I wasn't going to answer any more inquiries about Nappi, Jerry and Bud. "Tell me about the brakes."

Easy. Not much lying was required. Anything to do with the meeting with Bud could be covered by client confidentiality.

"Why didn't you take Lionel with you last night? He seems like a better bodyguard than Jerry."

Oops. Now I had to make up some story about Lionel's absence which didn't reveal he was searching for Nappi.

"I didn't need a bodyguard. I needed a driver."

"After last night, it appears you now need a bodyguard." Frida threw back her head and rolled her eyes at the ceiling. She'd been doing a lot of that.

We stared at each other for a long minute. I cleared my throat. "I don't know what happened to my brakes. When I slowed for the train, they felt mushy, so I pulled over. Then Bud showed up. Then you showed up. Then I threw up, went to the hospital and lost my calzone."

"Bud says he thinks those responsible for cutting your brakes followed you out of Indiantown and were about to pull over behind you."

"Bud might be right."

"Do you have any idea who might want to do you harm?"

"They could have wanted to harm Jerry, not me."

Frida gave another eye roll. "Be serious, Eve. You have a way of annoying people. Jerry is a klutz. Was there someone you might have annoyed into wanting you dead or injured?"

I'd have to tell Frida about the threat I received, but could I do it without letting her know about what was going on with Nappi? I needed to talk this over with Crusty. And with Lionel.

Frida and I did our silent staring thing again.

"I don't suppose I'll get anything more out of you now." Frida sighed, pushed back in her chair and looked down at me with grave disappoint-ment in her eyes. "I'll take you home before Grandy calls and gives me what for."

Frida was a good friend, and I felt guilty not being able to be honest with her.

"Maybe your guilt will get to you and make you talk to me."

"Don't start," I said.

"What?"

"The mind reading thing. Can't I have any private thoughts?"

She gave me a snarky little smile. "One more thing. I let it slip to Jay about finding a body because he seemed to need more convincing that the loss of his horse and the beating of his driver and a death, a homicide, was too much criminal activity in this county to be unrelated. You know how stubborn he is. Do you think I convinced him?"

"No. Jay does what he wants to do. You know him."

"You're right." She grabbed my arm and led me out of her office. The deepening worry lines on her face told me she was concerned Jay would do something foolish. I was also. Maybe I could find out if he intended to ship the horse to his friend sooner than he said he would. Simply because Jay Cassidy promised you one thing didn't mean he wouldn't go ahead and do whatever he wanted.

FRIDA DROPPED ME BACK HOME WITH A WARNING. "If you rethink your willingness to be honest with me, you know how to find me."

"I wasn't dishonest . . ." I got out of the car and turned to look at her. Instead she drove off in a cloud of dust without so much as a wave goodbye.

Crusty sat in my kitchen drinking a cup of coffee which Grandfather had prepared.

"This coffee is so much better than anything I make. Or you make, Eve. How do you do this?" he asked Grandfather.

Grandfather pointed to the coffeepot on the stove. It was an old bat-tered perk pot. "Toss the grounds into the pot with an egg shell to clarify the brew, and then boil it."

"For how long?"

Grandfather smiled. "For how long it takes. Want a refill?"

Crusty nodded.

I grabbed a glass of juice from the fridge and dropped into a chair at the table. "Where's Grandy?'

"She left to do some shopping. She also let drop she had a birthday coming up soon. I know she wouldn't want me to remind you about it, but with everything happening around here, I assume you forgot." Grandfather wiped his hands on a towel and looked at me, one eyebrow cocked, not accusingly, because that wasn't his way, but inquisitively because that was. "I'll leave you and Crusty to talk."

He left through the back door, and I watched him walk across the yard to his house next door. He was hiding disappointment because he thought I had forgotten Grandy's birthday. This was an important one, too. Her eightieth. I had talked to Sammy about it, but then hadn't followed up. As I watched Grandfather, an idea came to me.

I threw open the window and yelled to him. "I didn't forget. It's a big day, so it calls for a big celebration. I hope you're free Saturday."

"Evening?" he asked.

"Most of the day and into the evening. We don't want to miss the fireworks. We'll meet here at ten in the morning." I was so excited. I wanted to dance around the room. Instead I did a little jig over to the table.

Crusty gave me a puzzled look. "Your baby hormones making you looney . . . more looney?

I shared with him my birthday surprise, and then he and I got down to business.

Sammy drove in as Crusty and I finished talking.

"Any problems?" I asked as I threw my arms around him and gave him my very best cleared for public viewing kiss.

"Nope. What are you two up to? If it's detective stuff, I'm leaving anyway. I've got to return the trailer and get out to the game reserve. I wanted to stop by to reassure you and to see how you were doing." He gave me a squeeze, then held me at arm's length. "You look like you've been plotting. Have you? Or can't I know?"

"It's about Grandy's birthday celebration."

"I meant to remind you. I assumed you had forgotten."

Why did everyone assume I hadn't remembered Grandy's birthday? Well, it had slipped my mind a little until Grandfather gave me a gentle nudge.

I shared my plans with Sammy.

"Short notice," he said.

"It is. With the way everyone around here reads my mind, it has to be."

Sammy gave me a goodbye hug and was off.

"You and your gal can come if you'd like," I told Crusty.

"We won't ruin the fun?"

"Nope. A big party with all your friends is always more fun." Could Jerry be considered a friend? Did I have to invite him also? Nappi wouldn't be there, and that saddened me. I was certain Lionel, wherever he was, would find out about the party. I intended to invite Madeleine and family and Renata. If Lionel showed up, he and Renata would have to work things out and not spoil the fun.

Disney. I knew Grandy would be thrilled. I know I was.

"Okay. I see your mind is off on the party, but we need to finalize our approach to Jay's situation and to whether or not we bring Frida into the loop about the warning and our speculations about Juan Mateo, Nappi's disappearance and . . ."

His words cut into my thoughts about the party. We had left Frida in the dark about so many issues related to her murder investigation and Jay's case. Guilt almost ruined the joy I was feeling about Grandy's upcoming birthday celebration, but not quite. Maybe Frida would like to come along to the party. She could bring her kids. Or were they too old for Disney? Was anyone too old for Disney?

I brought myself back to the present. "I think we need to tell Frida everything we know and suspect."

"Including the situation with Nappi? By the way, what is his current situation?" Crusty asked.

"I don't really know, but I'm afraid whoever is behind all of this has found him. Lionel is out there looking for him. I seem to have lost track of both."

"They're big boys. They can take care of themselves."

I wasn't so sure. Nappi seemed so defeated when I saw him.

I heard a truck pull into the drive. It was Sammy, and he was pulling Jay's trailer.

I ran out the door, worried something was wrong. "Why do you still have Jay's trailer?"

"Jay said it was in better shape than ours, so he told me to take it to the coast and pick up the pony. I thought I'd stop by here for Jacob and let him drive since you promised him he could get the pony today."

"It was generous of Jay to let you use his trailer." It was generous. I wondered what Jay had in mind.

"Don't give me your suspicious look, Eve. I'm sure Jay was being considerate. Where's my son?"

I peeked at the clock. Jacob only had a half day of school today and was due any minute. "He's probably on his way home. I'll make sandwiches for both of you, and you'll be ready to go when he gets here."

"I'm off," said Crusty. "I can talk to Frida this afternoon. If I leave it to you, you might decide to leave out some details."

"I did all my lying to her this morning. I think I owe her an honest conversation. I'll do it."

Crusty got into his truck and rolled down the window. "I'll let you know about Saturday." He waved and drove off.

Sammy put his arm around me and gave me a deep look. "We're alone." His voice was low, and he ran his hand suggestively up and down my back, making me tingle all over.

"Not quite."

Netty ran down the steps of Grandfather's house. "My pony comes today, today, today," she sang, her entire face aglow with joy. "Goodie. Goodie. Goodie."

It was going to be a busy week: Netty getting acquainted with her pony, the Disney trip and whatever other situations might, probably would, arise.

Sammy grabbed her and tossed her into the air. "Here comes your brother. We're going to get the pony right now. Would you like to ride with us?"

She wriggled out of his arms and bolted for the truck.

"How about a little lunch first?" I asked.

"No." She climbed into the front seat and crossed her arms over her chest. "Hurry."

"Sammy, you can't take her in the truck. She has to ride in her car seat, and it needs to be in the back."

Netty's smile faded, replaced by a quivering lip, a sure sign tears and howls would follow.

"Tell you what, Netty. You and I can follow your brother and Dad in our van. Okay?" I held out my hand, she took it and climbed down from the truck. "A sandwich first?"

She shook her head.

I gave Sammy a helpless look.

"I'll make them for all of us and bring yours and Netty's with me. You and Netty can go ahead, and we'll meet you there. Netty can meet her pony and make friends."

Good. Netty might have been too excited to eat, but I was starved. As usual.

"Have you decided on a name for your pony?"

We were halfway down the Canopy Road to the coast. The day was perfect, the humidity low. The overhanging limbs of the live oaks were hung with Spanish moss, and sunlight and shade created light and shadow patterns on the pavement. I loved this road.

"I think maybe she should be named Twinkle." Netty's voice sounded very certain. The name would stick, unless Netty decided on another one before we met the pony. One moment Netty might be adamant about something, but the next she could do an about face. When I pointed this out to Grandy, she told me my mother said I was the same when I was her age.

"You're still like that," Grandy added.

I smiled to myself at the memory. "Okay, then. Twinkle it is."

"Of maybe Freckles."

Hmm.

"Or Sadie. Or . . ."

"It might be better if you waited until you met her."

"Okay."

There was a black van coming up fast in my rearview mirror.

"Stupid jerk," I muttered. "He's going too fast for this road."

The van pulled out to pass me, then swerved into me, making me jerk the wheel to my left. The road had no shoulders, only the trees and beyond them a deep ditch on each side of the pavement.

I got lucky because as I swerved, the gravel turnoff to a ranch opened to my right. I steered onto it and stomped on my brakes. The van pulled off the road ahead of me and backed up.

The driver stuck his head out the window. "Are you okay? Sorry, lady, but I dropped my cell phone and was looking on the seat for it."

I got out of my van and approached his driver's side door. The fact someone had gotten out of the passenger's side of his vehicle didn't register with me until I heard Netty scream. I turned to look back and saw someone had opened the back door and reached into my van. The man was trying to pull Netty out of her car seat. Whoever it was wasn't familiar with child restraint seats because he struggled to free her while Netty continued to yell. I whirled around to dash back to my van, but the driver of the other vehicle opened his door hitting me and throwing me off balance. I stumbled but regained my footing while he grabbed at my clothing as I fled. He got ahold of my shirt. I halted, turned on him and slammed my fist into his face. He clapped his hand over his nose, blood running between his fingers. His partner, struggling to free Netty, made a final effort to extract her. I continued my run for her and heard the guy with Netty yell out in pain.

He turned when he saw me coming, then yelled at the driver. "Let's get out of here."

I grabbed for him, but he sidestepped me, and ran to the black van. The driver hesitated a moment, and I thought he might come back for me. Or Netty.

Instead he wiped his nose on his sleeve. "I'm not finished with you. I'll be back." He jumped into the van, and it sped off.

"Netty, are you okay?" I reached in for my daughter whose face was white with fear, but when I gathered her into my arms, she appeared to be physically unharmed.

"I got him, didn't I, Meemie?"

"What do you mean, honey?"

"I bited him on his ear."

CHAPTER 13

—

THERE WERE A FEW DROPS OF BLOOD on Netty's lower lip. I extracted a tissue from my pocket and wiped it off.

"It sure looks like you did get him, love." I continued to hug her close.

"Too tight, Meemie." She wiggled in my arms.

We were safe. Or were we? Nappi had gone into hiding to protect us, but I now knew keeping out of sight was doing nothing to safeguard anyone. I was sure both Jay had been targeted and so had I the night I'd left Indiantown. And now Netty and me. It was silly to believe whoever was after us would back off if Nappi behaved and stayed out of it. He believed they had killed his grandfather. I believed they wanted all of us to suffer or to die. I needed to get more aggressive with finding out who was responsible. I wanted Nappi to see the situation as I did. Think, Eve, think. It was time to go back to the beginning. To Nappi's grandfather's death. Frida could get access to the autopsy report. Lionel said he would be in touch. How? Could he find Nappi again? I loosened my hold on Netty but didn't let her go. I never wanted her out of my arms, but I knew holding her close could not protect her. I had work to do.

Coming up behind me was our truck and the horse trailer.

Jacob was driving. He pulled over, Sammy jumped out of the passenger's side. "What happened, Eve?"

I quickly told him about my encounter. He took Netty from my arms and sat her back in her car seat, and after assuring himself she wasn't hurt, he turned to me taking my hand in his and looking deeply into my eyes.

"Ouch." I withdrew my hand from his grasp. "I think I damaged my hand when I hit the guy."

"Okay, then. We need to get you medical attention, and maybe it would be a good idea to have a doctor look at Netty, too."

"Don't want to go to the doctor. I want my pony."

"I think she's fine, Sammy, but we do need to call Frida and let her know what happened here. It's another part of a puzzle a very horrible person has been laying out for us."

I contacted Frida who was leaving Crusty's office. In less than twenty minutes she pulled up with a crime scene van behind her.

"We have to stop meeting like this." There were worry lines across her forehead.

I gave her a weak smile and tried to hide my hand behind me. I told her we were unhurt when I called. The last thing I wanted was another trip in an ambulance, but with the delay in picking up the pony, big tears rolled down Netty's face. I handed my cellphone to Sammy and asked him to call Grandy to pick up Netty and take her to the rescue facility. At least she could meet the pony and get to know Twinkle or Freckles or . . .

"Wanda. I think her name might be Wanda." Netty wiped the tears off her face with her hand.

She could meet the little gal while the adults sorted out the attack.

"Don't worry, honey. We'll let your brother get on the road soon, and you'll have your pony home in a few hours." Sammy pushed a damp ringlet off her forehead and took a tissue from me to blow her nose.

"I don't know if I want Jacob going off alone," I said.

"We'll stay here with you while you and Frida talk. I don't think these guys will try anything more." Sammy then leaned close to me. "What about your hand?'

"Is there something wrong with your hand, Eve?" Frida asked. "You said you hit the guy. Did you hurt yourself?"

"Maybe a little." My hand was throbbing with pain. I pulled it out from behind my back to look at it. Frida gave it a gander, clucked over me like a mother hen, and then called the ambulance.

"I've got something I should have told you," I said to her while we waited for the ambulance to show.

"Why am I not surprised?"

"Listen to this." I held up my phone to let her listen to the phone warning I had received.

"I know you're mad," I said.

"No, I'm glad, glad you're not hurt." She hugged me until my ribs hurt. The ambulance pulled up, and I got to reconnect with my EMT buddies.

I wasn't transported to the hospital again, but my friend EMT Deirdre recommended I have a doctor look at the hand tomorrow.

"I don't think anything's broken, but it's badly bruised and swollen. Ice will help."

Yes, it would especially if it was surrounded by a shot of Scotch, but booze was off the menu for me.

I WATCHED AS NETTY LED HER NEW PONY around the field next to our house. It was two days after I'd given the guy a bloody nose and the day before everyone was to go to Disney. I hadn't forgotten my determination to delve into Nappi's grandfather's death to discover the identity of the individuals targeting us. Frida promised to see what she could find from the discovery of the death and in the autopsy report. If there was foul play, something would show up.

"Or," Frida told me, "maybe there's been a cover-up with the police or the coroner's office."

"If you go nosing around, won't it arouse suspicions?" I asked.

"Give me some credit, Eve. I can be as devious as you about my sleuthing."

Both Crusty and I were anxious to contact Lionel in hopes he had a lead on where Nappi might be hiding.

"How does he keep in touch with you?" Crusty asked.

"The way he wants." I shrugged. "It's up to him. I don't push." No one pushed Lionel Egret.

Sammy wanted to hold off our Saturday trip, but I was adamant Grandy deserved a grand party and what better time than now. My hand was healing nicely. So far everyone had managed to keep Disney a secret from Grandy. She thought leaving for some unknown destination mid-morning Saturday was odd, but I lied to her and told her we were going to a museum in Orlando.

"What museum?" she had asked.

I couldn't think of the name of one, so I made one up. "It's an orchid museum."

"I've always loved orchids," Grandy said.

"And we'll have dinner somewhere there," I said.

"Where?" Grandy had asked. I shouldn't have embellished my reply to her.

"You're a nosey old thing, aren't you?"

"Orchids are nice. At least you're not taking me to Disney. That's for kids."

"Disney is for adults, too." Oops. I'd always thought she loved the idea of Disney. Was I making a mistake?

"I guess I think of the Magic Kingdom as Disney. Now that is for kids."

"Epcot. That's not just for kids."

"I don't think any of the Disney stuff is for me."

Had I miscalculated?

As we continued to watch Netty and her pony, who had been renamed several times, but was now known simply as "Ponygirl," I asked Grandfather if he thought Grandy was serious about saying Disney was only for kids.

Grandfather laughed. "I was there when you and she talked. Didn't you notice her expression? There was a twinkle in her eyes. She's putting you on. She's hoping it will be the Magic Kingdom and not some orchid museum. You know her better than to believe she wouldn't be up for a little fun." He left the room, muttering, "Orchid museum. What a dumb lie."

"What? She loves orchids," I yelled after him.

He stuck his head back into the room. "She loves Cinderella, Snow White and Mickey Mouse more."

I called to Netty and told her dinner would be ready soon. Until we built a barn, she knew it was her responsibility to take the pony into the corral and set up her feed.

"Can I ride her tomorrow?" Netty asked as she washed her hands for dinner.

"No. Remember? Tomorrow is Grandy's birthday celebration. The museum."

Netty smirked at me. "No museum. Disney."

"How do you know?" I asked. The last person I wanted to find out about the surprise was Netty. I knew she'd tell everyone including Grandy.

"Grammy told me."

What? How did Grandy find out?

"But it was supposed to be a surprise," I said.

Netty ran into the kitchen, giggling. "Everyone knows. Grammy wants to dress up as one of the Disney characters. And me too."

It was good to know I hadn't misjudged Grandy's fondness for Disney even though the surprise factor was blown.

WE HAD QUITE THE CARAVAN driving out of town the next morning. Frida was with us, but her kids weren't. She said they had something else on for the day, but I thought she hadn't wanted them along because she was being our police protective escort, unofficial of course. Crusty and Margie drove in his truck, and Grandy and Max accompanied Sammy and me in the van with Netty. Madeleine and David with the two twins drove their large SUV, our two youngest boys in the far back seat. Jacob was at the wheel of Sammy's truck with Grandfather as the passenger. Although I was certain Shelley would gladly have minded the store, Renata passed on the trip and volunteered to work. I wondered if she had somehow managed to contact Lionel and the two of them were planning to meet while the rest of us were away. If they did meet, it took the burden off my shoulders for talking to either of them about what was going on in their relationship.

"I know you found out we're not going to the orchid museum," I said to Grandy as we drove north. "And don't play coy with me by denying you know."

I turned in my seat to look at her. Her blue eyes were round with the look of innocence she was so good at feigning. Why couldn't I pretend ingenuousness? It must have been a gene that skipped several generations. I held up my finger to let her know I wasn't having any of her guiltless maneuvers.

"Are we having lunch with Mickey?" she asked.

I nodded.

"Will I be dressing up like Cinderella?"

"No. You'll be the fairy godmother" I said.

"I want to be Cinderella. You be the fairy godmother."

"I'm not fat enough."

"They can pad you." Grandy sat back in her seat, arms crossed over her chest. The only one who could dissuade her from her Cinderella selection might have been Netty, but she announced her choice as Snow White. Shucks. Snow White was my second choice. Sammy acted as if he was paying no attention to this gals' argument, but I caught the corner of his mouth twitch.

"You'd make a good Prince Charming, but I'll bet Max has dibs on it already," I said.

Sammy gulped and glanced in the rearview mirror as if to confirm Max's role. Max smiled, and Sammy tossed me a relieved look he wouldn't be the one wearing tights.

WITH THE HEAVY TRAFFIC NEARING ORLANDO, it took some maneuvering to keep the vehicles together so we could park near one another in the lot. By the time we got everyone ready to catch the train to the park, it was close to one in the afternoon. We were all hungry, and the younger kids were cranky from the long ride. We grabbed some lunch to go as soon as we got into the park. We had decided ahead of time what attractions we would go for. I had gotten us a fast pass so we wouldn't have to wait in lines. David, Sammy and our boys went with the rest of us for Pirates of the Caribbean, then departed to Epcot for the more "adult" adventures. Crusty and Margie wandered along behind us, seemingly more interested in each other than in what the park had to offer. We all arranged to meet at the Italian restaurant in Epcot. I'd made reservations there at six. Before we walked to any of the other rides, we stopped for ice cream and then had pictures taken with Mickey and friends. Netty, Madeleine's Eve and Grandy dressed up as princesses for the photo opts. I held back disappointment I couldn't be one also, but I didn't want to compete with the children or ruin Grandy's obvious joy at celebrating her birthday as royalty. Netty loved the parade, but probably not as much as Grandy did. Max grinned from ear to ear to see his wife's delight with her birthday present.

"I should have thought of this," he said to me as we watched Goofy and company ride past us on their float. Before we departed the kingdom for our dinner rendezvous, we let the kids choose a souvenir from one of the gift shops. Netty chose a huge stuffed Minnie Mouse, almost as big as she was.

Everyone was on time for our dinner reservation. I don't think we used up the kids' reserves of energy nor Grandy's, but the rest of us were more than happy to sit on a real chair and relax. Smelling the garlic and spices as we perused the menu made me think of Nappi and how he loved to cook for us. I teared up at the thought of my good friend and worried about where he was. Was he safe? Was Lionel wrong about Nappi seeking a new hiding place? Had someone taken him and hurt him? The worst was thinking he might be dead.

"Are you okay, Eve?" asked Sammy.

"Fine." I grabbed the napkin to stem the flow of tears and blew my nose.

"May I offer senora my handkerchief?" Our waiter gave me a brilliantly white linen handkerchief. So like Nappi's, I thought, and sobbed harder.

"No, I couldn't." I shook my head. How could I dirty this pristine square of cloth? I turned to look up into the waiter's chocolate brown eyes. I gasped in surprise.

"Nappi?"

He smiled and held his finger over his mouth. "Shh."

"Oh, no," I said. "They kidnapped you and forced you to wait tables?"

Nappi continued to grin and shook his head.

Sammy also recognized him.

"Old man. Good to see you. We were worried. About you."

"Let's be cool about this," said Nappi. "Would the table like to see a wine list? I'll send the wine steward over."

"Not for me or my Eve, but the other adults might like to choose something," Sammy said.

Nappi summoned another server from the corner of the room. The tall man approached the table and handed David the wine list. David pointed to the list. "I think we'll have this chianti."

"May I recommend something rounder, less sharp on the tongue? Perhaps this one." The wine steward pointed to another selection.

I leaned over to look at the choice.

"Oh, sure. It's the most expensive red on the menu. It's a ploy to get you to spend more," I said to David, but he brushed my comments away with a wave of his hand.

The wine steward directed his attention to me. "Perhaps Madam might like a sparkling cider, nonalcoholic."

"How did you know . . ." I didn't finish my sentence because his voice sounded so familiar. I leaned toward him to get a better look. "Lionel? How did you get here?"

He shrugged. "The usual way. I rode in a car. With him." Lionel pointed to Nappi.

We topped off our dinner with tiramisu. Netty gave her piece to me. It made up for my not being able to enjoy wine with my lasagna. After everyone at the table realized we were being waited on, not by two Italian natives, but by a friend and a relative, we settled down to an enjoyable meal, but I could tell Frida was as anxious to talk to Nappi and Lionel as I was. I glanced several times at Crusty, who gave me a curt nod, acknowledging he had recognized Nappi and Lionel, but he quickly turned his attention to Margie who was feeding him bites of bruschetta.

"We'll find you later at the pyrotechnic display," said Nappi. "We can talk there." He bowed as he took my credit card and left. When he returned, I checked the bill. Had I misread the amount when I first looked at it? It now read $5.33.

"Excuse me." I waved to our server. "There's been some mistake."

"No, madam."

The man who returned the bill and my card was not Nappi.

"The man over there paid for your meal." The server gestured to the back of the room where I caught a glimpse of another waiter and a tall wine steward retreat behind the kitchen doors.

"Do you know him?" I asked.

"No. He's new. Was there a problem with his service?"

"Not at all. It was perfect."

Everyone wanted to leave to get a good viewing spot for the fireworks. Although the food provided the fuel I needed to get through the rest of the evening, knowing Nappi was safe was better than a full rack of ribs and an order of slaw.

Crusty, Frida and I left the others to find their places for the fireworks while we stayed behind near the side of the restaurant. Nappi and Lionel met us, and we conferred about what steps we could take to find out who was responsible for the threatening note to me, the attempted abduction of Netty and threats against family and friends.

"Someone has it in for you," said Frida. "And I don't mean because of your in-your-face attitude. It's more like payback for something big."

I laughed. "I've solved a few murders, but those involved local folks. Well, except for my uncle who had ties to the Russian Mob."

The sky lit up in a blaze of brilliant colors, and explosions ripped through the air. Oohs and ahs from the crowd followed each display

"Meemie, come." Netty tugged at my hand to pull me over to where the others were watching the fireworks.

Frida and Nappi joined us to watch the display of lights and sounds.

I thought about my uncle's death and whether the Russian Mob would involve itself in revenge activities against me, my friends and family. Why would they care? His murder was more personal than about mob business.

I leaned over and spoke to Frida. "Maybe it's not at all about retaliation for a murder I solved. There are other criminal issues I've poked my nose into."

Nappi overheard me. "You've been a busy sleuth over the years, dabbled in all kinds of illegal activities. Think back."

"Are you going back in hiding," I asked Nappi, "or is this something you want to be a part of?"

"I'm in. It was a mistake for me to try to make myself invisible. I was giving in to their demands, and it only encouraged whoever is behind this. I apologize, Eve, for failing you." Nappi took my hand and kissed it. Now that was the Nappi I knew.

"Welcome back to the team. I missed you."

Sammy lifted Netty to his shoulder so she would have a better view of the light show. We were all one family.

In the silence following the finale of the light display, I felt the hairs on the back of my neck stand on end. I spun on my heel and searched the crowd behind me, but no one looked familiar and no one met my gaze. Was I paranoid or simply cautious?

CHAPTER 14

———

WATCHING A FIREWORKS DISPLAY with my family was not the time to figure out who was behind this payback play, if payback was what it was. Besides, I had used the word "team" with Nappi. Deciphering what was going on needed the input of others, not simply mine, so Nappi, Frida, Crusty and I arranged to meet the next morning at Crusty's office.

"Me, too. You leave me out of everything you do." said Madeleine. David scowled at her but said nothing. He didn't want her involved, but he knew better than to verbalize it to her.

I had promised her a few months back she could help with a case, but I hadn't followed through.

"And me," added Grandy.

Grandy had proved herself useful on other adventures, so how could I deny her this one? As for Max? His excitement was fishing.

I fell into bed exhausted when we got home but awoke in the middle of the night to the sound of a truck revving its engine on the main road. When I looked out our bedroom window, I saw taillights, four of them. Perhaps a truck hauling a trailer had pulled over. I yawned, thought no more of it and threw myself back into bed.

I was awakened early by Netty's scream.

"Meemie, Daddy! She's gone. Ponygirl is gone."

Netty stood by our bed holding a bunch of carrots in her hand, tears rolling down her cheeks.

"What happened, sweetie?" I pulled her to me while Sammy threw on his jeans and headed for the door to outside.

I followed with Netty in my arms. We both spotted the open gate to the corral and the absence of Netty's pony. The horses were there, but no pony.

"The pony does like her carrots, but someone got here before Netty did this morning. Look." Sammy pointed to a half-eaten carrot which lay on the ground outside the gate and the small prints of the pony being coaxed down our drive toward the road. We followed the tracks. but they ended abruptly at the main road.

"I heard something around three this morning. I think a truck and trailer pulled over out here."

"Yep. It appears they lured the pony here with the carrots and then loaded her into a trailer." Sammy stared down the road.

"I want my pony." Netty howled and struggled to get out of my arms as if she was intent upon trying to follow the kidnapped animal on foot.

"We'll get her back." Sammy took his daughter in his arms. "Netty, look at me. We'll get the pony back."

I shook my head at him. He was promising something he might not be able to deliver on. "I'm calling Frida." I walked back into the house. Sammy followed, hugging a now quietly sobbing Netty.

When Frida arrived, she confirmed what Sammy thought. The pony had been hauled off, taken to who knew where and to what fate?

"With the attempt the other day to kidnap Netty and now this, these people are getting close, too close." Frida slapped the side of her leg in frustration and anger.

My cell rang.

"If you decided you didn't want the pony, you should have contacted me, not dropped her in the early hours here at the rescue facility. What are you trying to pull, Eve?" It was Melissa Andrew, the manager of the rescue facility, and she sounded hot.

"I wasn't responsible. The pony was taken from us this morning. We learned she was ponynapped a few minutes ago. Is she okay? She wasn't hurt?"

"She's in good shape, but I don't understand what happened."

"I'll give you all the details when I sort out everything. Could you keep her there for the time being? I'm not certain how safe she'll be here. You have security cameras there, right?"

"Yes."

"Detective Martinez is here. She wants to see the tape. We might be able to get a lead on who did this," I said.

"Will do."

Frida signaled me she wanted to talk to Melissa. I handed Frida the phone.

"Good news, Netty. It seems your pony took a ride and is now back at the rescue place." I played down how frightened I was by the nabbing of the pony.

"Let's go see her. Now." Netty pulled me toward the car.

"Not now. We want to make certain she's okay. The people at the rescue place will check her over. For now, she's scared and needs to settle down. I'll take you over to see her this afternoon. Now let's go give those carrots to the other horses. No sense in letting them go to waste," I said.

Placated for a time, Netty took her dad's hand, and the two of them headed toward the corral.

"In isolation I would label this as a cruel prank, but given everything that has happened recently, it's no prank, and it's more than cruel. It's frightening. It's as if they are telling us they could have done something far worse to the pony. And they're now on our property. That's too close. When is this going to stop?" I said to Frida.

"Never, not until we find out who's doing it. It could go on for years if we can't flush out the responsible party. When I first started working on the police force, a guy came in after he experienced a series of pranks played on him. Not serious stuff at first, mostly annoying events like someone pulling out all his plantings in the yard or an intruder leaving the doors to the house open while he and his wife were on vacation. The intrusion ran up his AC bill, and their cat wandered off. Then he found a dead skunk in his car. By the time we began to investigate, the deeds had escalated to the garage burning to the ground and his daughter taken from school and dropped off in Miami. We made no headway on solving the case, and then the incidents stopped as suddenly as they began."

"Did the person get tired and quit for some reason?"

"Everything returned to normal right after one of his classmates from high school was killed in an auto accident. It seems they were best friends until our victim started dating the other guy's girlfriend and ended up marrying her."

"You mean the guy killed in the accident was so jealous and angry he engaged in all these acts?"

Frida nodded. "And I don't think he had any intention of quitting. In fact, we were worried the acts might escalate into taking the life of a family member. We need to stop these people before they kill someone."

"They already have. Nappi's grandfather. They're not escalating their crimes. They've already killed, whether we can prove his death was murder or not," I reminded Frida.

Frida didn't disagree. Her cell rang. While she took the call, I went out to the corral to check on Netty and to talk to Sammy.

Frida joined us as we fed carrots to the horses. She had an odd little smile on her face.

"The call was from an emergency room nurse who works in the hospital in Stuart. She's a friend who I check in with from time to time. She sees some interesting cases in her work, some aren't the kind requiring a report to the authorities like a gunshot wound or a stabbing, but they are suspicious like the one she dealt with earlier this morning. A guy brought his friend in who had a severely infected ear. He said he'd been bitten by a cat. The guy who brought him in had a large bandage over his nose and two black eyes. My nurse friend made friendly with him while his buddy was being seen to by the doc on duty. When she asked him what happened, he said he ran into a door. Broken noses rarely are because of a confrontation with a door. Usually it's the result of a punch in the nose. The bite didn't look to her like a cat did it either. And here's the kicker. She said the ear infection guy signed in under the name of Juan Mateo. She knew from me the name was the same one associated with the dead guy we found in the water. A popular name, don't you think?"

"I don't suppose the guy left an address, did he?"

"Sure, but I'm guessing it's bogus, but we may get a break because the doc said he needed to come back in a few days to have the ear checked."

"Do you think he will?" I asked.

"Maybe." Frida didn't look too convinced.

The guy was our best lead. If he didn't return to have his bite checked, we were out of leads. I felt defeated. The use of the name "Juan Mateo" was like a taunt. I had gone over and over how the death of Nappi's grandfather, the theft of his horse, the attack on Netty and me, the warning note, kidnapping of the pony and the use of the Mateo name were connected. I had enemies, but who was determined enough to do all of this to get back at me? And for what reason?

Frida seemed to be reading my mind. "Sit down and make a list of everyone you've been responsible for bringing to justice. There has to be some connection, and it has to be someone with a long reach and the ability to influence the people in Nappi's circle for him to lose all his connections and his money."

"Let's get into Crusty's office. We said we were going to meet this morning. Sammy can drive our horse trailer over to the coast to pick up Netty's pony soon."

"You need someone to keep an eye on this place. I can't offer you anything in the way of protection because my boss isn't convinced all these events are connected or even serious. You might consider hiring private protection."

I laughed. "We can't afford protection. Besides we have our own "security" people. All of us need to combine our resources. I'm sure Nappi and Lionel will be happy to provide coverage." I knew I was right, but there was the shop, Madeleine and David's ranch, their kids at kindergarten, maybe Shelley, Renata, Grandy . . . I wasn't certain how far reaching these horrible people would go to accomplish their ends. We needed an army. Every friend of mine was in danger.

"I don't have a plan in mind yet, but we need to figure out how we can coax these people into the open. I don't think we can sit around to wait for their next move. Time to bring in the offense." Nappi had tried to lay low, and it hadn't worked. I was certain he would agree we needed to act.

Meantime Frida was right. We had to protect ourselves. I told Frida I would meet her and the others at Crusty's office in a few minutes. I wanted some time alone to construct a list of my enemies. I put together my list in half an hour. I hadn't heard from my drug enforcement contact, Bud, so I decided to give him a call and give him some specific work to do, a few names he should run through his contacts.

He was at his desk when I called.

"It's not as if I've forgotten about you, Eve, but the grapevine hasn't provided much. No one knows anything about Nappi's grandfather except to say they were surprised at his death. I guess they expected him to live forever. When I suggested he might have been killed, everyone was surprised. 'The guy couldn't have been gotten to. He was savvy and surrounded himself with only the most trusted men.' I took another look at the autopsy report. There's nothing fishy there. The guy died of old age."

I filled Bud in on the latest "events" in my life, the attempt to kidnap Netty and the taking of her pony. "There's no evidence Nappi's grandfather's death was a homicide, but someone warned Nappi away and cut off all his resources, and I also got a warning."

"I ran everything by my contacts, and they were puzzled, but they came up with nothing."

"I've been making up a list of cases I've been involved in since I moved here. Some of them were before I became a PI, but the people in all of them are ruthless characters. Could I give you some names and you can see if anyone you know has information about them?"

"Sure."

Bud took down the names and said he'd get back to me.

"Anything would help, Bud. Any little piece of information. We're under attack, and we can't defend ourselves if we don't know who is behind it."

AT CRUSTY'S OFFICE what I'd come to think of as the posse gathered to review what we knew and to decide on how to proceed.

Frida cleared her throat to get our attention. "Before we get started, I think we should strategize about how to keep all your friends and family protected, Eve. We need to move people into safe locations. Renata is in a motel room with no one to protect her. And Nappi, where are you staying? What about Shelley and even Jerry?"

"I think Renata should move into one of the extra bedrooms in my old house where Grandy and Max are living," I said.

"I can take the other bedroom." Lionel's face lit up, and I knew why. He was suggesting he and Renata share the same lodgings. It might have provided the right situation for the two of them to work out their differences, but I thought it was as likely they end up in bed once more without a discussion preceding the lust fest.

"Nuh uh," I said. "Jerry can move in there and you, Lionel, will stay here with Grandfather as usual. Sammy and I will be in and out of here and home. We can use you on the premises looking after the kids, the horses and pony. As for Shelley, she left for up North. Jay has enough men on his ranch to keep the bad guys away or to handle them should they turn up."

"I think we're covered," said Frida, "But no one goes anywhere alone. Clear?"

"It feels like we're under siege." Madeleine's face was pale and lined with worry.

"We are," said Frida. "I can't provide you with police protection, but you can safeguard yourselves by remaining vigilant. I want to know where you are every minute." She made eye contact with everyone in the room.

I slapped my hand on my thigh. "Okay then. Let's get down to business."

"I'm with you, Nappi. We should set up a sting to bring these people out in the open, but it's hard to decide what would work if we don't know who we're dealing with." Any reluctance Frida had expressed in the past about working with Nappi was gone. She dropped her gaze, and I saw a blush arise on her cheeks. "It's nice to be working on the same side."

Nappi smiled. "We always were."

"You said your grandfather always surrounded himself with the most trusted men, but someone got to him. I think we need to know the identities of these men, their backgrounds and where they are now." Frida flipped open her notebook.

Nappi cleared his throat. "I've been thinking about my grandfather's bodyguards and having difficulty believing any of them would be involved in his death. They were four men he trusted, and all of them had been with him for over twenty years. His house was built like a compound. No one could get in there without clearance from his guards."

Crusty interrupted. "What you say might be true, but let's get their names."

"What about household help like a housekeeper?" asked Madeleine.

"Thelma?" Nappi laughed. "She was almost as old as grandfather."

"Perhaps someone got to her," I suggested.

"And did what?" asked Frida.

"You could take another look at those autopsy results."

Frida bristled at my suggestion.

"I wasn't criticizing your thoroughness, but we need something, so we'll have to go over everything we've done and look at it again."

Frida settled back in her chair with a sigh. "I'll take a copy of the autopsy results to a friend of mine in the next county who's the medical examiner there. Maybe she'll see something in those results we haven't seen."

"Okay," Crusty said, "we know the first step we should take is to find out who is behind all of these attacks. Then we can defend ourselves and develop a plan for trapping them."

"Frida will look at the autopsy results and continue examination of evidence in the other attacks. Crusty, Nappi and I will proceed with taking a closer look at the people surrounding Nappi's grandfather. And . . ."

"And what, Eve?" asked Frida.

"I'll continue to think. I gave Bud a list of the people I've dealt with in criminal cases here, but not all of them are capable of these attacks."

"I can think of a few who are, Eve." Grandy had said nothing throughout the meeting. "The Russian mob we ran into in your uncle's death is certainly a candidate for acts of cruelty."

"I thought of them also and gave that lead to Bud."

"I've known you since your first opened the store here. I feel somehow these people have to be connected to both of us," said Nappi.

"Many of them are behind bars, in institutions or dead," pointed out Madeleine.

"The daughter who was responsible for stabbing the woman found murdered the day of our store's grand opening is mad as a hatter." Madeleine gave a shudder, probably remembering the sight of the mother with the knife in her back lying on our dressing room floor.

"The daughter remains in the institution. I checked," said Frida.

"How could I forget?" I slapped myself on the forehead. "Duh. The mother may be dead and the daughter in an institution, but there is another connection there to consider."

"Ghosts? People coming back from the dead? A mad woman slipping notes directing these attacks out of the institution to underlings?" Madeleine said.

"No, no. The guy I didn't bring to justice." I picked up my phone and excused myself to make a call in the outer office.

"Bud?" I connected on the first ring. "These names go to the top of your list of folks to check through your contacts." I gave him two names. He grunted his assent and rang off.

I could hardly suppress a smile when I re-entered the office.

"Okay. You look like the proverbial cat that ate the canary. Tell." Grandy pushed me into a chair.

"I don't know if this makes sense to you, but here's my thinking. We said it had to be someone who I helped bring to justice, but what if it's the one who got away, but whose criminal enterprise I ruined?"

"You're talking about Eduardo Garcia, the guy who ran a polo opera-tion and brought illegal drugs into this country in the vaginas of the polo ponies he imported here." Grandy's face lit up, then as quickly her expression darkened. "But he left the country."

"He left, but maybe he's back." I was certain I was on the right track. "Jay, Nappi and I ran the guy to ground. He fled the country and returned to Argentina. We all worked to break up his smuggling ring. He certainly has reason to dislike all of us. That has to be it." I pumped my fist in the air in emphasis.

"He hated you enough to return and seek revenge?" asked Crusty.

I nodded. Now all I needed was for Bud to confirm my belief by using his contacts to determine if Eduardo was back in residence.

THE NEXT MORNING FRIDA STOPPED BY as I was leaving for the shop.

"Can anyone cover for you today? You might want to come with me to visit my friend, the emergency room nurse working in the hospital in Stuart. She had news of the two men with the broken nose and the infected ear."

Renata and Madeleine were working this morning. I called Madeleine to let her know I wouldn't be in until early afternoon and to tell her I had asked Jerry to sit on the store in my absence. He was eager to help. How much help he would be was a question, but the store was so public I couldn't imagine anyone making a move on Renata or Madeleine there.

I jumped in Frida's car, and she spun gravel as she punched the accelerator.

"I'm not certain how much time we have. My nurse friend Lettie called to say the same men came into the hospital again. The one with the infected ear wasn't doing well. The ear was red and swollen to ten times its size. The other one with the nose issue seemed to be healing, but she told him his nose wasn't doing so well and he'd need an X-Ray. He was waiting to be called in for the film. She stalled him by telling him the machine wasn't working, but they're repairing it. She made it sound as if his nose was more serious than it was. I don't want to lose these guys."

She put on her siren and lights, and we passed every car on the Canopy Road to the coast, turned and raced through Palm City and took

US 1 to the hospital. She parked in front of the emergency room, and we barged through the doorway. Only two men were in the waiting room. When they turned to look at us, I saw both the guy with a bulbous nose and black eyes and the other one with the reddest, largest ear lobe I'd ever seen. He looked like a human, but lopsided version of Dumbo.

They immediately recognized me, jumped out of their chairs and ran down the corridor out of the emergency room and into the hospital.

"Lock all the doors leading out," yelled Frida to the ER personnel. She and I pursued them into the main entrance waiting room and then down a hallway toward the first-floor patient rooms. Our culprits raced by a nurse exiting a room with a bedpan, almost knocking her to her knees. I grabbed the bedpan and threw it like a frisbee toward the ear fellow, and Bingo! I hit him on the back of the head. He yelped and fell to the floor and lay there unmoving. The other guy looked back for a moment to see what happened to his buddy allowing Frida, who was an even better runner than me, to catch up with him. She tackled him, brought him down and applied cuffs.

"You need help to restrain him, Eve?"

"Nope. He's out cold." I had been the frisbee champion of the sixth grade, and it appeared I hadn't lost my touch.

It was a double whammy for him—the bedpan had been full.

CHAPTER 15

B ACK IN POLICE HEADQUARTERS, Frida let me sit in on the interview with our perps. She chose to question the broken nose guy first.

"Name?" she asked.

"Not gonna give it to you." He sat back in the metal chair and crossed his arms in a posture of defiance.

"Well, it doesn't matter anyway. We've got your prints, and we'll run them through our data base. Somehow I have the feeling this isn't your first date with the law."

He shifted around in the chair as if he might be uncomfortable about having his prints run, but the insolent look remained on his face. "Hey, the hospital was about to X-Ray my nose. I have a serious injury here, and I need medical help. You refuse me, and I'll sue you."

"Fine. Go ahead. The X-Ray was a ruse to detain you until I could get to the hospital. Your nose is fine."

I gave a short laugh.

"What's so funny?" he asked.

"Have you seen yourself in a mirror? Your nose is about ten times its normal size, and you look like you're wearing black and green eyeshadow. Maybe it's not broken, but I wouldn't enter any beauty contests." I smiled and sat back in my chair. Oh, how I hoped his nose *was* broken. He deserved everything he got, pain and disfigurement, although I suspected his nose would heal and he'd look much as he did before I took my fist to it.

"And what's she doing here anyway? She's not a cop." Nose guy smiled, revealing missing teeth.

"She and I are working a case together, and you are in a position to help us. If you don't, there are a whole list of charges I'm going to throw at you."

"Go ahead. I can get a lawyer." He held out his hand and nonchalantly examined his fingernails.

"Murder is a serious charge." Frida slid a look at me as if to confirm how grave it was.

"Murder?" He dropped his posturing and slide forward in his chair. I could smell the nervous sweat pouring off him. "What you wanna know/"

Now it was Frida's turn to smile, and her teeth were perfect. "That's better. Now, I know you're not the kind of guy to want to kill anyone, so who are you taking orders from?"

"I don't know." Now he appeared to be sincere and willing to cooperate with us. "See, me and my pal there, the one you attacked with the lethal weapon . . ."

"Medical device," I interjected.

"Dangerous missile," he continued. "My buddy and I got a phone call offering us money to follow this woman" he gestured at me," and kind of scare ya. We weren't supposed to kill her or nothin.'"

"Did you get creative and decide to take my daughter? You could be charged with attempted kidnapping."

He looked down at his hands. "Not my idea."

"How much were you offered to 'kind of scare' Mrs. Egret.?" Frida asked.

"Five hundred bucks. Half before we did the job and half after."

"How were you paid?"

"The money was to be in the trash barrel at the junction of Attapatha Road and the Canopy Road. We collected the first half, but as we were about to get the rest early this morning, the county trash collectors came by and emptied the barrel. I don't know if the rest of it was there and is gone or what. I'm waiting to get another call."

Frida and I exchanged looks. I was certain the money wasn't there. The boys had completed their work. Why would those in charge bother to come through with the remainder of the money if they didn't have to and especially if there was no way to identify them?

"You weren't offered much money for beating up a driver, taking a horse, running her off the road, nabbing the kid and then taking her pony. You've been busy fellas for a measly five hundred bucks."

"Huh? We didn't do all that stuff. We only ran the broad off the road once, and my buddy was the one who decided to grab the kid. It turned out to be a mistake. I hope he doesn't lose his ear."

I snorted out a laugh. "I hope he does. And I hope the doctors are wrong and the shard of the bone in your nose is working its way into your brain and embedding itself there paralyzing you."

His mouth gaped open and a look of terror crossed his face. "Can that happen?"

Frida and I nodded.

"Wouldn't the doctors know if I was in danger?"

We shook our heads.

"It comes on slowly," I added. "It's not always obvious to begin with."

He dropped his head into his hands and began to sob.

"Oh, by the way," I said, "how did you come up with the name 'Juan Mateo.'"

He stopped his blubbering for a moment and his forehead creased in confusion. "Huh? They suggested it on the phone, kind of a code word to let me know it was them making contact. It seemed like a good name to use when I checked in for medical attention here."

It was clear to see whoever was behind all these acts hadn't hired the brightest criminal stars in the area.

Both fellas found an attitude of cooperation, but their information wasn't very useful. Frida took the nose guy's cellphone hoping she could trace the number the masterminds called from. It led back to a burner phone. It was all a dead end.

FRIDA DROPPED ME BACK HOME WHERE I got into my car, ran several errands and drove to the shop.

Madeleine was pacing back and forth in front of the clothing racks in the shop windows.

"Something's wrong. What? Are the twins okay?" I knew David had dropped them off at school and would pick them up this afternoon. We were reasonably certain no one could get to them in their classroom because Frida had alerted the school security officer to keep his eye out for anyone suspicious hanging around the school. We'd done the same with my kids at their school.

"Fine, fine, but we have neglected the shop because of everything happening and now two of the women we wanted to interview for the positions as clerk and tailor informed me this morning they are dropping out to take jobs elsewhere. Now we have only two candidates."

I thought about the situation. One of the them was Renata; the other a young woman Shelley had recommended but who had the least experience of any on our list.

"You have a recommendation?" I could have rushed in with my solution, but I wanted Madeleine, who had taken most of the burden of the shop on her shoulders in recent years, to have first say.

"I think we should hire Renata to fill the position on a temporary basis, and when things have settled down, we can re-advertise it. If we take on someone new, we'll also be responsible for the individual's safety. I don't think it's something we can afford to work out right now, and who in their right mind would take on a part-time job which might get them, uh, you know."

"The word you're looking for is 'killed.'" I wondered if Renata wanted to be in the same position. Maybe she'd find returning to casino work preferable. "You want me to ask her how she feels about taking on the job and all it might entail?"

Madeleine's face relaxed, and she stopped pacing and wringing her hands. "Sure. If she says yes, I'll handle the other candidate."

"We're putting off the inevitable, you know."

"As always." She smiled to let me know she didn't hold me responsible for this mess.

Later in the afternoon when we explained to Renata we feared her life might be in danger and we recommended she move into my old house with Grandy and Max, she dismissed our worries.

"Oh, don't be silly. I can take care of myself. I'm sure no one would try to get to you through me."

"It's not a choice, Renata. I can't have your wellbeing on my conscience. I can't take the responsibility."

"But I will be in the way."

"No, you won't," I assured her. "There's plenty of room there, and Jerry will be using the other bedroom, so he's another measure of safety for everyone there." To be honest, I had some questions about how useful Jerry might be, but sometimes he came through.

Renata turned away for a moment, then faced me again. "To be honest, Eve. I really need my privacy."

Oh, oh. I had a suspicion what she meant by "privacy".

"I thought you told me it was a mistake for you and Lionel to get involved again."

A red flush spread its way up her cheeks. "How did you know I was rethinking . . ."

"I know how persuasive the Egret men can be, so put the hormones on hold for the time being. You can always get back to whatever you two think you're doing later. I'll give you a ride to your motel after we close and accompany you to the house."

She seemed about to argue when David pulled up in front with the twins.

"Your ride is here, Madeleine." I left Renata and pulled Madeleine with me to the office to get her purse.

She shook her head and whispered we hadn't talked to Renata about the temporary position.

"I'll tell her before she leaves. You worry about your family." I walked her out the door to the car and stuck my head in the window to ask David if there were any problems arising at the school.

He shook his head. "I want to get these kids home. They're kind of fussy today."

I looked back into the shop and watched Renata as she began to tidy up the clothes racks. She looked more like she was punishing the clothes than tidying them. She shoved them back and forth on the racks causing some of them to fall off onto the floor.

"The twins aren't the only ones being fussy today. I'd better get back in there before she destroys the merchandise."

David watched as Renata hurled a chiffon dress across the shop. "What's with her?"

"She misses her boyfriend." I closed the car door and waved good bye as they drove off.

I re-entered the shop and got Renata's attention. "Are we making a mistake by offering you the position on a temporary basis? I thought you liked working here, but you seem to bear grudge against our merchandise."

She stopped her frantic movements. "You're offering me the job? But you haven't interviewed anyone else."

"Because of this 'situation' we're going to put off other interviews for now. Anyone close to me might get the attention of whoever is after me. How can I ask an employee to take such a chance?"

"But you're asking me to?"

"Sure. You told me you could take care of yourself."

"You're serious about what's happening, aren't you?" Renata began to pick up the clothes she had thrown and to straighten up the dress rounds.

"We are all in agreement. We think there's real danger for everyone surrounding me. Look at what's happened so far. We also believe it began with Nappi's grandfather's death, rather his murder."

"Okay. Now you've got my attention."

"Do you understand why I don't want you off in a motel room by yourself?'

"I get it."

"Will you take the job under those circumstances or would you like to go back to Las Vegas to your old job? It might be a lot safer."

"Safer, maybe, but I don't need to spend my days and nights being groped. If you say you can protect me, I believe you."

Did I say I could protect her? Or did I say I'd try?

"We've got the best team in place." I gave her a reassuring smile and hoped I wouldn't fail her or anybody else I loved.

We closed the shop, and I took her to her motel room where she packed up her things. "Everybody's coming to Grandfather's tonight for dinner, so I'll drop you at Max and Grandy's and you can ride with them. Jerry will follow in his car. All of you should be safe."

I tossed Renata's suitcases in the trunk. As we buckled up, she asked, "Do you have any idea who's responsible for what's happening?"

"I've got a few, and Frida and a friend of mine are following up on some leads."

"I don't expect you to do all the work, Eve. I told you I'm pretty good at taking care of myself. I also have a close friend nearby."

I looked across the car at her. "I didn't know you were in touch with friends around here."

She laughed. "No, not a human friend. I mean my pal, Rudy." She reached in her purse and pulled out a pistol.

Oh, no, no, no.

"Do you know how to use a gun? Better yet, do you have a permit to carry?"

"Oh, sure. Unfortunately, the permit is for Nevada. I couldn't carry Rudy 1 on the plane, so this is Rudy 2. I bought it when I got here. I applied for a carry permit, and it should come through any day now."

She seemed so confident, so nonchalant about the gun.

"Put it away. Guns make me nervous."

She let out a guffaw. "You? But you're a PI."

"Yeah, but I like to fire my weapon with my eyes closed. I hate guns."

She grinned and put the weapon back in her purse.

"I hope it's not loaded."

"What use is it if it's not?"

She had a point, but not one I felt comfortable supporting. "There will be kids at dinner tonight. I have a daughter who is snoopier than I, so I insist you not bring it with you in your purse tonight."

"Will do. I'll ask Jerry for a good place to secure it."

"Jerry is the last person to ask about guns. Give it here. I'll have Lionel take care of it."

"Lionel will be at dinner tonight?" She said it softly, a small smile playing on her lips.

"Maybe you could take time out late tonight to talk."

"About what?"

"About, you know, the two of you."

"Sure." She sounded as if talking was the farthest thing from her mind. I could almost feel waves of lust emanating from her.

"I thought both of you agreed you didn't like each other years ago. What's up with the recent revival? And didn't you tell me you thought getting together again was a mistake?"

"A gal can change her mind. Especially if the guy has reformed."

I snapped my head to one side to look at her. "Reformed? Lionel? Hardly."

"Well, softened a bit then." She smiled her tiny little smile again. "And, Eve?"

"Yes?"

"You might want to direct your attention onto the road. There's a truck heading straight for us."

"Yikes!" I jerked the wheel to the right and narrowly avoided hitting the approaching vehicle's driver's side. The driver honked at me and yelled something I was glad I couldn't hear.

"I don't understand why Sammy lets you drive with the kids in the car. You're a menace on the road." She sat back in her seat and pursed her lips in another stupid smile. Who knew Lionel could bring such a lovesick smile to a woman who should know better?

CHAPTER 16

—

IT WAS COMFORTING TO HAVE EVERYONE who was dear to me in one place, safe and happy, gobbling down the pizza, ribs and chocolate cake we had ordered from the Burnt Biscuit. After dinner, Lionel and Renata adjourned to the backyard to keep an eye on the kids playing by the canal while the rest of us sat around our kitchen table drinking coffee. I sneaked a peek out the rear window to see if the two adults had their heads together discussing anything. Renata sat in a lawn chair while Lionel gathered fire wood for evening S'mores. They appeared to be doing a fine job ignoring each other.

I tapped on the window and got Renata's attention, then signaled to her by pointing my finger at Lionel and mouthing the words, "Go talk to him." She ignored me and turned her attention back to the children.

"It's like having a lovesick teenager," I said to Sammy. "Can't you talk to your father?"

"Me? You've got to be kidding. Lionel doesn't listen to anyone much less me." Sammy shook his head and went to the fridge to refill the cream pitcher.

No one heard the car pull up in the drive or notice anyone coming up our steps until there was a knock on the kitchen door.

Conversation came to an abrupt halt, everyone on alert. I saw Frida's hand move to the gun she wore in a shoulder holster under her jacket, and Nappi mimicked her movements. Was he packing, too? Sammy gave a quick glance into the living room toward the gun cabinet in which the household weapons such as the rifles and shotguns used for hunting were locked.

"Who is it?" called Sammy.

"It's Bud," came the reply.

"It's my pal from the DEA." I went to the door and opened it. "You're in time for coffee."

"Sorry to disturb you, but I've got some news, and I was up here on business, so I thought I'd stop in. It looks like I'm interrupting a party, but this is important, so I thought you should know, Eve. Is there somewhere we can talk?"

"Come on in and have a seat. You can talk in front of everyone because these are the folks who have been impacted by whoever it is targeting me and mine."

Sammy offered Bud his chair, and Grandy poured him a coffee.

"Cream and sugar are on the table. How about a slice of cake?" She grabbed a plate from the cupboard, and before he could say no, she cut him a large piece and put it and a fork down in front of him.

"Thanks." He looked around the room, and I realized he didn't know everyone, so I made introductions.

"Ah, yes. The infamous Mr. Napolitani and the famous grandmother of Eve Appel as well as her posse of relatives and friends." His tone was friendly, and he seemed genuinely pleased to meet everyone.

"That's a nicer greeting than you ever gave me," I remarked.

"Yeah, but they haven't given me any trouble like you did." He shoved a piece of cake in his mouth and looked up at me, but there was a smile on his face.

"What's up?" I pulled up the chair next to his.

"I checked on that Eduardo guy. It seemed like a good lead for who might be making trouble for you. The guy certainly had connections here and back in Argentina. My contacts tell me he was a fellow who didn't like anyone who got in his way. He was powerful and mean with money and influence." Bud wiped his mouth with a napkin.

"You say 'he *was* powerful.' Did something happened to change his situation?" Nappi asked.

"Yeah it did. He's dead and has been for several years. When he arrived back in Argentina, the drug lords he was working for didn't like his failure with the drug operation here. They killed him, or so the story goes."

My heart almost stopped beating. I had been so certain it had to be Eduardo who was behind everything happening. "It all fit so well. Could someone have stepped in to avenge him? I played a role in breaking up the smuggling of drugs into the country, and Nappi, Jay and other friends of mine helped. So maybe the drug lords want us to pay also."

Bud thought for a minute. "I guess it's possible, but why wait a couple of years to take action? Also, I think the drug operation is more interested in plying their trade and making money. I don't think they particularly care about the past."

"The drug lords in Argentina must want someone on the ground here," said Nappi.

"Sure, but the person appointed will conduct an entirely different operation. No more smuggling drugs in in the vaginas of polo ponies. They'll use another approach." Bud covered his mouth and suppressed a burp.

"It might be possible the new person is worried we might interfere the same way we did with Eduardo," I said.

"Pardon me if I sound skeptical, but you kind of stumbled onto the polo pony scheme. It's not like you folks were drug agents or authorities." Bud tried to lighten this criticism with a rueful smile.

Frida had remained silent until now. "Bud's right. It was serendipitous we found out about the drugs. We were looking for a killer, not a drug operation. It turned out the two were somewhat related. Coincidence for us."

Bud got up from the table. "I'll tell you what I'll do. I'll take a closer look at Eduardo's death. I'm interested for my own reasons to find out who might have been set up to resume his work here. I'll get back to you. I'm not promising anything, and if there's an active drug operation we should know about, I can't let you in on the details and blow our operation, but I'll see what I can find out."

Crusty, Frida and I accompanied Bud to his car and waved him off.

"There goes our best lead," said Frida. "Eduardo has nothing to do with this unless you believe people come back from the dead for revenge."

I stared after Bud's car as it pulled out of the drive and onto the highway. "I guess it's time to take another look at who else I might have offended over the years."

"Most of them are dead or behind bars. Eduardo is the only one who got away." Frida kicked a clump of dirt with her boot.

"This might be a stretch, but let's think of who these bad puppies left behind, someone who felt obligated to take revenge or . . . "

"Someone who is being ordered to take revenge on us," Nappi had come up behind us without our noticing.

"You've got an idea?" Frida asked.

The baby gave a kick, giving rise to an interesting string of thoughts. "Someone who has money, a long reach and as good an organization as you had, Nappi."

Nappi and I both spoke at once. "Freddie the Bull."

"But he's behind bars," said Frida.

"But his organization continues," said Nappi.

"Who's running it?" I asked Nappi.

He shook his head. "I don't know, but maybe we can find out."

"Meantime," Frida said, "I'm going to do an in-depth examination of all the people surrounding your grandfather—his bodyguards and his house staff."

"All loyal," Nappi said with certainty. "I've already talked with them."

"I should get some information back soon from the medical examiner I asked to take a closer look at the autopsy results. My suspicion is we'll need a more complete toxicology screen."

"Isn't that like looking for a needle in a haystack, Frida? Don't you have to have some idea of what to look for?" I asked.

Frida turned to Nappi. "Can we get access to your grandfather's house? Maybe something might turn up there."

"We're looking for a possible poison, right?" I asked.

Frida nodded. "Look, let me find out what those autopsy results say to my friend before we jump the gun here."

"My grandfather's place is on the market, but I don't think it's been sold yet. I've got the name of the real estate agent. I'm sure you have the authority to go in and look around," Nappi said.

"Poison. You think he was poisoned?" I said.

"What else could it be? We'll know more tomorrow when I talk with my medical examiner pal."

"I always heard poison was a woman's weapon." I thought of the Nappi's grandfather's housekeeper. My suspicions must have registered on my face.

"She's been with him for over twenty years," Nappi said.

"People can be bought," Crusty said.

"Or threatened," I added.

Before we could say anything else, we heard shouts from the backyard.

"The kids!" I bolted toward the canal side of the house, rounding the corner in time to see all my children as well as David and Madeleine's standing unharmed near the firepit watching in shocked dismay as Renata and Lionel threw marshmallows at each other and yelled insults at the top of their lungs.

Netty rushed to get between them. "Stop it. You're ruining our S'more treat. Stop it!"

The alarm and dismay on Netty's face must have registered where sanity and reason hadn't worked. The two so-called adults stopped tossing the puffy treats, glared at each other for a moment, and then broke into laughter.

After I made them pick up the mess, Renata and Lionel wandered off down the bank of the canal. I watched them stop and gaze into each other's faces, then join hands and continue walking. I crossed my fingers their time alone together would result in a talk, not a touchy-feely session. The second time around seemed to be more hormone-driven than the first.

Sammy came up behind me and put his hand on my shoulder. "A truce then?"

"For now." I leaned into him. "The baby has been pretty active tonight. It either means he wants to join in the fun, or he doesn't like all the tension and upset."

"Well, he's your kid. I'm sure he's letting you know how eager he is to join in on the chase." Sammy hesitated for a moment. "We're referring to the baby as 'he'. Do you think it's a boy?"

"I'm certain of it." I extracted a sonogram picture from my pocket. "I had an appointment earlier today, but I forgot to tell you in all this confusion." I handed the picture to him. There was no doubt. Unless the kid had three legs instead of the usual two.

Sammy hugged me tightly. The baby gave a powerful kick. "Hey, I could feel that too."

We hadn't said anything to each other, but I think we both wanted this baby to be a boy. I could tell Sammy was thrilled. He would have been as happy with a girl, but a boy was the cherry on the top of the sundae, the extra sauce on the ribs, another helping of coleslaw, a bigger slice of cake. Whoa. I think I made myself hungry again.

MAKING CERTAIN THE NEXT MORNING no one was alone, but had a buddy to accompany them, we each set out on our assigned tasks.

Frida had talked with her medical examiner friend. She called me with some news while I was finishing breakfast. "From the description of how he died, my friend thinks our best bet is arsenic. Since he was so old, everyone assumed it was death by natural causes like a heart attack. She recommended we run more tests."

"Meaning we need to exhume the body?" I asked.

"Nappi will have to agree, but I assume he will. I have the papers for him to sign. Is he there with you?"

"Right here. He stayed last night and made everyone breakfast this morning."

"Right then. I'll drop them off on my way to the office in a few minutes. I must be in court this morning on another case, so I called the real estate agent and cleared your access to Nappi's grandfather's house. She'll meet you there with the key."

"But we don't know what we're looking for," I said.

"Anything suspicious. Since his death wasn't treated as a homicide, *anything* suspicious."

"I wish you could be there. Maybe we should wait," I said.

"I think we need to move quickly. Once we start with the body, the bad guys will know something is up and want to cover their tracks. I have faith in you, Eve. Take Nappi with you. Since he's familiar with the house, he'll make an easier job of it." Frida disconnected.

Frida's car pulled up minutes later. She left the engine running, put the papers in front of Nappi and shoved a pen in his hand. "Sign. Here. And here. And here."

He asked no questions but did as directed. Frida grabbed the papers and gave us a backward wave as she ran to her car.

"We've got our work assignment, it appears." I patted my rounded tummy in satisfaction. Pancakes, bacon and eggs for breakfast. I should be good for a few hours. In case hunger reared its annoying head again, I made Nappi and me peanut butter sandwiches. We jumped in my car and sped off for West Palm. I ate my sandwich on the way there and eyed Nappi's.

"No, you don't." H grabbed the sandwich away from me.

We pulled up in front of the house less than an hour later. There was no car in the drive or in front of the house, so we knew the real estate agent hadn't shown yet. I shut off the engine, and we settled back to wait. At the house next to his grandfather's a black SUV pulled out of the driveway and turned in our direction. A pale face looked out of the passenger's side and stared at me with an appraising look. I caught only a glimpse of the person through the tinted window as the car passed by, but I had the impression the individual had pale skin and long, dark hair. Man or woman? I couldn't tell. Something about the face seemed familiar. I mentally shook myself. With whoever it was trying to hurt me and those I loved, I was waiting for something else to happen. Was I being paranoid or watchful?

"Did you see that?" I tapped Nappi' arm to get his attention.

"What?"

"The car pulling out of the drive next door and passing us. Could you make out the person in the passenger's seat?"

"Sorry. I was looking in the rearview mirror. Here comes the real estate agent."

I shrugged away the creepy feeling between my shoulders. Nappi and I got out and met the agent on the sidewalk. He introduced me to her.

"Ms. Lowry, this is a good friend and a PI, Eve Appel Egret. Helena Lowry is the listing agent for the house. Any bites?" he asked.

Helena Lowry's attire called attention to her in ways her small stature couldn't. Her suit was a Chanel flamingo pink wool with large crystal buttons down the front of the jacket. She wore an aqua silk scarf around her neck and a three-strand necklace of faux pearls. Gold bangle bracelets sparkled in the sun and jingled when she put out her hand to shake mine. Her hair was long and abundant, and it looked to be the same color as mine, and like mine, it wasn't her natural color. Brown regrowth was visible. Everything about her said "look at me" from her capped teeth to her five-inch stiletto heels. I smiled to myself. She and I had almost the same taste in designer clothing, hair color and shoes, but the effect was different, at least I hoped it was. She seemed to be trying too hard to impress, while I couldn't have cared less what anyone thought about what I wore. But her smile was wide, and she seemed genuinely pleased to meet me and to see Nappi again. Why shouldn't she be? If she sold this perfect house in this perfect neighborhood, she stood to make a bundle of bucks in commission. Well, good for her. A gal had to make her way in this world.

"No interest yet. The place shows well because I've kept it in tip top shape. I even hired your grandfather's old housekeeper to come in and clean each week. But I'm a bit confused." At this point her 1000-watt smile dimmed. "I know you signed the papers as rightful heir, but then you also indicated the bank was the contact agency for any information on the house. Have you changed your mind? Are you now the one I should be in touch with? If so, we'll need to redo the paperwork." She stopped talking for a moment, then resumed. "Another issue. The police detective who contacted me, a Ms. Martinez, indicated there was something suspicious about your grandfather's death. I'm feeling a bit uncomfortable about all this."

I could imagine she was worried. Nothing chilled buyers' impulse to buy more than murder in the house they thought they loved.

I knew Nappi had put the bank in charge of handling the sale of the house because he had been "talked into it" by the people who were responsible for his loss of property and money.

I decided I should step in to reassure Ms. Lowry. "The bank remains the appropriate party to handle any offers. As you know, Mr. Napolitani was shocked and grief-stricken by his grandfather's death. At the time, he wasn't up to handling the matter of the house, but he's doing much better, and he may decide to take over the house listing and sale now. We'll see how he does back in the house today. The authorities are re-examining his grandfather's death, and, as their representative as I'm sure the detective told you, I've been instructed to look at the house. As a courtesy to him, I brought Mr. Napolitani with me. I'm sure you understand." I held out my hand. "You have the key with you?"

"About the matter of his death . . ." She began to dig around in her oversized bag for the key.

"I wouldn't worry right now." I gave her what I hoped was a reassuring smile.

I could almost read the thought running through her mind: I'd better move this house soon before the cops find blood splatter under the shag rugs.

"You don't need me to accompany you?"

"No, ma'am. It wouldn't be appropriate." Even to my ears, I sounded official and authoritative.

She pulled out the key. "Well, if there's anything I can do."

"No, ma'am, but thank you." Those 'ma'ams' really did hold the note of police business. I'd outdone myself. Out of the corner of my eye I caught Nappi trying to suppress a smile.

We watched her return to her car and waited until she drove off.

"Okay, Mr. Napolitani. Let's go."

"After you, Ms. Appel-Egret." He gestured in a courtly manner, managing a dip a titch this side of a musketeer's bow. No plumed hat, of course.

Ms. LOWRY WAS RIGHT. The house had been thoroughly cleaned recently, perhaps even today. I could smell lemon furniture polish in the living room. No white shag carpet, only grey marble tiles and an expensive-looking rug under the sofa table. The living area opened to the kitchen where the stainless-steel fixtures gleamed like mirrors, not a finger print or smudge on them. The smell of air freshener hung in the air.

"So where do we start?" I looked around the kitchen. "I'm guessing if he was poisoned, it wouldn't be sitting out on the counter."

"I'll look in the master bedroom and ensuite as well as the other bedrooms and baths. You can take the kitchen. If you have time, the attached garage is out there." Nappi pointed to a door in the kitchen.

While Nappi proceeded down a wide hallway to the bedrooms, I explored cabinets in the kitchen and pulled out items underneath the kitchen sink. Nothing looked lethal. In fact, all the cleaning supplies there were either "all natural" "biodegradable" or "green".

Nappi came into the kitchen while I explored the pantry. "Anything?"

I held the door open for him to see. The pantry was empty except for some canned goods which we examined carefully. The fridge had been unplugged and the shelves cleaned. "Nothing here."

"There's a closet in the third bedroom which is packed full of junk. Do you want to help me there?"

"I haven't gotten to the garage yet." I opened the kitchen door and scrutinized the attached garage. There were signs of oil on the floor, indications vehicles had recently been housed here. One car remained. It was an old Cadillac four-door sedan, black with shiny chrome accents. "Will you look at that."

"What did you find?"

"Come here." I stepped into the garage and began to walk over to the car.

Nappi stood in the open doorway. "Wow wee. It's grandfather's old Mafia car."

"Really? A mafia car?"

Nappi gave me one of his enigmatic looks, the ones he used whenever mafia or Family business was mentioned. "Well, it dates to the fifties. We grandkids always called it his mafia mobile because of the color and all the stories then about the mafia and their preference for giant hulking sedans with large trunks. You know, to hide bodies in."

I gave him a look filled with horror. "You're kidding."

He smiled and gave a dismissive wave of his hand. "Sure."

"So now I am curious about what's in the trunk. Is there a key?"

He moved toward a bank of storage shelves. A key lay in plain sight on the bottom shelf.

"He said there was no point in hiding it. Grandfather always left the key in plain sight. He didn't want anyone to tamper with this beauty, so he left it where it could be found with ease."

"Yes, and besides, who would steal a mafia don's car?"

We opened the doors.

"Real leather," Nappi said, "And burled wood on the dash. I didn't try to start it, but I'll bet it would start right up. He had a mechanic who kept it in tip top shape."

Before Nappi could slide into the driver's seat, I stopped him. "I want to see the bodies in the trunk." I gave him a playful smile.

He moved to the back of the car and inserted the key into the lock and lifted the trunk lid. There it was. A body.

"Only one," I said.

"You sound disappointed."

I shrugged. "It's certainly roomy enough for more." The baby gave a kick as if to punish me for my cavalier attitude. Suddenly, the world went green, then black.

CHAPTER 17

I AWOKE LYING ACROSS THE BACK SEAT of the mafia mobile where Nappi had carried me from the garage floor.

"I didn't mind seeing the body, but the baby seemed to object," I sat up with Nappi's help. Turning in the seat I noted he had closed the trunk lid. "Did you call Frida?"

"Yes. She's on her way."

"Did you recognize the, uh, the deceased?"

"I'm certain it was my grandfather's housekeeper. I'm equally sure Crusty was right. Someone got to her. I'm sad to say I think she might have been responsible for poisoning my grandfather, and when Frida questioned the autopsy results, the people who pressured her into killing him got wind of it and decided to silence her. Tying up loose ends. They'd eventually kill her. Our suspicions moved up the date."

I agreed. "I'll bet there's not a sign of the poison used. They must have made certain of that." I remembered the black SUV passing us as we pulled up in front of the house. "I think we missed them. Oh, toad's poo. If I had been more observant, I might have scrutinized the passenger in the car more closely."

"I'll get you a glass of water." Nappi disappeared into the kitchen and returned with my water.

"I hope we haven't disturbed the crime scene."

"The people we're dealing with are too smart to leave prints or any other evidence."

People always offer water to someone who has experienced some kind of trauma, and the gesture always seemed silly to me, but this time, I thirstily guzzled the water.

"Better?" Nappi asked.

I nodded, sinking back into the seat. Nappi leaned over, took my hand and gave it a pat.

"Maybe you should lie back, close your eyes and take a little nap until Frida gets here."

"I'm fine, really I am," but I must have dozed off because the next thing I knew I heard someone ring the front bell.

"Frida must be here. I'm certain she will have notified the local authorities, and they'll soon be on their way. I hope you don't mind, Eve, but if you're okay, I'll be on my way."

"Why? Frida knows you had nothing to do with this."

Nappi gave me a rueful smile. "Yes, but the other cops only know me as a 'Family' man. I'll be their first suspect, and the last place I need to be right now is in jail."

"But . . ."

Nappi opened the door to the kitchen and disappeared inside.

I found the remote for the garage doors on the dash of the car, punched it and the overhead door opened. Frida appeared in the opening.

"I thought Nappi called me. Where is he?" Frida looked around the garage in confusion.

"He had an appointment he just now remembered."

She raised one eyebrow in a skeptical look.

"Look, I'm not going to cover for him. I'm certain the West Palm police will be here soon. I'll tell them he was here and then left."

"They'll love it. He'll be their primary suspect." Frida's gaze took in the car and then focused on the trunk.

"Time of death might rule out his involvement. Listen, I need another glass of water."

"No need to go back into house. I've got a bottle of water in my car."

"Thanks."

Frida shook her head, but then shrugged off the remark. "You do look a little green. Are you okay?"

"The baby didn't like finding the body in the trunk."

"The baby's not the seasoned detective you are, huh?" Frida took my arm and walked me to her car.

FRIDA WAS RIGHT. The police out of West Palm liked Nappi Napolitani very much for the bludgeoning death of the housekeeper.

"And you let him walk out of here?" The officer who asked the question of me sounded incredulous at my unwillingness to stop him, but Frida interceded and mentioned I had fainted when I saw the body and was in no condition to stop Nappi.

"Besides, he's a friend," I added before Frida could stop me.

"Actually, Ms. Egret is a PI, and Mr. Napolitani was assisting her. On my orders." Frida took the officer to one side and explained the situation to him as I sat in her car and sipped my water while I called Crusty on the phone to let him know what we had found.

"A guy stopped by the office this morning and wanted to talk with you. Short fella, looked Hispanic, smelled a bit like a horse stable. He was nervous, kept looking over his shoulder every few minutes. Does he sound familiar? He wouldn't tell me his name or leave a number where he could be reached."

I searched my mind for someone I knew of that description. "Carlos. It had to be him. He's one of the stable hands at Homer Smith's horse farm. He knew the guy who called himself Juan Mateo, the first Juan Mateo. Carlos must have something important to tell me if he took time off to drive all the way over to the office."

I hated to show up at Smith's stables on the off chance he would recognize me as the wealthy woman who asked to buy polo ponies. I could blow my cover for any future snooping as her, but I needed to find out what Carlos had to say to me.

I disconnected and walked over to Frida. "I hate to interrupt, but if you don't need me here, I've got some business in Port Myakka at a polo farm."

Frida signaled the officer she would be right back. She walked me to my car. "You're going to visit Homer Smith's place? Why?"

I told her about Carlos dropping in at the office to see me. "Crusty said he was scared, so it had to be something very important. I don't think I should wait."

"Look, I'll be along right after I finish up here. The crime scene folks from West Palm are on their way. I'll vouch for you, but the local authorities will want to get a statement from you. And from Nappi, too."

I shook my head. "You know he won't want to chance coming in to give it to them. Jail is no place for a mafia don, especially one whose grandfather's murder could have been set up by a rival enterprise."

"He's in the wind again." She stared off toward the horizon and her shoulders slumped in a posture of dejection. "The man lives by his own rules, doesn't he?"

"Yep. Listen. I want to protect Carlos, so when you get to the polo farm, arrive as if you're doing more follow-up on Mateo. Don't let on I'm snooping around."

She nodded. "Be careful."

I said goodbye and sped off.

It took me less than a half hour to get to the polo farm. I parked my car in a grove of trees outside the gate to the stables and used the cover of the live oaks lining the drive to work my way toward the barns. I approached the second stable where I'd seen Carlos the day I had come here with Jerry posing as a rich gal with too much time on my hands.

I saw him mucking out a stable and caught his attention. "Psst. Carlos."

He looked up and recognized me with a small wave of his hand and a smile. He nodded toward an empty stall which was being used to store bedding material, and I moved into it to talk with him.

"You are taking a chance, Senora, coming here. You should stay away. There are bad people here."

"You took a chance taking time from your job to visit me. What bad people?"

"A man came yesterday and talked with Mr. Homer. I overheard the conversation between them. He asked if Mr. Homer had any files on Juan Mateo and, if he did, he should destroy them. Mr. Homer said he tried to deny Mateo worked for him, but the cops had already looked at the files when Juan was found murdered.

"The man told Mr. Homer to stick to his story the body wasn't Juan's, He then asked if anyone had showed up, a tall, blonde woman asking too many questions. Mr. Homer said no."

"But now it looks as if a blonde woman has shown up and she's snooping around, asking questions and bothering my workers." The voice was Homer Smith's who had come into the stall without Carlos and me noticing his arrival.

I decided to play it cool. I stuck out my hand. "Hi there. My name is Eve Appel, and I'm a private investigator working with Detective Martinez. And you must be Mr. Smith. We're not only working on the Mateo murder, but we also have two other murders we think are connected to Mr. Mateo's. Let me assure you we don't think you're involved, but the detective sent me here to make certain no one had come here threatening you. But I guess someone had. Want to tell me what the visit was all about?"

Most of what I said to him was either exaggeration or an outright lie, but I was practiced at bending the truth. I had no idea how much of Carlos' conversation with me Homer had overheard. I'd pretend he had heard only the last part of it.

Homer Smith wrinkled up one side of his mouth in a look of disbelief, but there was something else in his expression also. The man was frightened, really frightened.

He ignored my outstretched hand. Instead, he gave me a dismissive wave of his hand. "So is my stable boy here a PI also?"

I laughed. "No, no, no. I've known Carlos' family for years. I happened to see him when I was looking for you, Mr. Smith. Here's my card. I'd like to talk to you if you have a minute. If someone threatened you, the authorities would like to know about it."

He took the card, looked at it for a moment and then turned on his heel. "Get back to your work, Carlos. You, Ms. Detective, you come with me." This was certainly a different man from the one the faux rich gal I'd portrayed had encountered. Gone was his bonhomie and smooth manner, replaced now by a dismissive and rude demeanor.

He led me out of the barn and toward another building. It housed his office and several rooms which were probably used for meetings and storage of additional equipment. He slid behind a battered desk and gestured me to a straight-backed chair across from him. The lack of decoration or comfortable furniture said this was not an operation wasting money on amenities or luxury. This was a working polo farm dedicated to the sport, and to breeding and raising the horses who made the game so exciting.

"You look familiar." His chair squeaked in protest as he eased back into it.

"Really? I can't think why."

His pose of relaxing in the chair was misleading. The way he held his body said he was on guard.

"Carlos likes working here. He says you treat everyone well and you respect the horses you train. He's worried about what happened yesterday. He overheard a man threaten you. Other polo farms would love to have a worker so loyal. It speaks well of what you do here." Maybe I was laying it on too thick.

"He must have misunderstood. His English is not so good."

He was playing with me, and I didn't have time for it. "Let's cut the horse doodoo, Mr. Smith. One of the men who worked here was killed whether you want to own up to having employed him. I just came from another dead body. The two are probably connected. Some very bad people are responsible for both murders. I'm sure you're worried about your safety and your operation, and you should be. They won't hesitate to kill you and burn this place, horses and all to the ground." I was blowing smoke at him, but it seemed to be having an effect.

He ran his fingers through his dark hair. "Fine. You're right. A man did come here yesterday, and you don't have to tell me he's dangerous. His mere appearance was menacing."

"I don't suppose he gave a name?"

Smith laughed. "I'm glad he didn't. This is a guy I don't want to know any better than I do right now."

"Describe him then."

Smith stared over my shoulder as if he was remembering the meeting. "He wasn't very tall, shorter than me. He had a bull neck, dark, thinning hair, and he wore an expensive suit, but it was such bad taste, shiny black with a pin stripe and a gray silk tie." Smith stopped and gave a short snort of a laugh. "I know this sounds silly, but he reminded me of a stereotypical mafia boss."

"Anything else? His car?"

"What you would expect. A black SUV with some goon behind the wheel. I thought I'd been invaded by a crime syndicate."

I arose from my chair. "You've been very helpful. I'll let Detective Martinez know. If you think of anything else, get in touch. You have my card or call her. We'll keep you posted. I know you don't want to get any more involved, but if the guy returns, call us immediately."

"If he returns, I'll be leaving the country." Homer Smith didn't look any more relaxed than when I came into his office. If anything, the fear written in the lines on his face had deepened.

As I walked down the drive to my car, I felt a sense of déjà vu. Maybe all mafia guys looked alike, but Smith's description fit one I had met only a few years before—Freddie the Bull. But Freddie, I said to myself, was in prison. Or was he? Even if he was, I felt certain the people behind the murders and those responsible for what had happened to me and my family and friends including the incident with Jay's horse were connected with Nappi's family ties. I didn't get why they would try to steal Jay's horse, hurt me or what the motive was for the attacks on Nappi and his grandfather. Was there something Nappi wasn't telling me? I opened my car door and got in, mulling over all Smith had told me and my own attempts to make sense of it. Someone tapped on my window. It was Smith.

"I thought you'd like to know. There was something else about this guy, something that didn't fit with the rest of him He had long slender fingers like a concert pianist."

Aha. "How old was he? About fifty or sixty maybe?"

Smith shook his head. "No. He was in his thirties, about the same age as you."

Oh, rats! The man couldn't be Nappi's and my old nemesis Freddie. Freddie was older, much older. I was left with no idea who this guy could have been or why he was certainly involved in the murders and the other threats to me and family. I was no closer to identifying the person behind all this than I was before. I watched Smith retreat up the long drive, his head moving back and forth as if worried someone was there watching him or lying in waiting to attack him. He was one terrified man.

Frida pulled up behind me as I was about to leave the polo farm.

"Anything I should know?" she asked.

I told her what I had learned about Smith's visitor. "Doesn't the description sound like Freddie the Bull, the man who shot Nappi?"

She nodded. "But this guy is too young."

"Maybe Freddie is out of prison and got a face lift."

"I'm going to check on this." Frida tapped into the computer in her car and waited for information. "Got it." Her brow wrinkled in disappointment. "Dang. I thought we might have had a lead, but Freddie is still behind bars."

"He had himself cloned then."

"Don't be silly. Smith's description could be of anyone who likes to dress like an old-fashioned mafia don."

But with the hands of a concert pianist? A coincidence? I wondered. "I thought we were onto something."

"Go home and get some rest, Eve. You've had a long and unpleasant day. I'll drop by Madeleine and David's ranch to check on them."

"If anything was wrong, I would have heard, but I'd better stop to see Renata and Grandy at the shop to be certain." Worrying about people important to me was draining my usually abundant energy reserves. I waved to Frida, did a three point turn on the road and headed out to the highway back home. I hadn't heard from Nappi, which didn't surprise me. He didn't want to hide, but he wasn't interested in making his presence obvious. He'd pared his life down to the bare necessities. I hoped he might have fled to Grandfather's and I would find him there enjoying a chat on the front porch of Grandfather's house.

When I pulled up to the consignment shop, I saw Jerry sitting out front in the SUV Nappi had given him. I was surprised to see Nappi sitting in the car's passenger seat.

I walked over and tapped on the passenger's side window. "What a relief. I was worried about you. The West Palm cops would like to have a talk."

"Once time of death is established for my grandfather's housekeeper, I'll be in a better position to talk them out of arresting me especially if they believe I was with you and we found the body together. I'm giving the authorities time to digest all of this."

"Sure. Fine. I'm on my way home. Why don't you hop in and come with me? Lionel is probably around there someplace and the two of you can have a jaw together."

"I can drive him," said Jerry.

"No, you cannot. Your job is to keep an eye on Grandy and Renata and take them home after they close up here."

Jerry stuck out his lower lip, sulking. "This babysitting job is boring."

"It's not babysitting," said Nappi. "It's protection, and it's important. Take it seriously."

Jerry straightened up in his seat and put some starch in his back. The pout disappeared, and he stuck out his chin in an attitude of alertness. "Yes, sir."

"Do you want to pop into the store before we leave?" asked Nappi.

"Yep. I'll be only a minute. I have something important to tell you about a visit I paid to Homer Smith's polo farm." I went into the shop. There were several customers who were finishing up a purchase.

I greeted our clientele with a smile. "I see you found something you liked. So," I turned my attention to Renata, "business must have been good today."

Renata and Grandy exchanged wary looks. I saw the exchange but didn't want to say anything until the customers were gone. Instead I wandered around with an eye to determining if our inventory needed to be increased. Perhaps a trip to the coast to our consignors was something I could fit in tomorrow.

The clients left with their purchases.

I walked into the back storeroom and signaled for Grandy and Renata to follow. If there was trouble it wasn't something to talk about in front of anyone entering the shop.

"You tell her, Grandy," Renata said.

Grandy crossed her arms over her chest, always a sign what she was about to say was serious. "We had a woman in here earlier this afternoon. I was busy with other customers, so Renata waited on her. She tried on several outfits, some blouses, slacks and dresses and then looked at our jewelry and shoes. Renata was certain she was going to buy all of it, but she asked if you were in the store today. When Renata told her no, she looked disappointed and said she wouldn't buy anything from salesclerks . . ."

I interrupted her with a laugh. "You must have wanted to punch her."

Renata smiled and continued the tale. "I did, but my job here is to sell stuff, not teach customers manners, so I let it go. She asked if you would be coming in later. I told her I wasn't certain. She then asked if I could get in touch with you. I tried your cell, but . . ."

I slid my hand into my back pocket. My cell was missing. Where had I put it? "I don't know where my cell is." I thought back to the day's events. "I guess I could have left it at Nappi's grandfather's house." Perhaps it had slipped out of my pocket when Nappi lifted me into the car seat.

"I told the woman to leave her card, and you would get in touch, but she said no. She told me she would stop back here right before closing this afternoon," Renata said.

"You were very restrained." I admired her control. If she had acted that way toward Grandy or me, neither of us would have exercised that degree of control. "Listen, both of you have put in a long day."

"By the look on your face, so have you," said Grandy. "Do you want to tell us what happened?"

"It's a long story. You two go on home with Jerry. Nappi's in the car with him right now. Would you tell Nappi I'm tied up here and ask Jerry to drop him off first? I'll stay until five and see if the woman shows. I promise I'll close then and head home. If she doesn't come by, she'll be back some other time."

Grandy reached out and put her arm around my shoulders. "I didn't like this woman's attitude. She was haughty, cold and unpleasant to Renata. You promise you'll go right home in an hour?"

"Yep. This gives me perfect opportunity to survey our inventory and see what we might need. I'm thinking a run to the coast tomorrow is in order. You've done such a bang-up job over the past few days the store is looking bare." I probably should have told them what had happened at Nappi's grandfather's house, but I knew Nappi would fill them in on the way home.

After they drove off, I considered what the store needed and called a few consignors in West Palm and Stuart to see if they had any items we could take on. Picking up merchandise from our consignors was a service no other shop in the area provided, so it made us special and drew the high-end merchandise from the wealthiest patrons. I arranged for a few stops tomorrow, and by the time I finished with the calls, it was after four thirty. A smell like swamp gas permeated the store. Oh, oh, I thought, the unusually warm weather and wind off the slough had blown the funky odors off the slow-moving water. This end of town was often the worst hit. I should leave and forget about waiting for the shrewish client Renata had dealt with. Instead I slid back in my office chair and put my feet up on the desk. I was more exhausted than I realized and fell asleep in a few minutes.

I awoke with a jerk, the smell of the swamps overwhelming. Something was wrong. I could hardly move, and someone was standing over me with a handkerchief to their face.

"Sleep tight," the person said. I heard the side door open and close. I was alone, and a blackness enveloped me.

CHAPTER 18

—

"Eve, Eve. Wake up. We've got to get out of here." Crusty's voice seemed to come from a great distance. I wanted to move toward it, to free my nostrils of the marshy wet smell, but I my body wouldn't move.

"I can't . . ."

I felt arms reach under me and lift me out of the chair. Cool, fresh air rushed over me as we moved out the front door of the shop and I was laid down. I opened my eyes to see Lionel's face. Behind him red and yellow lights of a fire engine flashed, and I heard its siren.

"What's going on?" I tried to get up, but Crusty and Lionel pushed me back to the ground. They had propped me against a tree on the grassy area on the other side of the parking spaces.

"Boy, am I happy you talked me out of smoking. I was in my office, and I smelled gas. I wouldn't have noticed if I hadn't quit smoking." Crusty took an unused hanky from his pocket, poured water on it from a bottle and wiped my face. "Feel better?"

"Gas?" I was too groggy to understand.

"Here's some folks who want to take a look at you," said Crusty.

I looked up into the familiar face of EMT Deirdre.

"How long was she in there? She seems pretty groggy." Deirdre shined a light into my eyes and pressed her stethoscope to my chest.

"Not long, I don't think," said Crusty. "I was about to leave my office for the day when I smelled something funny."

"I smelled it too, but I thought it was the swamp." My head was clearing now. "What are you doing here, Lionel?"

"I came by to see Renata, but instead found you in the back room. Crusty was already trying to get you out. If you weren't so heavy with all your baby fat, he could have moved you by himself."

I guffawed at his remark. Fat? Me? Not even with some extra baby in me. Typical Lionel, but I was glad he was here. "Thanks for helping."

He grumbled something and turned away.

A firefighter approached us. "Someone cut the gas line leading into your hot water heater. Lucky Mr. McNabb smelled something or there could have been an explosion."

It Crusty hadn't stayed after the other businesses closed, the explosion would have taken out the building and ended my life. And my baby's life.

"Intentionally cut the line?" I asked the firefighter.

He nodded.

"But the line is in the utility room. How did someone get in there?"

"It appears they broke into the shop through the side door. We found the wood around the lock splintered," said the firefighter.

Too close. Too, too close. This had to end. I had come up with only two people capable of this kind of evil. One was dead; the other in prison, but somehow I knew I was right about one of them. Ghosts or someone who could walk through prison walls? Unlikely. But I had another idea, and I knew I couldn't be wrong.

After a brief examination by my friendly EMT and a refusal on my part to accept a ride to the hospital after she assured me the baby seemed fine, Lionel called Sammy against my insistence he not make contact. I win very few arguments with Lionel. Sammy pulled up in his truck and ran to me enveloping me in his strong arms.

"Eve. What happened? Are you okay?"

I looked up into eyes as brown as dark chocolate and twice as luscious and pulled him close to me. "I'm fine. Really. But this is all going to end. And soon."

"You know who's behind this? he asked.

"Maybe. I need to talk with Nappi. Let's go home."

Frida pulled up in her SUV and jumped out. After a few words with the fire officials and a quick check with the EMTs, she came over to me, a worried look on her face. "Maybe it's time you left here for someplace safer."

"And where would a safe place be? And who should I take with me? These people seem to be after everyone whose lives touch mine."

"I guess we could tether you up like the sacrificial goat who brings the tiger out of hiding." She gave a quick smile and then seemed to realize how inappropriate her remark was. "Oh, I am so, so sorry. Cop humor, I guess."

"Maybe it's not such a bad idea." I let Sammy help me into the truck, and we took off for home.

SAMMY PULLED UP IN FRONT OF OUR PLACE, and I jumped out of the truck, no longer tired, but energized by the plan I had hatched.

"Nappi here?" I said hello to Grandfather and checked on the boys and Netty who were in her room playing a board game.

Netty jumped up from the floor, scattering the game pieces. "My pony is like you, Meemie. All she wants to do is eat."

"Pick up those game pieces, my little love, and get washed up for dinner." I gave her a quick squeeze and smiled at the boys who all were at the age they felt a hug from their mother was "icky."

Nappi called to me from out back, and I bounded out the door.

Sammy followed in my wake. "Don't you think you should sit down, Eve? I'll bring you a lemonade."

Lemonade? I could already taste it and feel its coolness. "And maybe some cheese and crackers and salami. I didn't eat lunch, and I'm starved."

"Sit." Sammy pointed to one of our lawn chairs. "If you're hungry, then I know you're fine. You'll spoil your supper, you know."

"No, I won't."

Sammy laughed. "No, I guess you won't."

Nappi got out of his chair and hugged me, looking deeply into my eyes as if he could discern there if I was putting on a front or really okay.

"You heard about the gas?" I said.

He nodded.

We both sat and gazed for a moment across the canal where the sun was beginning its decent into the western sky.

"I've got a hunch, Nappi. Call it Eve intuition. Maybe you don't have this information, and this is a wild guess, but does Freddie the Bull have any relatives?"

Nappi raised one eyebrow in curiosity. "He had four kids. Two sons and two daughters. One son is a doctor in Boston, the other a lawyer in Hartford, Connecticut. The girls are married. One keeps books for her father and the other is a stay-at-home mother. Why?"

I told Nappi about the man who threatened Homer Smith.

"I think one of the sons or perhaps both has a deep need for revenge against both of us. You helped put Freddie the Bull out of the murder for hire business, and he tried to kill you, but failed. Now he's paying for that and his other crimes by life in prison. I think he believes removing all your influence and power is payback for what you did to him, but, more important, he knows the worst he could do to you would be to sever your ties with what you really love, your grandfather."

Nappi nodded. "Don't forget. Freddie also blames you as much as he does me. You were as important as I was in taking Freddie down. He's arrogant and a fool, but smart enough to know that I also love you and your family. If Freddie can come at me through you, well, that would delight him.

"We need to find out if I'm right. Frida suggested an approach I might consider."

Sammy handed me a lemonade and set a plate of snacks on the wooden log we used as an outside coffee table.

"Thanks." I grabbed several crackers and piled salami and cheese on them, then stuck them into my mouth and chewed. "You need to hear this, Sammy. Tell me what you think." My words didn't come out quite so clearly, and I puffed out cracker crumbs all over Sammy's shirt. "Sorry." I took a swallow of lemonade and cleared my throat.

"I think I need to get away."

Sammy smiled and nodded. "A rest is a good idea. With everything happening, you could use a break."

"Frida suggested it earlier."

Sammy's smile disappeared and suspicion clouded his face. "Wait a minute. Frida suggested it? What's going on? What do the two of you have in mind? You've cooked up some plan, and it doesn't include me, does it?"

My time away didn't include Sammy. He was right, but I hoped Frida would make him see the plan wouldn't put me in any danger and would keep the children safe.

"Let's get Frida out here and see what she thinks would be best." I stroked Sammy's arm to win him over, but it didn't work.

"I already don't like it, whatever it is." Sammy walked back into the house.

"He feels you're leaving him out. Why don't you leave whatever you're planning for tomorrow? Take a little time tonight to recuperate from the day." Nappi said.

"I'm trying to keep everyone safe. I'm trying to bring this whole thing to an end." I reached into my pocket for my cell phone and realized I didn't have it. I probably dropped it in Nappi's grandfather's car this morning.

"Durn. I think Frida has my cellphone. I need to get it back anyway. I'll be back in a jiff." I ran into the house to use the landline.

Sammy gave me a dark look when I picked up the receiver and dialed.

"I think Frida has my cell. I'll be only a sec." I knew he didn't believe me.

She answered on the first ring.

"It's Eve. Do you have my cell?"

"You called me for that?"

"That, and I'd like to talk about the goat thingy you mentioned." I couldn't help myself. Once I had a plan of action, why wait to execute it?

Unfortunately, my enthusiasm for putting my plan into action was curbed by Frida who I had counted on to jump at the idea of trapping the killer of Nappi's grandfather and housekeeper and the person responsible for the attempts on my life.

"Can this wait until tomorrow morning? I promised my kids I'd take them out for pizza and a movie. Don't you think it's a good idea for you to take a break tonight, too, especially after the day you've had?" Frida sounded eager to get me off the phone and to get on with her plans for the evening.

"I thought you'd want to hear about the talk I had with Nappi. I think I've got a line on who's behind the killings and the trouble aimed at me."

"Yes, but not right now. How about first thing tomorrow? I'll drop by the house. Gotta run."

"Before you go. Do you have my phone?"

"I had to turn it over to the West Palm detectives as evidence."

"Of what? It's my phone."

"It was part of the crime scene. You can go get it tomorrow. Gotta run."

"But . . ." I was talking to dead air.

Tomorrow? Why did everything have to be put off until tomorrow?

Sammy had been standing at my side when I made the call. "I apologize for my attitude earlier. I want to get to the bottom of this situation as much as you do, Eve, but let's have dinner now and then we can talk. I know you've hatched a plan to take out the people who have made our lives miserable and are responsible for at least two murders. Settle back and enjoy the kids. Nappi, you and I can discuss this after dinner." He reached out and touched my face. "Okay?"

I was being selfish, and I knew it. If I hoped to win over Sammy and the rest of my family to what I had planned, I needed to think this through carefully and work through all the details with the Frida's help.

I leaned into him. "Okay. In fact, let's put off discussion until Frida arrives tomorrow. We'll strategize then. For now, let's enjoy what Grandfather has made us for dinner."

Good food, a board game with the kids, Grandfather, Lionel and Nappi capped off a pleasant evening. Sammy and I tucked the kids into bed, and then joined the rest of the adults sitting out back enjoying the moon coming up over the quiet waters of the canal. I couldn't help worrying if this night would be the last relaxed one I would spend with my family and Nappi.

"Don't stay out here too long," I told everyone when Sammy and I left for our bedroom.

Nappi reached up to hug me and whispered in my ear. "If you're right about who's behind the murders and trying to harm you, you may be looking at more than you can handle."

I SLEPT POORLY THAT NIGHT, tossing and turning, re-examining every aspect of what I knew or thought I knew about Freddie the Bull. I arose before dawn, made coffee for Nappi and Sammy for when they got up and an herbal tea for myself. I knew it was too early to make the call, but I couldn't wait any longer. I punched in Bud's cell phone number.

"Are you in your office yet?"

"What time is it? And who is this?"

"It's Eve. You didn't recognize the number because it's not my cell. It's a long story, but it can wait until later."

"Can this intrusion wait until later also? I haven't had my coffee yet, and I'm mean as an old bull moose in rut when I'm not caffeinated."

"You're meaner than that under the best of circumstances. I'll give you fifteen minutes. Call me back. It's important, and we need to talk."

I was surprised when he called back in ten.

"I heard all about the murder at Nappi's grandfather's house yesterday as well as the gas line incident at your shop, so I figured something was up. Dare I hope you're getting in touch because you have information I can use? Some drug related stuff maybe?"

"Huh?"

"I'm a drug officer. I assumed you were getting in touch because yesterday had a drug association, and you wanted to let me know about it." His tone of voice held a note of hope which barely concealed the underlying tone of aggravation.

"I need your help again."

"Don't you always? I respect your boss Crusty McNabb, and he's why I'm being tolerant. You, I still find annoying."

"And yet here we are talking like civilized folks. You've heard of Freddie the Bull?"

Bud replied. "His operation had been heavily into transporting drugs, at least until he went to jail. Now it's hard to get a line on what's happening."

"It would make sense that with him behind bars someone in his operation, maybe a family member, is carrying on for dear old dad. Right?"

"Maybe."

"I may know who could be following in his father's footsteps. Can you send me a picture of his sons?"

"According to my information his sons are professional men. You think they're involved in continuing his operation? You're reaching, Eve."

"Look. Can you send pictures of them to Frida's cell phone?"

"Not yours?"

"Mine is in the hands of the West Palm cops. I haven't gotten it back yet."

"How did the cops get your phone?"

"As I said before. Long story. Send me pictures, and I'll owe you." I disconnected before he could say no.

"Up and working already." Sammy came into the kitchen, shrugging into a tee-shirt. He nuzzled my neck. "Do I smell coffee?"

"In the pot." I leaned back and touched his face. "Don't start what you can't finish."

"I can make some eggs and toast if you're interested," Sammy said.

"I think I'm more interested in the other." I got out of my chair and stepped into his arms.

Later, there was a knock at our bedroom door. "If it's one of our brood, we'll be out in a jiff," called Sammy to the intruder.

The door opened and Netty poked her head in. "What's a 'brood?'"

"Never mind, sweetie. Come on in. Your dad and I were talking."

"You sure do talk loud." Netty ran into the room and jumped into bed with us. "I'm hungry."

Sammy laughed. "She certainly does take after her mother. I'll make those eggs now."

Sammy never got the chance to make the eggs because by the time we got dressed again, Nappi stood at the stove stirring food in a frying pan, an apron tied around his waist.

He held a spatula up in the air. "Frittata okay with everyone?"

Grandfather and Lionel entered the back door. They carried a loaf of freshly baked bread. By now the boys were out of bed. The entire family stuffed themselves on a vegetable frittata and warm bread spread with homemade strawberry jam. I think I ate twice as much as everyone else, but I was eating for two, so no one complained when I reached for the last piece of bread.

NAPPI AND I LEFT TO MEET WITH CRUSTY, but first, I stopped by the store to check on Renata and Grandy. I called to let Madeleine know about the gas line break, which I said was an "accident." I didn't want her to worry. I don't know if she believed me.

"I don't get how a gas line can 'break,'" she said. Yep, she didn't believe me.

"It ruptured. Too much pressure is what the fire department said." I held my breath. Would she believe my tale?

"Okay. But it's safe to open the store today?"

"Sure. I'm at the shop with Renata and Grandy right now. I called the gas company, and they're sending someone to repair the line. The fire department shut off the line at the tank last night. Everything is fine."

"This happened last night? And you didn't call me then?" Now she sounded mad as well as suspicious.

"No need. It was nothing."

"I'm coming in after I pick up the twins from their half day of kindergarten."

"Great. How about the two of us pop over to the coast and pick up some merchandise? I need to stop by the police department in West Palm on our way."

Madeleine sounded pleased with the idea of the two of us getting away from the shop. After I hung up and turned, two pairs of curious eyes were fixated on me.

"Something's up other than a trip to the coast, isn't it?" Grandy stood with her hands on her hips, her mouth screwed up in one corner, her usual look when she caught me up to something. Renata nodded in agreement. I was no good at playing innocent with people who knew me well.

I saw Frida's car pull up in front of the shop "We'll see. Ah ha. Here's Frida now."

Frida entered the store, holding up her cell. "What's this all about?"

"A gift from Bud. He sent them, did he?"

"Yep, but no message, only the mugs of two guys who look familiar to me."

"There's no need for a message. Let me see the photos."

She handed me the phone, and I scanned the pictures. "One looks as if he could be a clone of Freddie the Bull. I think we have some answers."

CHAPTER 19

—

Nappi, Frida and I adjourned to Crusty's office to talk strategy.
"I'm certain Freddie the Elder has been directing this operation from his prison cell and has found a willing accomplice in his son, Freddie, Jr, the attorney. From what Homer Smith said it had to be the younger Freddie who threatened him recently. The description he gave me fits the picture. He looks like his dad." I showed the picture on Frida's phone to Nappi and Crusty.

"Are you certain you want to set yourself up this way?" Frida asked.

"I'm setting up both Nappi and me to tempt Freddie boy. I want to make certain everyone else is protected and make it look as if you're busy elsewhere."

"There's a law officers' conference in Orlando this coming week. I'll make certain the word gets out I'll be attending," Frida said.

"Instead you'll be keeping a discrete eye on Nappi and me."

Crusty cleared his throat. "There's one problem. What does Sammy think of all this? Or haven't you told him?'

"I told him this morning I needed to get away."

Nappi let out a harrumph of disbelief. "He might have agreed you need a break, but I'll bet you didn't fool him about what you were up to?"

"He's one hundred per cent behind my taking time away from here."

"But?" Nappi said.

"Okay. You're right. He thinks something is up. And so do Grandy and Renata." I paused. "And Madeleine's suspicious."

Frida drew her eyebrows together in a look of concern. "Everyone has to act as if you're taking time off because of the pregnancy and believes Sammy can't get away so Nappi will be keeping an eye on you. Do you think the plan will work?"

I nodded. "Sammy won't be coming along with us because David has a full schedule of hunting clients and needs his help on the hunting ranch. Everyone will be assured of our safety if you can point out to them that we'll be safer if there aren't more people involved in my little 'vacation.'"

"True. This had to be a small, tight operation. I'll take Crusty with me, making only four of us. I suggest you take your pistol with you, Eve."

I groaned inwardly. I hated to carry a gun. I was so bad at shooting. Frida read my mind. "Go practice this week at the range. No one will find it odd given your propensity to aim with your eyes closed."

For my time away we decided to go to Nappi's houseboat on Card Sound road.

"My only concern with the boat is the guy who lives next door. He impressed me as a shady character when he insisted on barging in when Lionel and I were there." I remembered how obnoxious the guy was. If we could get him out of our hair, it would help.

"I also think he followed me when I went into Key Largo to get rid of all my stuff," Nappi said.

"Including your watch which I'm certain he was wearing."

"I'll get in touch with the Monroe County Sheriff's department which has jurisdiction there," said Frida. "I'm sure they can find a reason to remove him from the area."

We were certain Freddie Jr. had eyes on all of us, so it was a sure bet he would see Nappi and me leave for the houseboat. He would know we were setting a trap for him, but it was the kind of trap I knew would appeal to Freddie's ego. Nappi and me against whatever he would throw at us. Freddie had to believe he could take us on. His sources would let him know about the law officers' conference and of Frida's attendance there. As for Crusty, we decided Jerry could dress as Crusty and spend the time in his office. Disguise was something Jerry was good at, and this time he didn't have to dress up like a woman as he had in a previous ploy to fool Freddie the Elder. We arranged for several of Sammy's cousins to keep an eye on our kids during the day, and Grandfather would also be at our house. We assigned Lionel the job of sitting on the shop to make certain Grandy, Renata and Madeleine were safe at work. I was certain he would have preferred to be with Nappi and me, but it appeared protecting Renata appealed to him.

Grandy, often my sidekick in chasing down criminals, understood the plan and knew she would have to take a back seat this time.

"There will probably be other occasions where I can tackle a few bad guys," she said. She was probably right.

David kept an eye on the twins at school while Sammy worked with clients at the ranch. Sammy would be with our kids after work. As for Jay, whose driver and horse had been the original targets, we let him know of the plan. He assured us he was safe. He had his foreman Antoine and other workers to keep watch over his place. Everyone was on alert; everyone was as safe as we could possibly make them. Best of all Freddie would notice nothing different, only Nappi and me leaving for the houseboat. Freddie would follow like a predator stalking his prey. In the end we intended to make him the prey.

I knew everyone, despite our precautions, would feel anxious about the approach. Even I had misgivings, not so much for my own safety, but I was asking friends and relatives to take a chance Freddie and company wouldn't make a move on them despite my conviction that Freddie preferred getting at Nappi and me. The person hardest to convince would be Sammy, but I trusted Frida would convince him it was a sound approach and one ending the uncertainty we had been living with for weeks.

"I'll call the station in West Palm and tell them you're dropping by today for your cellphone." Frida rose from her chair and started toward the office door. She paused for a moment, hand on the knob. "Are we certain this is the only way?"

I looked around the room at the uncertain looks everyone had on their faces, but there was something else there, too: courage and the determination to put an end to the evil Freddie and family were perpetrating on us. "This is the only way. Between the four of us we can make everyone understand."

Our plan wouldn't go into effect for several days giving us time to make certain there were no holes in the defenses for our families. Until then we were on high alert, not knowing if Freddie had more immediate moves in mind.

On the way to West Palm in the afternoon to pick up merchandise from our best consignors, I explained to Madeleine what was afoot. "You and the kids will be safe. David and the others will be with you."

"I don't like the idea of your going off to Nappi's houseboat with only him, Crusty and Frida for protection. You have no idea how many men Freddie has at his side. Can you be sure he'll get wind of where you are? Maybe he won't show, and this will be a bust." Madeleine nervously fiddled with the scarf around her neck.

"It will work. Freddie will know it's a setup. If he's anything like his father, it's the kind of challenge he'll like. Don't forget, I'll be there too. With my trusty gun."

Madeleine snorted. "Oh, that will be a big help."

"I intend to practice this week."

"Sure." She rolled her eyes.

I shot her a dirty look. "You have no faith in me."

"Yes, I do. You always manage to come out of these messes on top, but never according to the original plan. This will be no different."

"You aren't mad I didn't include you in on the action? I know I promised you I would use your help on one of my cases."

"Maybe not this one. Anyway, I think I'm better at the thinking part of detective work. Not the action part."

I was relieved to hear her express reservations about being in the middle of the action. From the time we were kids I'd always treated Madeleine like a little sister, protecting her from the larger, more aggressive kids. Madeleine was a girly girl, one I loved better than anything, but she wasn't the physical take charge type. Brain work and sheer stubbornness were her approach to sleuthing.

I looked over at Madeleine and saw worry line her forehead. I showed and pulled the car onto the side of the road.

"Part of the reason I have the courage to do this PI work is because of you, you know."

"Me?"

"You taught me I should think first, then take action. If I've become more patient, it's because I've learned to follow your example."

Before she could interrupt me, I hurried on with my explanation. "I'll never have the social acumen you have, but I try to keep my mouth for a few nanoseconds before I hit someone with my thoughts. And I include others in my plans and don't try to do it all alone."

"That's true, I guess."

"This community would have tossed me out on my ear if I hadn't followed your example. I'm more of a lady now."

Her mouth fell open in an expression of disbelief. "Don't push it, Eve. There is nothing ladylike about you, and, if there was, I would have you looked at by a competent head doctor. I'll give you a smidgen of maturity and more tolerance of others, not much mind you, and I appreciate your saying I served as some kind of role model, but there's only so much a person can do with someone with as bold a personality as yours. As for me, if you hadn't come into my life and saved me from being bullied as a child, I'd never have learned to stand up for myself."

I thought about what she had said. "You're right. You stand up well to me, and that's no mean feat. I guess I did teach you something."

"Actually, having a daughter who seems to be a carbon copy of you has taught me more." Madeleine sighed and slumped down in her seat. "Now little Eve thinks she's old enough to gel her hair into a punk style."

"I wonder where she got that? Do you want me to speak to her?"

"Nope."

"I know, I know. You can do it."

"Nope. I had David talk to her. I know how to delegate as well as stand firm."

"I love you, my sweet dear friend." I reached over and hugged her. She hugged me back harder. She handed me a tissue from her purse, we both had a slobbery cry and then laughed a bit at how "girly" we were acting.

"Not to change the subject, but all this crying is ruining my mascara and giving me the hiccups. So, you and Frida think the murder of the guy who worked at the pony farm, Juan Mateo, was also Freddie's doing? I don't get the connection, do you?"

I thought back on what Carlos had told me about Juan. Let's see. Carlos overheard someone talking to Mateo, asking questions and wanting to see Homer Smith who wasn't there. Jay's name was mentioned. The individual who approached Mateo was worried he might blab to someone.

"Mop-up," I said to Madeleine. "Leave no possible witnesses behind. Freddie junior is as ruthless as his father."

I pulled up in front of the West Palm Police station and jumped out of the car. "Be back in a second. I've got to pick up my cell."

However certain I was about Mateo's murder, something nagged me about the situation. I hesitated for a moment as I made my way up the steps of the police station. Something. Something. I shook free of my doubts and continued up the steps. If I focused on other matters, it would come to me.

AFTER I GRABBED MY PHONE, Madeleine and I stopped by several of our consignors and picked up clothing and a few small household items which I stashed in my trunk. I had been on alert the entire trip down to West Palm and back, checking my rearview mirror and watching every car behind me and all the ones I passed or passed me, but it was a trip without incident. The constant vigilance was exhausting, and I looked forward to bringing this to an end.

Back at the shop, Grandy told me the gas line was repaired and business had been brisk. "I think people heard about what happened and were curious about the incident. They came to gawk, but once they were here, Renata and I convinced them to buy. I also told everyone we would be getting in new merchandise tomorrow."

"It's a novel advertising ploy: 'Come tour the shop where the owner was almost blown to tiny bits.' Catchy."

Grandy tsk tsked at my attempt at humor. "You look exhausted, Eve. Renata can unload the items from your trunk, then you can go home and take a nap."

"Good idea. I'll inventory what we procured on our trip, and we'll get the merchandise out on the floor by the end of the day." Madeleine pushed me into a chair.

I tossed Renata the keys to my car and slid down in the chair. Before I knew it, Grandy was shaking me. "Maybe I should drive you home. You fell asleep."

"Nope. A few winks. I feel fine now, but I think maybe I should go home and check on the kids. I haven't spent much time with them lately because of all the upheaval in our lives. I'll open tomorrow. The rest of you can take the morning off. I'll let Jerry know he doesn't have to be here either."

"Who is going to be here with you then?"

I reached into my purse and pulled out my gun. "Me and my little friend. We'll be fine."

Grandy rolled her eyes. "Loaded?"

"Never mind. I'll take care of the gun. It's my responsibility." I dropped the gun back into my purse and left the shop. When I stopped at Jerry's car to tell him about the plan for tomorrow morning, I caught him sleeping.

I rapped on the window and startled him awake. "We give you a job, and you can't even handle the simplest task."

Jerry rolled down the window. "I heard about my upcoming assignment, doubling as Crusty. Why am I always the one who must dress up as someone else? Why can't I be myself for once?"

I wanted to say, "Maybe it's because being you is usually useless," but I reconsidered. Jerry wasn't always incompetent. He tried hard to do the right thing, but often got it wrong. Maybe if I wasn't so hard on him. Maybe I should try to help build his confidence. "It's an important job, Jerry. We want Freddie to believe Crusty is here keeping an eye on things. The plan wouldn't work without you."

"Really?"

"Yes, really."

"If someone comes into the office and wants to hire me as a PI, can I do it?"

"No."

"Okay. I understand. I don't have a license. Can I carry my gun?"

Jerry was more incompetent with a gun than I was, but if packing would make him feel more on top of the job, it might be good to have him armed. In case.

"I'll tell you what. I'm going to the gun range this week after work to do some shooting. If you come with me and handle your weapon well, then you can carry it while playing Crusty."

The worry lines on his forehead disappeared, and his eyes lit up. He looked more like the old Jerry I had once fallen in love with.

I patted his arm. "Deal?"

"Sure."

I walked to my car, got in and drove off. I'd made Jerry so happy I could see him beaming at me in my rearview mirror. It took so little to lift his spirits and get his cooperation. Maybe I should have tried this approach years ago. I thought back to all the aggravation he had caused me throughout our years of marriage and mentally shook my head. No. Not all of Jerry's irritating behavior was my fault. He was congenitally annoying as well.

The boys were home from school and along with Netty were out back with the horses. Grandfather had saddled Netty's pony for her, and she was merrily riding around the perimeter of the corral. He had told the boys they could ride up and down the canal, but not out of his sight.

When he saw me, he waved. "Home so early?"

"I was tossed out of the shop and told to take a nap. I think I will."

"Meemie." Netty halted her pony and held her arms out to me.

"Stay on your horse, honey. Mommy needs to take a nap." I gave her a big hug and then patted the pony's rump to get her going again.

"Watch me. I can go fast," called Netty.

I watched for a moment, then yelled to tell her I was leaving. She was so wrapped up in the horse, she ignored me.

In our bedroom, I stretched out on the bed. I hadn't been asleep long when I felt something soft on my neck and thought Netty's pony had gotten into the house and was nuzzling me. "Get this pony out of here."

"I'm not a pony." The voice was Sammy's, and he had settled in the bed next to me. "I arrived home a few minutes ago. Grandfather told me you were here taking a nap. I didn't mean to wake you up, but now I see you're awake, how do you feel about takeout from the Biscuit?"

"Only if it's ribs and slaw and only if it arrives in less than an hour." I yawned and stretched. "I got enough shut-eye to take the edge off. I think I'll take a shower."

"Me, too." Sammy laughed and took my hand. "A quick one. Frida said she was dropping by with something important to discuss with all of us."

"A quick what exactly?" I asked.

Sammy laughed and pulled me into the shower. Soon the water grew cold, and someone was knocking on the bathroom door.

"Me, too," shouted Netty through the closed door.

"We'll be out in a minute, honey," said Sammy.

"Hurry," said Netty, not a plea, an order.

Sammy and I laughed, jumped out of the cold water and toweled off.

Frida showed up at the same time the food arrived, so we invited her to eat with us.

"I ordered plenty, unless Eve decides to eat for more than two." Sammy usually commented on my appetite in a joking manner followed by a smile, but this time Sammy dropped the rib he was eating. "Maybe the ultrasound was wrong, and there's more than one baby."

"Don't be silly. I'd be a lot hungrier in than I am now."

After we'd finished eating and were drinking coffee out back by the canal, Frida set down her cup. "I'm here because Nappi, Crusty, Eve and I have developed a plan to flush out the person behind everything happening."

Sammy sat back in his chair and crossed his arms over his chest. His black hair fell forward onto his shoulders and his eyes darkened. He looked exactly like a warrior from the past Seminole Wars. I could almost read his thoughts. He would hate what was coming.

Frida laid out the strategy in terse terms. She wrapped up with what I hoped would make the approach ironclad. "You can see everyone has to be in place or this won't work."

Sammy hadn't moved a muscle nor blinked once. "I don't like it."

It was what I expected him to say. I leaned forward to add persuasive words.

He held up his hand to silence me. "I don't like it, but I understand your reasoning. I can't forbid Eve from doing this, but I know she wants my approval." He looked at me, the love in his eyes almost more than I could bear to see. "I have only one change to make."

I held my breath. Somehow I knew what Sammy was going to say.

So did Frida. "If you're going to suggest you come with us to the houseboat, I have to veto your idea. You're needed here with your children, father and Grandfather and out on the hunting ranch. Besides, this is something for us professionals."

Sammy turned his fiercest look on Frida. "Professionals? "His tone was mocking. "A PI, a pregnant apprentice PI and a mob boss. Professionals. I don't see it."

"You think you could do better?" Frida said, her tone of voice taking on an angry edge.

He ignored her question and directed his attention to me. "I have always supported you, Eve. This time I think you're wrong about this scheme."

"Do you have a better idea. Sammy?" asked Nappi.

Sammy seemed to retreat a bit. His look became softer and his shoulders lost their tenseness. "Okay, let's try this. Take me along with you. David can manage the ranch and protect Madeleine and the kids on his own without my help."

Frida thought for a moment enough time for me to insert my opinion. "I don't want Sammy with us for very selfish reasons. You love me, and you'll be distracted by your feelings and probably at the wrong time. You can't take part in this."

Sammy rose from his chair. "If I don't take part then you don't, Eve."

"I'd like to see you stop me." I jumped out of my chair and hurried into the house.

I FELL ASLEEP WITHOUT SAMMY AT MY SIDE. When I awoke the next morning, his side of the bed hadn't been disturbed. It was so unlike Sammy not to come sleep by my side. We'd had disagreements before, but never had we let them come between us. Where had he spent the night?

I smelled coffee. Oh, good. He'd probably slept at Grandfather's next door, not wanting to awaken me, but now he was making coffee for all of us. I grabbed my robe and went to the kitchen. Grandfather stood in front of the stove heating water for tea. Nappi and Lionel sat at the table drinking coffee.

"Oh, I thought Sammy was out here," I said.

"He's not with you?" Lionel looked surprised and a line of concern creased his usually smooth forehead.

Nappi got up and went to the window. "I thought I heard his truck start up earlier this morning. It's gone. He must have already left for David's ranch."

I grabbed my cell and called the hunting ranch.

David hadn't heard from him or seen him. "I was about to call your place, Eve. I've got clients coming in soon. I asked Sammy to be here early, but he hasn't shown."

That was so not Sammy.

CHAPTER 20

—

I GNAWED AT MY THUMBNAIL AND CALLED FRIDA.

"He was pretty steamed last night. I'm sure he's driving around calming down. He'll show up, Eve. Give him time."

"You don't understand. This is something Sammy would never do. He is the most responsible man I know. He'd never not show at the hunting ranch when he knew David counted on him. And he'd never worry me this way even if he was angry at me. Something is wrong. I know it."

"I'll tell you what I'll do. I'll alert our officers and the county sheriff's people to be on the lookout for his truck. Meanwhile, I'll take a ride around the lake area in my car and see if I can spot him."

I wasn't completely satisfied with her plan for locating Sammy, but I knew it was all she could do. "Call me back every half hour or so. I let David know what's happening, but he's stuck at the ranch with his clients today. Lionel and Nappi are out looking also. Grandfather called Sammy's cousins who are sitting on the school where the kids go. I'm taking Netty with me to the shop today."

"We're covered then." Frida paused for a moment. "I know what you're thinking, so let me say it. If Freddie has gotten to Sammy, he'll be in touch with you. Don't get crazy if he does. Call me."

"Yeah, right."

"I mean it, Eve. Call me." She disconnected.

I called Grandy to let her know about Sammy.

"Do you want to go look for him? Renata and I can open the store today."

"No, I think I should be with Netty. Working in the shop will distract me from my darker thoughts. If you want to come in, fine, but make certain Jerry comes also."

"Who's looking after you?" Grandy asked.

"I'm looking after me, me and my trusty little gun."

Grandy laughed. "Oh, sorry, but you haven't had the opportunity to get out to the range yet, have you?"

"Jerry and I were going this week, but gun practice can wait. Sammy comes first." My cell indicated an incoming call. "Gotta run. It's Frida. Maybe she has news."

Frida did have news, but it was not the kind I wanted to hear.

"I found Sammy's truck on one of the dirt roads west of the lake. He's not in it, and I don't see any sign of him."

I reconnected with Grandy, told her Frida had located the truck and I was on my way to meet her there. "Grandfather will keep an eye on Netty."

I gave Netty a hug and told her I was going out to meet her daddy. "You stay with Grandfather. Don't give him trouble and don't run off."

She stuck her thumb in her mouth, something she did only when she was upset. "There's nothing to worry about, honey. I'm certain Daddy is fine."

She looked up into her great grandfather's face as if she wanted confirmation from him of what I'd said.

Grandfather put his hand on her shoulder. "Your daddy wouldn't want you to worry about him, but he would be unhappy if you didn't go out and feed your pony this morning."

Netty's face brightened. "Then I can ride her, huh?"

Grandfather held his hand out to me and cocked one eyebrow in a questioning look.

I smiled and nodded. "Yes. I have my amulet. I never go anywhere without it."

"And Sammy always wears his, too," Grandfather assured me.

"Me, too." Netty grabbed the rawhide thong around her neck and pulled the amulet Grandfather had made her from under her shirt. "See?"

Safe. Everyone was as protected and safe as could be given the uncertainty of the threat from Freddie. We didn't know how many men he had with him, and we had no idea when he would strike, at whom and in what way. I didn't want to believe he had moved on Sammy, but why was Sammy missing?

I hugged both Grandfather and Netty goodbye and jumped into my car. I fishtailed out of our drive and onto the road south around the lake.

I missed the dirt road and had to make a U-turn. I spotted Frida's car only a half mile down the road. Sammy's truck was pulled off onto the grassy shoulder. A small canal ran alongside the road.

"I've called in one of our crime scene people to take a look." Frida walked to the truck with me. "The truck door was wide open. I couldn't see any tracks leading off in the dirt because it's so hard packed, and there's no sign of another vehicle, but it looks to me as if someone walked toward the canal."

I scanned the inside of the truck cab. "Sammy's twenty-two is missing from the gun rack." Did he take it with him, or did someone take it from him?

A crime scene van pulled up, and a man I knew from Frida's work got out.

"Hi, Georgie," I said. "I'm happy you're here and can tell us what you see."

Georgie walked around the truck, then up the road and back down it. He explored the area off toward the canal. "Someone came this way. The grass is all disturbed. Maybe there was more than one person. The area is heavily trampled." He bent down to more closely examine the grass. "Blood here, too."

My heart did a series of skips. Sammy, where are you? Are you hurt? Did someone harm you?

Frida turned to me and must have seen the expression of fear on my face. "You've gone all pale, Eve. Are you okay?"

"I'm fine. It's the smell." I sniffed the morning air which smelled fetid and heavy. "Reminds me of the other night at the shop. Like gas. I hate that odor."

Frida knew me well enough she understood the swamp gas was a reminder Freddie the Bull Jr. had almost gotten to me and it might mean he was responsible for Sammy's disappearance. "Don't jump to conclusions. It might not be Sammy's blood. It might be an animal's."

"Then where is Sammy?" My voice broke with emotion. I struggled to hold back my tears and to remain calm.

"We'll leave Georgie here to do his job. Let's round up Lionel, Nappi and Crusty for a meeting. Georgie will call as soon as he has some answers."

I looked out over the small canal and into the dense vegetation on the other side. Was someone watching us from across the water and smiling because they could see how upset I was? Did they have Sammy with them? Could he see me and know how I was feeling? Or was he dead, his body hidden somewhere in the swamps he so loved?

Frida was right. There was nothing we could do here. I needed the input of the people I most trusted to help me find who was behind Sammy's disappearance. It had to be Freddie Jr, and we had to flush him out and now.

I PACED NERVOUSLY AROUND CRUSTY'S OFFICE while Crusty, Nappi and Frida watched me, their faces a sea of worry.

"We can't move on our plan to ferret out Freddie with Sammy gone. We have to find him." I felt so impotent. There was no one to yell at, no one to physically threaten. I threw myself into a chair and ran my hands through my hair.

"If we could get in touch with Freddie, we might be able to make some kind of a deal," said Crusty.

"You don't deal with the like of the Bull's family," said Nappi. "He wants to bring us down."

"What do you think he intends?" Frida asked.

"I think he means to harm the ones we love most, let us watch and inflict as much suffering as he can," Nappi said.

"He's certainly done a great job of it so far." I jumped up from my chair and began my pacing again.

"We need to remain level-headed and think this one through." Frida turned to me. "You had a threatening message sent to you on your phone earlier, but he did make contact."

"Yes, but nothing since then and there's no way to call back. It was a blocked number, and I'll bet it was a burner phone to boot. It's probably at the bottom of some canal." I thought for a moment. "Wait a minute. I'll bet we can get a message through to Freddie Jr. by contacting dear daddy."

"And say what?" asked Frida.

"Tell him we'd like to meet, we know he holds all the cards, but we'd like to see what he has in mind. Say we'd be willing to do what he wants if he sends Sammy back." I thought it was a brilliant idea.

"He likes keeping us up in the air. He's not going to play," Crusty said.

Nappi got up from his chair and walked to the window where he looked out for a moment. "Maybe he will play. If he's like his father, Freddie Jr. thinks he's smarter than anyone else, so he'll like us groveling because he'll think he's got the upper hand, assume we're defeated. He'll want one final meeting to make things as bad as he can. We can use our original plan but bring Freddie Sr into the picture. The arrogance of the two of them may encourage them to make a stupid move."

Frida flipped her notebook closed. "Let's do it. We've got nothing to lose."

Freddie the Bull Senior resided in the federal penitentiary here in Florida. A high security facility, it housed a variety of inmates including terrorists, murderers, sex offenders and gang members. It was reputed to be one of the most violent federal detention centers in the US. We decided Frida should pay a visit to Freddie and while there check to see who might have visited him in the last year. I begged to accompany her which no one thought was a good idea.

Nappi pointed out to me we should appear as if we were defeated by his moves, not enraged or frightened. "It's too much stress for you and for the baby. Let Frida play this hand. You should be here in case someone from Freddie's people tries to get in touch about Sammy."

Much as I hated to admit it, he was right. Although I was torn between seeing Freddie the Bull's ugly face looking out from behind bars or searching for Sammy in case he was somewhere near, I knew I couldn't leave here. I could feel Sammy somewhere close by.

Nappi came over and put his arms around me. "I'm sorry for all this, Eve. If you hadn't been my friend, you would never have been involved in helping put Freddie behind bars, and his family wouldn't be seeking revenge."

How could I weigh the price of Nappi's friendship? All friends came as they were, people with flaws, people with pasts and people who had other people in their lives. "We don't ask for a resume when we take someone into our lives. Friendships aren't like that, Nappi."

He smiled and, for the first time since we had met, I thought I saw his eyes fill. "You're not going to cry, are you?"

He withdrew a handkerchief from his pocket. It wasn't the usual carefully folded and pressed white linen monogrammed hanky he used to carry. "I think my allergies are bothering me."

Frida arose from her chair. "I guess I'd better call the prison and make the arrangements, but I'd like to have you come with me, Nappi. I think there's some psychological advantage to having Freddie see defeat in your eyes. Do you think you can fake it?"

Nappi focused his brown eyes on her face. He wouldn't be playacting. His eyes, usually sparkling with life, seemed dulled with pain. "I can."

"IS DADDY HOME YET?" Netty ran into my arms as I stepped out of the car. Her three brothers were right behind her, their faces solemn with worry.

"Not yet." How could I explain to her and our sons what was happening?

Grandfather came around the corner of the house. "I've been sitting beside the canal thinking. I told the children we were concerned their father had been taken captive by some bad men, the men who were responsible for taking Netty's pony and who tried to hurt you and her."

I could have been angry he had told the children about their father, but I wasn't. I trusted his instincts. "Thank you for talking with them."

"These are strong children, Eve. Their ancestors fought for their land, for their way of life. These are the children of Miccosukee warriors who never gave up and were never defeated." Pride showed in Grandfather's face and was reflected in the faces of Netty and her brothers.

Someone tapped me lightly on my shoulder. I turned. It was Lionel making one of his unannounced appearances.

"White folks are certainly stupid. I went to look at the place where Sammy's truck was abandoned. Frida's crime scene guy read only part of what was written there."

"Well, he's not finished with gathering all the evidence," I said.

"He'll never find what I did." A small smile tickled Lionel's lips.

"You think you can pit your native skills against forensic technology?"

"No, but I know pigs."

I had no idea what he meant but Lionel insisted I go with him back to where Sammy's truck had been found.

As we were about to leave, Frida called me. "My crime scene guy said he saw signs of feral pigs in the area and it was possible Sammy's truck hit one of them. The blood we found was not human. It was animal's blood."

"I already knew it was an animal's blood." I glanced at Lionel who gave me a smug smile. "Lionel was out there, and he wants me to return with him. Maybe you'd be willing to meet us there?"

"Sure. If he's seen something and made sense of it, I'm game. I'll bring Georgie with me. Maybe he and Lionel can exchange information."

"Georgie would be willing to talk to Lionel?"

Lionel tipped his head back and let out the bark of a laugh.

"I think Lionel might enjoy the exchange," I said to Frida

BACK AT THE PLACE where Sammy's truck had been abandoned, Lionel led Frida, Georgie and me down the canal for over a mile.

"This will get a little muddy." Lionel stepped into the canal and waded across at a point where the water was shallower and where the muck on both banks was torn up by animal tracks. "Feral hogs." Lionel pointed at the tracks. "And one man."

"I can't see human tracks here, only pigs," said Georgie. Frida and I nodded in agreement.

"A boot ridge." Lionel pointed to the ground where there was the faint imprint of what might have been the toe of a boot. "And blood." He indicated a droplet on a leaf. Lionel continued down the far side of the canal, and we followed until we came to a path leading away from the water and into the dense vegetation beyond. "I followed the path to this point and then lost track of the blood and any sign of a human. The pigs have been all over this place, a large group of them. Sows, boars and piglets. Protective mamas."

"What are you saying, Lionel?" I asked.

He turned around and settled back on his heels. "I think Sammy tracked a pig through here. It would take some doing, but I think I might pick up his track if I worked this area for several hours."

I was exasperated with Lionel. "Why would Sammy want to run down a pig? He had to know we'd be worried when he didn't return. You're not making sense."

Frida held up her hand as if to signal me I needed to listen to Lionel. "Tell us what you think all of this means, Lionel."

"There are limited signs near the truck, but there are a few blood stains. I think Sammy turned off on the dirt road because there was a car behind him. I think it passed him and in the process of trying to run him off the road, the car hit a pig and injured it. Sammy got out of his truck with his rifle in his hand and may have shot at the people in the car. His action was probably enough to chase them off. I assume they were a few more of the incompetent men Freddie hired to do his work. Knowing the pig had been hit by the car and it was likely a sow, he began to follow her to see how badly she was wounded. My son respects the ways of nature and of our tribe living within the rules of nature. If a mama pig is wounded, you track her and if it's serious you put her down. I'm sure he's following her track. I can find them. I thought I'd let you know Sammy is in all probability safe." Lionel turned and began walking into the trees.

"What do you mean 'is in all probability safe?'" I yelled at his retreating back.

"I told you. Feral pigs. They're mean and bad tempered. You go after a hurt one carefully."

"What about those men who were after Sammy. Aren't they a threat?"

Lionel stopped and turned for a minute giving me a look filled with disbelief.

"They're city goons. They won't want to be back here among the snakes, gators and pigs."

No. They wouldn't. I didn't like it either.

Frida pulled one of her feet out of the sucking mud and almost lost her boot. "Let's get out of here. I say we leave Lionel to his tracking. Unless you want to go with him, Georgie?"

"If I won't get in your way, I'd love to learn how you do this." Georgie's eyes lit up with eagerness.

Lionel signaled Georgie to follow him.

I hoped Lionel was right and Sammy would return to us as soon as he had taken care of the pig hit by his pursuers. I hated to admit it, but Lionel was smart, swamp wise. His son was like him.

After Lionel and Georgie disappeared into the dark undergrowth and dense trees, I stood motionless and listened to the sound of the wind rattling the palm fronds and sniffed the swamp odors. I could almost feel Sammy's presence. He was working his way into the depth of the swamps to do what he was born to do: follow the call of what nature told him was right. Come home soon, Sammy.

CHAPTER 21

—

CAREFULLY CHOOSING MY WORDS, I told Grandfather and the children Sammy was out in the swamps tracking a feral pig hurt by one of the bad guys. I wasn't one hundred percent certain Lionel was right, but for my family, Lionel's word on what happened was fact. Deciding their father would be home soon, the boys and Netty ran off to the corral to feed the horses and the pony.

Grandfather could tell I was worried about Sammy. "Lionel reads sign better than anyone I know. Well, anyone other than me. I taught him. I shouldn't brag, but Sammy's safe."

I rolled my shoulders to release the tension in them. "I so want to believe he is."

Crusty's car turned off the main road and started down the drive toward the house.

Nappi got out of the passenger's seat. "Any word on Sammy?"

"I was about to call both of you." I told them what Lionel had found, or what he had surmised. Nappi and Crusty nodded and smiled in relief. What was I worrying for, I asked myself?

"Frida left word she arranged for a visit with Freddie the Elder at the penitentiary tomorrow afternoon. Freddie the younger may be holding Sammy or not, but we think talking to Freddie Senior is a good way to challenge him and his son into making a move on us." Nappi rubbed his hands together, signaling his eagerness to get on with our sting operation, although right now it felt like less of a way to flush out Freddie and more of a way to put all of us in danger.

"I'm uncomfortable about this. Do we really think we can outmaneuver this guy? So far we haven't been able to stay one step in front of him," I said.

Nappi put his arm around me and patted my shoulder. "We know what's coming. Freddie doesn't. We have the upper hand on this one."

Did we? I tossed and turned all night in bed, starting at every sound, thinking it was Sammy coming home or worrying it was someone sneaking up on the house intending to do us harm. If Sammy didn't show up by morning, I would insist we go look for him. I had no idea where Lionel was. Maybe the swamps finally did him in or perhaps Freddie had hired some old swamp guides to take after both Lionel and Sammy and . . . My fears went on and on until I finally dropped into a troubled sleep.

The sun hadn't risen yet when I heard a twig snap under the bedroom window, and I sat up in bed. "Sammy?"

"It's me. Lionel."

"I don't want you, Lionel. I want Sammy."

"Don't get all snappy with me. I came back to tell you Sammy is on his way home and he's got a present for you."

A present? He had worried the stuffing out of me, and he stopped to get me a present?

"I don't want any stupid present. I want Sammy." I jumped out of bed and pulled my robe on over my nightie. By the time I got to the door and had turned on the back outside light, there was no one there. "Lionel?" Had I been dreaming?

Lights shone on the side of the house, and I heard a vehicle pull up in front. I ran back inside and grabbed my gun, then peeked out the front windows. Sammy's truck was there. A man got out, but I could see it wasn't Sammy. The shadowed figure looked familiar.

"Stop right there. I've got a gun." I leveled my weapon at the person.

"Don't shoot. It's me. Georgie."

"What the . . . Okay, I keep asking. Where's Sammy?"

"Oh, sorry. Sammy had me drop him off in town. He didn't want the meat to spoil. I thought Lionel would have stopped by and told you."

Why was it so hard to get a straight story out of anyone? I should shoot the lot of them for being so annoying.

"Meat?" What language was he speaking?

"Here comes my ride," said Georgie.

One of the crime scene investigation vans pulled up and Georgie jumped in. They drove off without another word to me about what was happening. I stood outside gazing into the distance as the sky lightened. No Sammy.

"Eve?" said a voice from behind me.

I turned. Sammy stood there a grin on his face, but there was also doubt in his eyes.

Instead of stepping into his arms as I had intended to do when he returned, I punched him on the shoulder.

"Hey! That's no way to welcome the hunter back from the hunt."

"Why, oh, why won't you carry a cell phone so you can stay in touch with me? I was worried sick about you."

"Dad said he told you and Frida what he thought was going on. Didn't he get in touch with you to say I'd be home after I stopped by the meat packer?"

"He came to the window and said something I didn't understand." Why was I being so silly? I didn't care what had gone on. I only cared Sammy was here. I threw myself into his arms and buried my face in his neck. I smelled something . . . rank. "What is the malodorous smell?

"It's pig. Feral hog to be exact. My present to you."

My beloved Sammy was back in my arms bearing the gift of swamp piggy stink.

WHEN SAMMY EMERGED FROM THE SHOWER, once more my sweet-smelling man, he explained how he had tracked down the pig hit by the men who had tried to force him off the road.

"I had seen the tracks of a number of the piglets, and I worried the men had hit their mother, but it turned out to be a young boar hog. It took me all day to track him down. He was in bad shape. I don't know how he managed to drag himself through the rough terrain. He had several broken ribs, and he was scraped up and bleeding. I put him out of pain, then knew I had to field dress him and carry him out. Lionel and Georgie ran into me as I was heading back. We took turns carrying the pig, but I had to get it to the butcher and cooled down before the meat went bad. We took my truck into town, and I had Georgie drop me off at Lowell's Butchering. It's lucky Lowell lives right next door to his shop. I woke him up and told him what I needed. Georgie called police head-quarters then drove my truck here to tell you I would be home after I talked with Lowell about how I wanted the pig butchered. I got here as soon as I could. Didn't you get the message? Lionel took a short cut across the swamps back. I assumed he'd stop by and let you know what was happening."

"I got two messages. Lionel said you had a present for me, and Georgie told me you didn't want the meat to spoil."

"Oh, good." Sammy grabbed jeans and a tee-shirt from his drawer. "I'm hungry."

I slugged him in his shoulder again.

"Why are you hitting me?"

"Where's my present?"

"Tonight you'll get it. Tonight we'll have the best ribs you've ever eaten, wild boar ribs. Yum."

"Why didn't Georgie call on his cell?"

"Lionel said he and Georgie hadn't gotten far tracking me when Georgie dropped his cell in the swamp when a mama pig and her young'uns charged him and knocked him down. He was about to dig in the water for it when Lionel saw a gator approaching. They got out of there fast." Sammy chuckled. "Now how about breakfast for the hunter?"

How could I stay mad at a man who spent hours tracking a wild ani-mal through the swamps and remembered to bring his wife a gift? I made love to him and then fed him pancakes.

WE DINED ON RIBS, and they were tasty, a stronger pig taste than I was used to, but juicy and meaty. It was good to have the entire family includ-ing Nappi gathered at our table. Sammy sent a couple of pig roasts to Georgie to thank him for his help and some ribs to Frida for having faith in Lionel's take on the scene. Sammy hadn't gotten a license plate on the vehicle that tried to force him off the road, but Frida used the vehicle's description to put out an APB on it.

Still stuffed from ribs the night before, Frida, Lionel, Crusty and I gathered the next morning in Crusty's office to put the final touches on our plan to trap Freddie. Nappi and Frida planned to take off at noon to pay their visit to Freddie Senior in the penitentiary Northwest of

Orlando near the central Florida town of Wildwood. They would toss what we knew in Freddie's face and challenge his son through him to confront us "like a man."

"That should get under Freddie's skin. "I can hardly wait to see the expression on his face." Nappi rubbed his hands together in anticipation, an eager smile on his face.

"We're not telling him where the showdown will be. It will be an additional challenge to the Freddies, to see if they're clever enough to find us," Frida said.

I knew they would be. They probably had their goons stationed outside the office right now keeping an eye on us.

Sammy stuck his head in the office. "I'm on my way to David's ranch. I thought I'd see how things are going."

I knew exactly what he meant by 'see how things are going.'" "No, you cannot go with us."

Frida got out of her chair and put her hand on Sammy's arm. "You're worried, and you think you're not doing anything to help, but you are. It's your responsibility to keep the children and Grandfather safe. The Freddie organization has a long arm as we've seen. I'm worried he might take the opportunity of my absence and our set-up to decide to strike elsewhere, at the family."

I swallowed the lump lodged in my throat. I knew Freddie might attack the family instead of taking our bait, but the way she said it made it seem so real. Was I abandoning my family to challenge Freddie one on one? Was I as ego-driven as he was?

"I understand. We're all in danger and will continue to be until we take this guy and his operation down." Sammy bent over and gave me a kiss on the cheek. "Go practice at the shooting range." What he hadn't said was what I already knew. My inability to hit a target shouldn't be the weak link in this strategy. He hadn't given me his blessing to go ahead with our plan, but I sensed he had come to grips with my part in it.

I spent the afternoon at the shooting range with Jerry. I don't know which of us was the worse shot, but I was determined to improve. I tried to keep my eyes open when I aimed. I was successful half the time.

Jerry was reloading his weapon after a round of shooting. "I'm getting better at this. How about you, Eve?"

"A gun will never be my weapon of choice. I do better slinging my shoes at my adversary."

"Imagine the bullet is a strappy Manolo Blahnik." Jerry aimed at his target and fired.

Maybe he had a point. I envisioned one of my stilettos as I took aim. No, it wouldn't do. I missed the target entirely. I was hopeless. I was saved from a continuation of this incompetence by my cell ringing. It was Frida.

"I thought I'd give you a call and tell you what happened at the prison."

I turned away from the gun range to hear Frida better. "Tell me. I can't wait to hear."

"He didn't say a word but listened to what we had to say with a smug look on his face, then threw back his head and laughed as if we'd told him the best joke he'd ever heard."

"He said nothing?"

"Yeah. Nappi says it's a good sign. We're a go."

ON MONDAY I KISSED THE FAMILY GOODBYE and left in my car with Nappi. Frida called me on her way to Orlando to tell me she was checking in at the conference hotel. "I'll be slipping out the back and be in position by this afternoon."

"I hope no one notices Jerry isn't in his usual place outside the shop and doesn't notice he's playing the part of Crusty."

Frida chuckled. "Lionel will take his place outside. They'll focus on him as more of a threat and not worry about where Jerry is, and if the Freddie people think he's left his post to come down to Nappi's houseboat as protection, I don't think they'll see him any risk."

"Maybe they saw the two of us practicing at the gun range."

Frida chuckled again. "Then they'll know how little danger they're in."

I let her remark slide by. "Okay, then. We're all set. You arranged with the Monroe Sheriff's department to have Nappi's neighbor picked up?"

"I did. Now let's focus on what we're doing. All the loose ends have been tied up."

Had they? I wondered. There was a niggling thought I had missed something, something important.

WE ARRIVED AT NAPPI'S HOUSEBOAT in midafternoon. The day had been sunny when we began our drive, but as we neared the coast, clouds built offshore, and it looked as if we were in for rain and wind. I checked the weather on my phone and noted there was a storm off the coast blowing in with a series of squalls and a forecast of rain throughout the night.

When I told Nappi about the impending weather, he looked out at the building cloud bank. "Not good. The storm will make it difficult to hear anything happening outside, and we'll find it difficult to see through the darkness. They have the advantage on us now."

As we unloaded our supplies from the trunk of my car, I glanced over at Nappi's neighbor's place. It looked shuttered and empty. "His truck is there, but it looks as if he's not."

"The Monroe County jail is his home for now." Nappi grabbed a bag of groceries we'd stopped for in Homestead. "I'll make us a nice stew with the chicken I bought. You sit back and relax."

How could I relax when I worried men with guns might storm in? I connected with Frida to see if she was in place in one of the live-aboard boats she and Crusty had rented closer to the restaurant but in walking distance to us.

She answered immediately. "We're here. Are you getting settled?"

"I'm worried about the incoming storm."

"Hunker down. It might make the conditions unpleasant for Freddie's gang. I don't see Freddie as the kind of guy who likes to be out in bad weather."

"I don't like it either especially when it rocks the boat. I don't have my sea legs with this pregnancy." A gust of wind off the water made the boat roll and pitch. "I may be in for a bit of nausea."

Nappi began preparation for dinner, and my stomach settled after I had some of his delicious chicken stew. The wind continued to blow, and rain pelted the boat's windows. I stood at the sink overlooking the water and dried dishes while Nappi washed. Suddenly, the boat rolled toward the shore, and the window over the couch behind us shattered.

"Get down!" yelled Nappi. He pushed me to the floor and dove after me. Rain blew in the broken window.

"A shot?" I asked.

As quickly as the night had been rent by the noise of breaking glass, silence descended. We both lay on the floor listening for the sound of another shot or someone slamming through the door. My phone lay on the counter. I couldn't get to it to contact Frida without exposing myself to the shooter.

Nappi saw me glance at the cellphone. "I'll get it. You stay down."

With the light from inside the boat and the darkness outside Nappi made an excellent target. I waited for the inevitable bullet and hoped it would miss him. He grabbed the phone. I winced in anticipation, but nothing happened.

"Call Frida and let her know what happened but tell her not to make a move yet. We'll stay put for a few more minutes to see what their next move will be." Nappi worked his way into the back cabin where the lights were off. I saw him get up onto the bunk there and take a careful peek out of the window.

Absolute silence settled in. After the howling winds and rain of the storm the calm was eerie. It continued for several minutes, then was broken by the sound of a knock on the door. My heart took a leap and then seemed to stop.

"You folks okay in there?"

It was Darby Dunlop, Nappi's neighbor and the guy who was supposed to be spending a few days as the guest of the Monroe County Jail.

CHAPTER 22

—

"Well, Mr. Dunlop," Nappi opened the door a crack, "I thought you were gone. We didn't see any signs of life when we pulled up this afternoon." Nappi was making pleasant. I guess he didn't want to act as though we were ungrateful he was concerned or give away our surprise he was in residence rather than in jail.

"I got dropped off right after this storm came in."

"We noticed your truck was there, but we didn't see any sign of you."

"Nope. Darnest thing. There was some kind of a mix-up, and the police hauled me off to jail. By the time it was straightened out, I'd spent last night in a cell with some drunks." Darby smiled as if being taken to jail for something he didn't do was no big deal. He peeked around the door and saw me get up of the floor. "Scared ya, did it, the tree limb flying through the window? Anybody hurt?"

I shook my head.

"I got some plastic if you want to button 'er up for the time being."

"Thanks, but I can take care of it." Nappi began to close the door.

"Well, if you need me, I'm right next door."

He stood outside the door for a few minutes before we heard him step off the boat deck.

I connected with Frida on the cell. "Darby Dunlop was here."

"What? No. Impossible."

"I don't know how he got out of jail, but there he was offering to help repair the window shattered when a limb punched it in."

"I'll get back to you."

"I'm going outside to repair the window. I've got some materials in the shed. How about a cup of tea for us?" Nappi opened the door and stuck his head out, looking to make certain no one was there.

My cell rang. It was Frida. "I called the Monroe County Sheriff. They told me they had heard from me earlier today with the message I wanted them to let Mr. Dunlop go, and I would pick him up later at his residence with a charge from our county."

"Someone posed as you? Freddie must have a woman working with him."

"Probably a relative. Do we revise our plan or do you and Nappi feel you can handle him along with whatever Freddie hands you?"

"I can't understand why someone would pose as you to get Dunlop out of jail. I don't think Nappi ever suspected his neighbor in the boat was in the employ of whoever killed Nappi's grandfather and then came after all of us. Maybe Dunlop was put here to keep an eye on Nappi from the very beginning." I hadn't felt completely secure in our plan, but now I understood we might have underestimated Freddie all along. The guy had tentacles everywhere.

I shook off doubts about the way forward. "Nappi's outside repairing the window. I'll ask him when he gets in, and we'll get back to you. My instinct is we go ahead despite Dunlop." I disconnected and waited. The presence of Dunlop and his possible connection to Freddie wasn't something we'd counted on, but at least we knew he was there. Cool night air continued to pour through the broken window. Where was Nappi?

I wondered if I should go outside and look for him, but after several minutes, he stuck his head through the window. "Sorry I took so long. The shed is a mess. It took me while to find the materials. Now, where is my hammer?" His head disappeared and then reappeared. He placed thick plastic over the window, and I heard him nail it into place.

A few minutes later, the door opened and Nappi appeared. He hesitated a moment, then seemed to stumble into the room.

"Are you okay?" I reached out to steady him.

"He brought a friend," said a voice from behind him. A short fat man with a round face looking as if it had been molded from clay and left unsmoothed by a potter's hand, stepped into the room behind Nappi. He held a large handgun in his hand, his beautiful long fingers incongruous holding the ugly weapon.

How could I mistake him for anyone but Freddie the Younger? He had those hands, narrow, graceful with well-manicured nails. Like Freddie the Father.

"Let me introduce myself..."

"You don't need to. You're the man who's behind everything that has happened to Nappi, me and our friends and family. You're doing your father's bidding, revenge for our putting him in prison."

His face flushed red with anger. "Not my father's idea at all, but mine."

"Aren't you a clever boy." I was baiting him and knew I shouldn't. Nappi shot me a look warning me to back down.

Freddie waved the gun at me, the universal bad guys' signal for "move to one side." He pushed Nappi toward me. "The two of you might like to sit down. I see you've made tea. We can chat for a few moments, then I'll be leaving you."

I held my cell in my hand, hidden behind my back.

"Put the phone on the table," Freddie said. "You think I didn't see it? Stupid woman."

I tossed the cell onto the table, and it slid to rest partially covered by the towel I had been using to dry dishes. My purse with my gun rested beside the towel. I darted a glance at Nappi who acknowledged with a tilt of his head he knew what I had in mind—distract Freddie.

Nappi and I took chairs at the table. Freddie continued to point his gun, but his body seemed to visibly relax. His eyes remained fixed on us, but he turned his head slightly toward the door. "C'mon in, darling."

The door opened to let in a rail-thin, dark-haired woman. The moment I saw her face, the piece of the puzzle eluding me, the bit of memory lodged tightly in the recesses of my mind broke loose. How could I have been so stupid? The warning on my phone came from a woman, and a woman visited Homer Smith's polo farm and talked with Mateo. Carlos said he hadn't seen her face, but her voice sounded familiar to him. It would. He'd heard it the times Eduardo has visited the stables. She was Eduardo Garcia's personal assistant, the woman who accompanied him out of the country when he fled back to Argentina to avoid being indicted for trafficking drugs into the country inside polo ponies. She must have been the woman on the phone with the Monroe County

Sheriff's office posing as Frida, and she was probably the woman in our shop insulting Renata and who came back later to cut the gas line. My mouth dropped open in shock.

"I see you remember who I am." Her thin lips twisted in an evil smile.

I returned the smile. "I suppose you're now the head of the drug smuggling operation since we know Eduardo is dead. He must have taught you all the tricks he knew."

Her smile disappeared, replaced by a darkening of her eyes in anger.

"I taught him, not the other way around. I wouldn't have been so stupid to have gotten myself killed by the Argentinian bosses."

"But if you fail this time, the same fate awaits you, unless we discover your operation first."

"No one knows I'm even in this country, and none of your drug enforcement agencies are onto my plan to begin drug shipments once again."

"Besides," Freddie interrupted, "she has our family behind her. Huh, Babe?" Freddie leaned his body into hers and put his arm around her shoulders.

She gave a small shudder of revulsion at his touch.

"How did the two of you connect?" I asked. "You're an unlikely pair."

"I needed someone as bent on making you and your mob buddy pal here pay for what you did to Eduardo. It was better than paying people to help me out. I used my resources to learn about you in detail. When I read about Freddie the Bull and how the two of you put him in prison, I knew I'd found my man. He offered me the services of his 'family.'"

"This is a perfect match. I get to tap into her expertise on drugs."

"What does she get out of it?" I asked, "other than an association with a crime network that's not very good at what it does; witness your father paying for his crimes."

"Hey," Freddie said, moving toward me with his arm raised.

"Forget her." The evil witch stepped in front of Freddie. "We've got better in store for her than a slap in the face."

"Eduardo and his vet treated those horses horribly, and you want to follow in his footsteps?" I said.

"Don't be silly. We're not going to repeat the method he used." She ran her hand through her hair and then flipped a lock behind her ear with her fingers.

"What then?" I asked.

Confronted now by two enemies, distracting both wouldn't be easy, so I was doing the next best thing—trying to get as much information as I could from them.

Freddie rose to the bait. He might have been a lawyer and supposedly educated and smart, but he couldn't resist showing off how clever he was and how in control of this operation. I knew who was calling the shots, and it wasn't Freddie.

"Beef," he said before she could stop him. "Imported beef from Argentina. The drugs are hidden inside the sides of beef." He threw back his shoulders and produced an arrogant smile.

"Obviously not your idea. Hers?" I asked.

Her eyes snapped with irritation at what he said. "You fool." She slapped him.

Shock spread over his face and for a moment, the two of them focused on each other. I made a dive for my purse and my gun, grabbed it and got off one shot, eyes open for once. Freddie fired at the same moment. His shot went wide of both Nappi and me, but mine lodged in her arm.

Freddie was a bad shot but faster on his feet than I expected from someone so short and fat. He grabbed Nappi and pointed his gun at Nappi's head. "I'll kill him. Drop the gun."

I lowered it to the floor.

"Are you okay, Selma?"

Ah, she had a name.

"I think you'd better get your girlfriend to a doctor," I said as if there was any chance they would leave us to seek medical attention.

"Never mind me." She grabbed her arm where the bullet hit her. "It's not serious, but let's finish up here and go. No more talking. I'll leave this for you." She set the oversized purse she was carrying on the table, reached in and seemed to fish around inside as if she was searching for something. In less than a minute she extracted her hand. The purse began making a ticking sound. A bomb!

Without a backward look, she opened the door and walked out into the night. Freddie grinned and stooped to pick up my gun off the floor, but Nappi dived for it as Freddie turned to aim his weapon at Nappi. Nappi came up with my gun in his hand and fired at the same time Freddie got off a shot. Nappi's shot hit Freddie. He cried out in pain and dropped his weapon. Freddie's shot again went wide. Wow, the man was worse with a firearm than I was.

I moved toward the door to open it, but it wouldn't budge. "Your partner wedged something in there when she left. We're all trapped here. I don't think she has any regard for you, Freddie. The woman is pure evil."

Nappi yelled at me. "The window, Eve. Go out the window."

"No. I . . . "

"Now. I've got this. I know bombs. I'll handle it. I'll follow you."

"What about him?" I pointed to Freddie.

"Don't worry about Freddie. Go." Nappi gave me a thin smile of encouragement and moved toward the table and the ticking purse. Freddie lay on the floor, groaning and looking terrified.

On impulse, I removed the amulet from around my neck and handed it to Nappi. "This will help."

I kicked at the plastic over the window with my boot, tore it open and wriggled through, intending to move toward the door of the houseboat and open it for Nappi.

"Oh, no, you don't," said a male voice as I ran for the door. Dunlop grabbed me by my neck and propelled me off the boat.

"Don't let her get to the door," said Selma who waited on the dock "Let's get out of here fast. The device is going to blow."

Dunlop shoved me away from the boat. I struggled with him, but small as he was, he was wiry and strong.

He dragged me toward the road, and then flung me down onto the sand. I turned back to see if Nappi had followed me out the window, but I didn't see him or Freddie.

"They're toast," said Selma. "Here." She handed Dunlop a gun. "Kill her and then get me out to my boat. I need medical attention."

Dunlop's jaw dropped. He backed away from the proffered weapon. "I ain't shootin'anyone. I didn't sign up to do no killin'."

"Fine, then I'll do it." She fired the gun at Dunlop, and he crumpled to the ground.

"And now you, my dear."

Before she could fire, I threw myself down, grabbing at her feet and knocking her off balance. The gun flew from her hand and landed somewhere among the weedy areas dotting the sandy area.

I needed a weapon but knew there was little chance of finding the gun, so I grabbed for her foot and tugged. Her heavy boot came off in my hand. I looked at it for a second, then slammed it hard against her face.

"My nose."

I was getting good at breaking noses. I looked at the boot. Hmm, maybe there was something to recommend Wellingtons after all. I couldn't have delivered as powerful a blow with one of my stilettos.

I jumped up to run back to the boat. Too late. It exploded, raining debris, flames and charcoaled timbers down. I covered my head with my hands to protect myself.

Nappi. Oh, no, not Nappi.

Tears welled up as I watched the houseboat burn. A hand touched my shoulder, and I whirled thinking it was Selma, partly recovered from the blow I landed on her, but it was Frida.

"Nappi was in there," I sobbed, my body shaking with shock and grief, my mind not wanting to believe what I knew to be true.

Frida grabbed me and hugged. We stood there for a moment watching the boat burn.

"I'm sorry, Eve. We tried to get here, but we were too late. You were smart, Eve, connecting to my number when you set your phone on the table. I heard everything. We came running but stumbled onto a few of Freddie's men in our way. It took a while, but we disarmed and cuffed them." Frida continued to hug me while I shook with sadness and rage. Crusty walked up to us and encircled both of us in a giant bear hug. The boat continued to burn down to the water line. There was no sign anyone had managed to get off her before the explosion.

Gone. My loving, smart, funny friend was gone.

CHAPTER 23

—

"I HEAR SOMETHING OVER THERE." Frida pointed to the mangroves lining the banks.

"Have a look. I'll take care of these two." Crusty cuffed Selma and checked Dunlop. "I'll call 911 for this one. He'll make it."

Frida and I rushed down to the water's edge.

"Nappi?" My heart pounded in anticipation. Maybe he'd gotten out and was badly hurt.

A man lay tangled in the roots of a mangrove, but it wasn't Nappi.

"Freddie. Where's Nappi? Did he get out with you?" I reached down and gave him a shake.

"Hey, you're hurting me. I need a doctor." Freddie tried to wriggle out of my grasp.

"Not until you tell me what happened to Nappi."

He looked into my face and then smiled. "I got nothin' to say."

I was about to punch him in the arm where he had taken the shot, but Frida stopped me. "Look at this, Eve." She reached out to a branch of the mangrove. Something hung there.

"My amulet!" I grabbed it out of Frida's hand.

"And this." She plucked a strappy sandal off the same branch. I recognized it as the one which had gotten stuck in the mud the first time Lionel and I visited Nappi at the houseboat.

"Never mind, Freddie. You don't have to say anything. I don't believe you were smart enough to get yourself off the boat before the bomb blew, but Nappi was, and I suspect you're alive because he dragged you out the forward hatch with him."

I hung the amulet around my neck again and grabbed my shoe. When I heard a splash in the water, I turned back to look. Maybe a dolphin diving out there? Or perhaps . . .

Humming a tune under my breath, I slung the tattered, mud-soiled sandal over my shoulder and walked toward the road. The sandal might not have been repairable, but I'd keep it as a souvenir of how we took down Freddie and Selma.

"Nappi never hangs around for the arrival of the cops, does he?" Frida's voice carried a note of conviction indicating she was also convinced he was alive.

"Aside from you, cops aren't his favorite folks. He knows if they found him, they'd be distracted by his reputation rather than focusing on Freddie and friends. Nappi likes to make things simple for the authorities by keeping a low profile."

She nodded. "He'll be back in our lives when it's more convenient for all of us." If Frida had said this years ago, it would have been with sarcasm in her voice, but now she seemed to accept Nappi's style of operating.

We heard sirens coming over the bridge from the south. "Monroe County Sheriff's Department. Nappi skedaddled just in time." She held up her ID and waved at one of the officers who slammed on his brakes and jumped out of his cruiser. "Hey, I need another pair of cuffs here."

I sat under the shade of scraggly palm tree while EMTs loaded Dunlop and Freddie into an ambulance. Crusty came over and squatted down beside me. "You and Frida seem convinced Nappi got out before the boat exploded."

"And got Freddie out with him. I wouldn't have been so kind."

"Selma and Freddie were in on this together?"

"Freddie thought so. Selma thought she was running the show. My bets are she was. She is clever and evil. Remind me to call Bud and tell him about her plans to take over smuggling drugs in here from Argentina. Could I borrow your cell? Mine was in the boat. I need to call Sammy."

I DROVE BACK HOME IN THE EVENING, traveling west into the setting sun, home where everyone I loved would be glad to hear how well our plan went, everyone except for Nappi. I hoped he wouldn't stay away too long. I wanted to thank him for returning both my shoe and the amulet. He must have spotted the shoe on the bottom when he dived off the boat.

Dinner was, you guessed it, ribs and slaw from the Burnt Biscuit. As happy as everyone was about the outcome of the day, Sammy was quiet and left the celebration. I found him on the shore of the canal.

I leaned my head on his shoulder. "You were worried about me."

"I was."

"Do you want me to stop my detective work?"

"Do you want to?"

I thought about his question and remembered those days when I was simply the co-owner of the consignment shop.

"When I wasn't a PI, what was different? Aside from not knowing how to shoot a gun."

"You still don't."

"Not true. I shot Selma, didn't I?"

Sammy leaned in and kissed my lips, a gentle kiss like a breeze rising off the water. "With or without a PI's license, with or without a gun, you'd snoop. You can't help yourself. I know you. I married the nosiest woman in the swamps."

My Sammy. He did know me oh so well.

"For the time being I'd like to focus on incubating this baby if you don't mind."

The baby kicked as if to second my desire.

FIVE MONTHS LATER, almost to the day the doctor determined would be my due date, our baby boy was born after only two hours of labor. He came on time, he came easy, and I hoped this meant he would be a less difficult child than Netty, but one can never tell.

All my family and my friends crowded into the hospital room to greet our perfect little man. The only family missing was Renata who had returned to Las Vegas several months before. The casino where she worked had been sold, and the new owner offered her the job of manager at a salary too good to turn down. I don't know if she and Lionel ever talked about the one night they had together, but it wasn't any of my business. When Lionel said he might fly out to see her, I was surprised, but maybe a long-distance relationship would work well for them.

Madeleine and I hired a young woman Shelley had recommended as a tailor and shop clerk. Kimberley was working out well, but I missed having Renata in the shop, and Sammy, our boys and Netty missed her, too. Lionel seemed restless and began spending more and more time in the swamps. I hoped he wouldn't' return to them full time, but there was never any predicting Lionel's behavior. Perhaps a new grandson would keep him closer to home.

Throughout the pregnancy I had waited anxiously for Nappi's return or for word from him but heard nothing. Some nights when the baby was particularly active and woke me from my sleep, I wondered if I had imagined Nappi had escaped and had left the sandal and amulet. I wanted to believe he would walk through the door of the consignment shop any day, dressed as he usually was in his linen shirt and jacket, silk slacks and wearing another Rolex watch. He'd kiss Grandy's hand and mine, and we would gather at the Burnt Biscuit for drinks and ribs. I believed my amulet had been instrumental in saving Nappi's life, so I asked Grandfather to make Nappi one of his own. I could hardly wait to give it to him

Freddie had said nothing about the night on the exploding boat and neither had Selma or Dunlop. For people who were so loquacious before they were taken to jail, they were surprisingly quiet now.

"What's the baby's name?" asked Frida, breaking into my thoughts.

I looked down at my bundle of boy for a moment, but my attention was diverted by the scent of expensive cologne drifting into my room. In the doorway holding a bouquet of red roses was Nappi, looking as I had imagined him, a grin on his face, his dark hair brushed back from his high forehead. I caught the gold from his cuff links and watch gleam as the sunlight from the window caught them. So, Nappi had his watch back. From his manner it appeared he had more than that back.

"It's been a while." I shifted the baby in my arms as he squirmed and started to fuss.

"Getting back my old life took some time."

"What's your name?" I asked him. Sammy put his arm around my shoulders and our eyes met in silent agreement.

"You know it. Nappi." A look of confusion crossed his face.

"No. I mean your given name, not your nickname. This boy needs a name."

He handed the roses to Grandy. The baby began to cry, something he had been doing much of the morning. Nappi bent and kissed me on the forehead. I handed the baby to him, and the boy quieted.

"My name is Leonardo."

"What a perfect name for my son." Little Leo, certain to be a lion of a man when he grew up.

THE END

Lesley retired from her life as a professor of psychology and reclaimed her country roots by moving to a small cottage in the Butternut River Valley in Upstate New York. In the winter she migrates to old Florida—cowboys, scrub palmetto, and open fields of grazing cattle, a place where spurs still jingle in the post office, and gators make golf a contact sport. Back north, the shy ghost inhabiting the cottage serves as her literary muse. When not writing, she gardens, cooks and renovates the 1874 cottage with the help of her husband, two cats and, of course, Fred the ghost, who gives artistic direction to their work.

She is the author of a number of mystery series and mysteries as well as short stories. *Fatal Family* follows the first seven books in the Eve Appel mystery series, *A Secondhand Murder, Dead in the Water, A Sporting Murder, Mud Bog Murder, Old Bones Never Die, Killer Tied and Nearly Departed.*

CPSIA information can be obtained
at www.ICGtesting.com
Printed in the USA
BVHW070116140421
604815BV00008B/426